Of Melanesian and Scottish heritage, the author was raised by his extended family on the island of Ranongga in the Solomon Islands. He attended Kingsland Intermediate school in Auckland New Zealand before reuniting with his family in Honiara. His story "Kōpura Rising" was published in 2018 in the Anthology *Cthulhu: Land of the Long White Cloud* and was selected as a finalist for the 2018 Australian Aurealis Awards for Best Horror Novella. The author's third published story: "The Phobia Clinic", was included in the IFWG anthology *SPAWN*, edited by Deborah Sheldon. *Bedding the Lamia* is Kuraria's first collection. He is an Australian resident and currently resides on the mid-north coast of NSW, Australia.

Bedding the Lamia

Tropical Horrors

By David Kuraria

Bedding the Lamia: Tropical Horrors

All Rights Reserved

ISBN-13: 978-1-922556-34-9

Copyright ©2021 David Kuraria

V1.0

'And He Shall Suffer for His Art' first published 2011 in *Midnight Echo* volume 5, the magazine of the Australian Horror Writers Association. 'The Gods of Mwaia' first published in *Dimension 6* issue 12, 2017. Published by Keith Stephenson.

Printed in Palatino Linotype and Komikazba.

IFWG Publishing International
Gold Coast

www.ifwgpublishing.com

For Arthur Machen and Catherine Moore

Table of Contents

The Gods of Mwaia

"For some, rapid movement from a large tropical insect or arachnid can cause dread. Limbs of crawling things, appendages arranged for locomotive precision repulse certain dispositions. The individual stares with perverse pleasure, frightened yet unable to look away. Touching the bark of a tree only to find under fingertips, movement, turns casual exploration of nature into a frightening experience. It is the camouflage, a perceived malevolent deceit of the hidden, the disguised that horrifies."
–Astrid Bërgëson
The Hidden Realm, Oslo University Press 1926.

In a shabby second-floor waterfront boarding house room above the Honiara fish markets, Renai sat on a packing crate facing his friend, Alan O'Connor. The hulking New Zealander had been a guide-for-hire in New Guinea for a private security firm, protecting tourist adventurers from kidnappings. He looked freakish in the gloomy confines of the small room. Alan's skin was grey and his pupils were black.

Over the babble of voices haggling seafood prices from the docks below Alan's room, Renai explained his situation.

"You already know about the tribes on The Beast, my friend."

Renai jerked his head towards the south wall of the room, indicating his island home of Mwaia.

Alan shook his head. "You still having problems with those Kwaio landowners?" He paused for a moment. "You never did tell me why you call it *The Beast*."

Renai stared at his friend. "Doesn't matter. What matters is our displacement. Three generations have passed and we are still not allowed back on ancestral lands; no land for crops and forced to build our coral islets out in Bina lagoon, poor soil stolen from the farms. Alan, we can't continue this. My people starve on a diet of fish, skinny tubers and coconuts."

Alan looked at Renai, his friend's blonde afro catching the light of the morning sun shining through the small window.

"What's happening with the local government in town here?"

Renai growled. "Useless. They keep saying it is out of their jurisdiction. I have no choice. I am going to have to deal with this my way."

"Now I'm liking it. What have you got in mind?"

Renai leaned forward on the rickety chair. "I have to make a trek up to the highlands to plead my case to the upland Kwaio, the hereditary owners of the coast. These uplanders are secretive and aloof with many *tambus*."

"Okay, I'm in, who else do you have?"

Renai explained where he was up to with organising the trek.

"Two interpreters you say? Friends of yours, Ren?"

Renai felt stifled in the sweltering confines of the tiny room. "I've met them a few times, decent fellows. La'akwai is a lowland Kwara'e. He's fluent in Kwaio dialect, but he enjoys his weed. The other one, Luti, is coastal Kwaio and knows his bushcraft. From what I've seen he's good with handling local youth disputes."

"I'm not getting paid for this, am I?"

Renai grinned. "Of course you aren't. You're here to help a friend in need."

"You know we're going to need first aid kits and vaccines before we go up."

Renai looked at the corridor through the open door of the room. "Ahead of you there. I have spoken with the medical staff down in Kirakira hospital on Makira. They are interested in collecting some upland plants for research. I said if they could spare someone to come with us, we could provide them with safety to do their work."

"So, the hospital is financing this?"

"Well, they've promised me a small budget and medical supplies, but we have to provide our own food and gear. I'm taking the ferry down tomorrow to meet with the intern who will be coming with us."

"At least it'll get me out of here for a while." Alan looked about his dismal lodgings. "When do you want to make a start?"

Renai was anxious to get out from the confines of the room.

"Day after tomorrow, we should all meet at the Bina markets."

Renai sat drinking a sour coffee in the Kirakira hospital cafeteria. He looked up to see a tall, athletic young woman sitting opposite.

"Hi, Mr Renai. I'm Tatau. Dr Mahia has given me a brief."

She smiled. "Not what you expected?"

Renai laughed. "Well, I was expecting someone with a white coat who would be complaining once we got into the mountains."

Tatau tapped her fingers on the sides of the table. "Well, you have me instead."

Renai pushed his coffee cup aside. "So you know where we are going?"

"Yes, into the highlands. I can have my equipment ready in about two hours." Tatau leaned forward. "How organised are you? How many people will be with us?"

Renai appreciated her enthusiasm, liking her no-nonsense attitude.

"Two interpreters, local boys and a Kiwi fellow, for protection."

"You know I will be using you to further my research. I just want to get that straight."

Renai laughed. "I fully understand."

Tatau stood. "I guess I should go and pack my gear."

It was market day on the foreshore of Bina Lagoon. Stalls had been erected to sell fruit and seafood and bright-coloured cloth; animals were put into hastily built corrals. Runabouts chugged across the lagoon, their owners nearly hidden by sale goods piled high.

On a grassy bank facing the lagoon, Renai sat with Tatau waiting for Alan to arrive on the Honiara ferry. They had been studying the terrain of the mountainous expanse of Mwaia on Tatau's laptop. Renai pointed to an upland section of the island.

"We have to be careful when we get up near cloud cover. There are sinkholes and caverns all over the upper reaches. Most of these are hidden by thin coverings of moss."

Tatau began one last run through of her medical supplies, which included a first aid kit and malaria vaccines stored in a chilled container encased in bubble wrap. Luti and La'akwai returned from the markets carrying bags of rice and salt as gifts to the upland Kwaio.

Renai sat up. "Here's the ferry."

Tatau's first sight of Alan startled her. "Look at the size of him. What's wrong with his skin?"

"Yes, he does turn heads. Alan used to work at a factory that refined precious metal, silver mostly; he worked at it for too long and absorbed it into his skin. Permanent, sad to say, but not harmful. He told me it's called argyria. Look at his pupils when I introduce you, he won't mind—they're jet black." Renai looked about the busy marketplace.

"You know, Tatau, this time of year it will be heavy rain every day on the upper slopes, with mudslides and falling rocks. Alan is the only person I know who could get us out of trouble should that happen—should anything happen. No helicopters to get us out."

She spoke in a whisper. "Strange, the locals aren't even staring at your friend."

"Alan's a local as well, these people have seen him before. They call him the shark man because of the grey skin."

Alan stepped up and whacked Renai on his shoulder. Renai staggered a little.

"Alan, this is Tatau, our doctor for the trip."

Tatau smiled. "Hey, nice to meet you."

So that's what silver does to a person.

Alan grinned. "Good to meet you, too."

Renai looked at his companions.

"Okay everyone, check your packs and pick up what you think you may need from the market. We are going to need food for three, four days."

Mid-morning of the second day Renai could no longer see the ocean. He realised that in Papua New Guinea, a lost trekker could be assured of eventually coming across a mining or logging camp, unless rebels found them first. On Mwaia there were no camps. Rich in old-growth hardwoods, the island had never been logged. Upland tribes fiercely protected their privacy. Up in the mist and torrential rain, the Kwaio lived a life unknown to the modern world. Theirs was a culture of strict tambu. To enter their world was dangerous, and Renai had long suspected what he might encounter when he arrived to plead his case for land rights.

At eight hundred metres the expedition was tired and drenched. The sun was a dim orange ball through the cloud covering. Renai leaned against a hardwood tree of the old-growth forest. He sipped tepid water from his canteen. His sago palm raincoat sat high on his reddish-blond Afro, protecting his head and shoulders from the downpour. He looked at each of his companions as they scratched themselves and brushed away bugs crawling on their exposed skin, seeing nothing of their faces underneath the palm hoods of their leaf coats. Luti, the Kwaio interpreter, was speaking with Tatau. Renai had noticed they had been in conversation quite a lot since leaving the Bina markets. He wondered if there was something between them. Luti looked at Renai briefly, then went back to discussing something with Tatau.

Alan was a little way down the trail, wearing his heavy back pack while doing push ups. La'akwai stood nearby smoking weed and grinning inanely at the tree canopy.

Renai walked down the trail and stood next to Alan as the big man stood.

"He keeps staring and smiling his dopey smile," Alan said. "Does he need to be high all the time?"

"Look, I'll have a word with him about his smoking. As for

the staring, you are a sight, and he's not met you before."

Alan stared into the wall of green. He craned his head to stare up at the cloud cover.

"What ever happened to that fella Lomu who was here studying the fish?"

Renai felt an itch on his neck and absently checked for ticks. "Marine toxins in sea snakes."

Alan frowned, turning to his friend. "Why d'you have to correct people all the time, Ren? You know who I mean."

Renai stopped poking about his neck. He hadn't realised he did that to people. "He went back to Auckland digging for Moa bones."

Tatau walked past Renai, her clothes sodden and the plastic covering her backpack dripping rainwater. Renai decided it was time for the second meal break of the day. "Let's take a rest, people."

Tatau leaned up against a tree and looked up the trail where rainwater was carving a channel. Runoff from the recent downpour cascaded from a muddy slope overhead. Through the spray, she could just make out the stocky form of Luti.

Renai checked the cloud cover. He knew he had to be careful on the ascent. Well-worn trails were washed away by flash floods. For many, attempting to scale the back of The Beast proved too hard—it broke them. What looked to be a flat rock at the side of an upward track could easily be a grey crust of limestone with a mesh of roots underneath, covering a hidden cave or narrow ravine.

Renai wondered what would happen once he met some of the Upland Kwaio. He hoped Luti was all he claimed and could help him and the others avoid all the social faux-pas which came with the strict societal ways of the Kwaio. He took his GPS from its plastic bag and switched it on. A moment later La'akwai and Tatau came to stand beside him, the plastic covering their packs being smacked by the heavy rain. Luti stopped next to him and shrugged his shoulders to adjust his backpack. Alan stepped up beside him and looked at Renai's GPS.

"How high are we?"

"Eleven hundred and twenty metres. We should start seeing bamboo forests and cycads a bit higher up."

Swathes of fern and scattered banyan trees covered the hillsides. Orchids of many colours reached for sunlight filtering down into small glades. A flock of bright-coloured parrots squawked and wheeled above a gap in the canopy. Luti looked down and idly picked a small lizard from La'akwai's plastic backpack covering and set it on a nearby tree trunk.

"We're close now to Kwaio outskirts," said Luti.

Renai looked at him. "How close?"

"Half a kilometre, maybe less; I saw crop gardens through the trees about a hundred metres back."

"You each know what's expected of you. What we say and how we behave in the first few moments will mean success or failure. To be sure, Luti, a quick run-through again please, so we're all straight on this."

"The Kwaio know of the outside world," Luti said, "but they have chosen to reject its ways. Don't think we are walking up to talk with a bunch of ignorant indigenous backwater folk. These people just want to keep their life and religion of their ancestors—magic and sorcery. When we are with them, we have to act as if we believe their ways. Watch their facial expressions. If we don't fit in straight away there will be trouble for us. There are strict rules. Don't laugh. Don't take photos. If you have to... um...urinate, ask someone. Point at yourself and they'll know and show you where to go." Luti looked at Tatau. "Unmarried girls and women go naked and married women cover their vaginas. Women visitors must go naked when entering a Kwaio village and are not accepted when they have their periods. I think once you have entered their space in the right way, someone will cover you, but I'm not sure."

Renai saw Alan and La'akwai look at Tatau.

"I don't bleed right now," she said and smiled at the gathered men, strangers only two days ago. "I'm a doctor, these things don't bother me." Tatau joggled her heavy backpack containing, among other things, the bags of salt she had brought as gifts. She smiled and looked at Renai. "You don't think I have come all this way without doing my homework, do you? I know what needs to be done."

Luti leaned in and spoke a few words to her. She laughed. Again Renai wondered what was going on between them.

"You might see some of the elders act strange, but do not speak with them," Luti said. "They have sacred rituals which we won't be allowed to see. The elders eat fungus and they see things. They go to sacred groves with stone circles up in the high country and speak secrets with things—the Ramo. I have to say again: do not speak with these elders. Remember, things will turn nasty if we break any of these tambus."

And there it is, thought Renai. *Ramo.* But Renai remembered the other word, the one not even spoken aloud by the coastal peoples, *the* word. He remembered the time on the cable ship *Sumatra Queen,* when he and his submarine winch crew, Marina and Fulcrum, had bought something strange up from the depths clinging to the winch arm. He recalled detention in a Guam military facility; the debriefing sessions and the warning of silence—the breaking of that silence with the story he had told Lomu, the New Zealander. It all came back to him, memories he'd tried to put behind him.

"Damned thing—damned memories following me."

He walked a few metres up the track and checked the cloud cover. Looking back, he noticed the men were watching Tatau. She held something yellow in one hand. Renai heard one of the men respond to something she must have said.

"Strange. I've not heard of that."

"What we have here is the honey mushroom fungus. I've read articles. For a sighted person, the licking of this fungus causes partial temporary blindness. Takers hallucinate and the brain tries to make sense of partial information. The eyes send messages and the brain is trying to fill in the gaps." Luti stared at Tatau. "I hope you are not thinking of finding the stones where the elders go. You can't go to the stones. Didn't I say they were tambu?"

Tatau spread her hands.

"Well, we'll have to find some samples elsewhere."

Luti pursed his lips and slowly shook his head.

"I am not liking this. No. It is said that when the elders take the rock fungus, they see the Shadow Men—the Ramo. Legend has it, Ramo wear people alive as cloaks sewn to their own bodies, flesh to flesh. The living human is left in agony with no food or water to keep it alive, so the victim dies slowly, being flapped about whenever the Ramo moves. The victim dies in terrible hunger. Another Ramo scoops out the organs, leaving only a rattling cloak of bones and dried skin." He looked at each of the assembled group. "But if we talk about collecting fungus or mention this spirit race to our hosts, we will have our throats cut."

Tatau wrinkled her nose. "Charming."

Renai beckoned the group to him

"People, everything aside, when we get to the outskirts, we stand at the edge of their village and wait to be invited."

Thunder accompanied the thickening rain. Renai felt a tap on his arm. Turning, he saw Luti trying to see through the close-pressed trunks of the hardwood forest. Luti straightened and sniffed the air. He smelt strong herbs.

"We have company."

Two copper-haired warriors led Renai's group into the village. With just the backpack containing medical supplies hanging from her shoulders and a bag of salt held in one hand, Tatau walked naked into the village. Renai followed and could not stop staring at Tatau's behind. He noticed La'akwai looking at the village huts and saw Alan's discomfort. Renai knew Alan was trying to look anywhere but at Tatau's nakedness.

The compound area was surrounded by huts and meeting houses of various sizes which sat on raised stumps amid enormous banyan trees, their arboreal roots falling to the ground like the wooden bars of prison cells. Tatau paced across the packed earth. Renai could see how she was taking this in her stride. She kept her pace regular and her head held high. She managed to take in her surroundings while she walked a little unsteadily towards a group of elders in traditional wear—feathers and local weavings—waiting for the group to approach. Off to one side were a group of women, tall, bare-breasted, the elder ones wearing colourful twisted cloth around their hips, bound around their vaginas. Renai saw how straight they stood, stately and obviously proud. Behind them children peeked out. Tatau saw a lean people, taut-muscled and well-nourished with healthy skin. Full-length leg and torso tattoos were on display, the green and black ink making the Kwaio an intimidating sight. Luti stepped up to Tatau and whispered to her.

"Remember what I said, okay?"

Renai followed Luti and Tatau. Looking ahead at the elders, he saw them conferring and staring at something behind him. Turning, Renai saw they were discussing Alan.

The two warriors leading the group stopped and stood to either side. Renai stepped up to stand beside Tatau. One of the elders, a tall lean man with a parrot-feather headdress and a woven loin cloth, stepped forward. The man leaned to one side and regarded Alan. Ignoring the others, he motioned Alan forward. Alan didn't hesitate. He stepped forward and stood eye to eye with the elder. Renai saw Alan bow his head for a few seconds and then look up. The elder smiled and turned to the other men behind him. One of them said something and the elder facing Alan grinned. When he spoke, Renai was surprised to hear English words.

"Grey man, shark man, hmmm." The elder smiled, showing stained teeth. He looked at the gifts bought by the group and nodded approval. He raised his arm and with a flick of his fingers motioned the others of the group forward. Renai stared at Alan

'Who would have thought he would be the one to get us accepted?'

Another Kwaio stepped forward. This man was old, with a mane of white hair and a posture suggesting great fitness. He pointed to Alan and La'akwai and motioned them to him. Renai knew La'akwai was stoned and a little paranoid. He went with Alan and stood beside the white-haired elder. The old man glanced at him, looking unimpressed. He looked at Alan and reached out and touched his skin. Alan remained still. The elder leaned closer, looking into Alan's eyes, studying the black pupils. The old man smiled, nodding approvingly. Alan seemed to have no idea what was happening. The elder lightly grasped Alan's arm and led him towards some women and a curious group of chattering children. The elder jerked his head indicating La'akwai should follow.

In a long lodge constructed from banyan and thatch, Tatau, Renai and Luti sat cross-legged on woven mats. Opposite, the tribal elders faced them. Fruit and water skins were bought in by a young warrior and placed on the mat between them. Renai saw Luti nudge Tatau. She spoke, and Renai was surprised she did not speak English—she was speaking to the elders in Kwaio. Renai had his mouth open and stared at Luti.

"So that's what they've been discussing. He's been teaching her Kwaio."

He cursed himself for not having prepared better. He watched the elders nodding as first Luti and then Tatau spoke Kwaio. Renai saw Tatau indicate with a finger the symbol of a needle going into her arm. Tatau held her hand flat with palm down, indicating a small person. The elders nodded and one turned to Luti and spoke a few words. Luti nodded. There was silence for a few moments as the elders conferred. Finally one looked directly at Tatau. He held his hand above the ground to suggest something small. He nodded and Renai saw Tatau's shoulders drop a little as if she was relieved. He knew then she had been given permission to inoculate the children of the village. Luti had been right. These people did know what went on out in the world; they simply chose to ignore that which did not directly affect them.

Renai nodded, smiling. He was not being upstaged or forgotten at all. The elders were simply getting other business out of the way before seeing to his needs. Renai felt relieved. Tatau shuffled backward. She bowed her head for a moment and smiled at the elders. Tatau said something which Renai guessed might be "thank you" and then she left the lodge.

Luti motioned to Renai. "It's time, my friend. Let's do this. I'll interpret."

Renai shuffled across and joined him. They both looked expectantly at the elders before them. One stared for a moment at Renai. With a flick of his hand he motioned for the discussion to begin. A few times during the negotiations, Renai regretted not having had the foresight to learn a few basic phrases of at least one Kwaio dialect. He had been planning this for so long and he had not even given thought to the one thing he so needed right then. As he spoke, he listened to Luti interpret. Each time he waited for a response and when it came, Luti related back to him what was said. Negotiations continued for half an hour. Luti and Renai waited tensely for a decision from the elders. It was Kwaio ancestral lands. Even by the coast, Upland Kwaio held dominion. Luti held out his hands, palms up, towards the elders. Even Renai knew this signified a certain defeat. He felt saddened that it had come to this—all the effort and stress had come to nothing. He heard Luti speaking to him.

"Hey, don't look so down. They agree."

"What—*What?*"

"It's okay, Renai. You have your land grant. It's just not that big."

Renai stared at the elders. Without turning, he spoke.

"How big are we talking?"

Luti thought for a moment.

"Ninety longhouses, that's about…um…twenty acres."

Renai turned to him.

"Twenty acres? That's not"—he thought for a moment before speaking— "twenty acres." He laughed and stopped short. He looked at the elders and saw them watching him. He turned to Luti.

"Hey, that's actually pretty good." Renai felt a great relief settle upon him.

Outside the elders' lodge, Luti and Renai met up with Alan and La'akwai. Tatau joined them, wearing a twisted coloured cloth covering her hips and thighs. Renai checked the time on his GPS.

The group was provided with dried meat and cooked taros and yams. They took their gifts and were escorted to the edge of the village, and there Tatau was able to retrieve her clothes and boots. Alan and Luti shouldered their backpacks. Renai realised they would have a couple of hours of hard travel back down the island trail before they set up camp for the night. He turned to his companions.

"I can't thank you enough for all you have done. Without—" He looked at Tatau and Luti. "Thank you." He glanced up and saw clouds promising more rain. "So, let's go home." He turned and started down the muddy track.

Tatau walked up behind Renai
"Let's take a little detour before we go down."

Renai shrugged his backpack into a more comfortable position. "Sure. Where do you want to go?"

Tatau stared ahead. "Up, just a little way."

Renai saw where she was looking. "What, up there? There's no trail."

Tatau looked at her boots sinking in the mud. "I'll make one. You have a good result. Now I need mine. Let's go up there and find a level place to make camp."

"Fine, let's go. But you're cutting the path."

Tatau pointed to the machete in Renai's belt. "I'll take that."

Alan stopped behind them. He looked up the slope Tatau had pointed to. "Oh, now that's nasty. Nice job today, Tatau. I'll make camp when we get up there. We can go home tomorrow."

Renai struggled up the muddy slope and followed Tatau onto a flat expanse of short highland heather with a surround of cycads. Luti and Tatau discarded their backpacks. Renai watched La'akwai pull a rolled smoke from his shirt pocket. He lit up, blowing a mouthful of strong dope which clouded the air about the faces of the group.

"There's no stopping you," said Alan.

La'akwai grinned and inhaled.

Tatau smiled as she looked up at the canopy. "It's just an extra day, Renai. I'm sure I can find some fungal specimens before we leave."

Alan and La'akwai were busy folding tents when Renai woke. He left the tent and saw the cycad forest and thought it looked like something from a dinosaur movie. Clouds had gathered and seasonal rain fell. Renai heard a swish of someone walking through grass bordering the camp. Turning, he saw Tatau walking with some plastic bags, her sago palm rain hood flapping from its string tie around her waist. She smiled.

"Morning. I've samples—not honey fungus, but these should tell me something when I get back to the hospital."

Renai nodded and stretched, then began helping break camp.

Alan packed the tents. He saw Luti coming back with a container of spring water.

"I found a path over there leading down through some rocks," Luti said.

The way out was a ravine leading the explorers through a cliff-lined path, funnelling them out onto a flat grassy field. Luti walked out into the space. He stopped and stared at a circle of enormous standing stones. He recalled what had been mentioned regarding the Kwaio elders and he knew they had stumbled upon a sacred site. Some vague warning flitted through his consciousness. He looked at the weathered petroglyphs covering the rock faces and at the yellowish green mossy substance clinging in patches to the carvings.

La'akwai wandered out from the ravine. He dropped his pack on the flat ground and hurried across to one of the standing stones. Without hesitating, he put his face up to the surface and licked a patch of moss.

Renai followed Tatau, Alan and Luti out onto the flat expanse, a natural amphitheatre with five-metre cliffs. Renai saw what La'akwai was doing. "No. Come on!"

La'akwai grunted. "This stuff is supposed to make you able to see the afterlife."

Renai glared at him. "A hallucinogen?"

"So I have heard."

Renai wiped rain from his face. "Come on. Stop that!"

Luti looked at Renai. "We should not be here, it is tambu. If we're caught, we're all going to see the afterlife."

Renai looked at the massive stones of the circle.

"One of the sacred places. I grew up on the coast hearing of this."

Alan had dropped his backpack onto the ground inside the stone circle and was wandering about looking at the surrounds. Tatau took a zip top plastic bag and a penknife from her jacket. Renai watched her take a scraping from a mossy growth on one of the stelae. He was going to say something when he felt Luti poke him in the ribs.

"Why do hospital people have to pick and poke?" Luti asked.

"They want to know how things work."

Tatau bagged the sample. Renai saw Alan with his face up next to one of the standing stones, tasting the yellow-green mat.

"Oh, come on, Alan, not you too. We need you to watch out for us."

La'akwai spoke. "We need to leave. This is not a place for us."

Tatau nodded with her back to him. "Yes, yes. Just give me a few minutes."

La'akwai became insistent. "Now, Doctor, please, we have to find our way back."

"Yes. I'll only be a moment."

Alan looked up one of the huge standing stones. He ran his hands over the pitted surface and the weathered carving, his fingers tracing the lines of the petroglyph. He looked at Renai.

"Yeah, alright, we should go. I don't want to get caught here by our Kwaio friends".

Tatau shrugged out of her backpack and placed it on the muddy ground. Rain thickened. She walked around inside the stone circle. At a point farthest from the ravine entrance, she knelt on a limestone outcrop on the lip of a large hole. She lay on her stomach and peered down into the darkened depths, thinking there might be fungus growing near the top. Below, she could see a series of serrated edges, sharpened in a spiral caused by flowing water from the frequent rain. Beneath an overhang she could see vines and creepers poking out from hidden recesses. The edge of bushes scraped against her arms as she leant further into the hole.

Alan spoke from above her. "Hey, careful, you'll fall in. Here, I'll hold your ankles."

Tatau nodded. "Thanks. I want a quick look to see."

Alan knelt and held her as she leaned over the now muddied edge and peered down. She felt the rain spatter across her back. With her head below ground level, Tatau looked for growths. She heard a noise and lifted her head. She blinked and stared at the opposite wall, just below eye level. Something flickered across the far wall. Tatau stared at the wall and thought she saw a shadow pass back and forth over a lighter patch. A slithering sounded to her left. A shadow appeared a little closer, as if something furtive was travelling unseen around the wall toward her. She felt a sudden panic and cried out.

"Pull me up. Pull me up."

She felt Alan's hands tighten about her ankles and she was pulled forcefully from the opening. As her head left the edge of the pit into open air, Tatau saw the entire far wall of the opening just below ground-level ripple, like a jelly mould poked by a questing finger. Tatau sat on the ground and breathed deeply.

Alan stepped closer to the edge of the cliff face, trying to find a little shelter from the rain. A rumble and a crack sounded from above. A section of the cliff detached and slid down towards where Alan was standing.

Through the driving rain, Renai saw the cliff face seem to split. A deluge of water cascaded over the lip. A scraping rumble sounded. Tatau backed away from the cliff face and stood with Luti and Renai.

Alan stepped forward away from the wall and peered up into the rain. "What *is* that?"

Renai shouted his warning.

They watched a grey shape slide over the edge of the rock face. The boulder hung for a moment and fell. Part of an inside edge caught the side of the cliff and the boulder, weighing many tonnes, flipped outward, turning as it fell.

Alan turned to run. He slipped on the muddy ground. His leg

slid sideways and he heard a snap. He cried out in agony and a red-smeared white bone tore a jagged hole through the side of his left calf muscle as he slid across the muddy ground, feeling the spatter of spray from the outer edge of the cascade. He heard voices in the driving rain shouting his name. Through the pain he managed to look up in time to see the huge boulder falling. Next moment he felt a great weight as he was pressed into the mud. There was nothing for a moment. Alan felt numb. The pressure of the boulder had turned him over a little and now his face was half submerged in the water and mud. As he tried to breathe he felt water go up his nose. He exhaled with a snort and mud and a bubble of water were ejected. He struggled and managed to lift his head. Water flowed into his mouth. Another wave of pain hit him. The weight of the boulder pressed his body further into the mud. Under the weight, a section of ground near the mouth of the hole dislodged and fell. Alan was washed over the edge and down in a rushing river of water and mud. Through his pain he glanced back over his shoulder and in the dim light and pouring rain, he saw the forms of his companions swept with him over the edge into the surrounding darkness.

Tatau's fall had been softened by the deluge of mud and shingle. She'd landed on the moss at the bottom of the recently opened cave. With the roof now collapsed, earth and muddy water swept down into the lightless depths. Tatau was able to see out of the opening some metres overhead. The rain was thinning and the cloud cover parted to show clear sky. She felt as if she was lying at the bottom of a wide chimney. She heard someone babbling and turned to find the source. She recognised La'akwai's hair. He was curled up into a ball and talking to himself. She saw him jerk a shoulder, then again. To her it looked as if someone had poked his shoulder and he was shrugging away from the touch. She thought is must be the effects of the hallucinogen.

He shouted something and turned to her. La'akwai's face was contorted, as if he was terrified of something. He thrust his hands out in front of him in an attitude of defence. Behind her Tatau heard another sound, a kind of gurgling moan. She sat up and, in the light filtering down from above, she saw the shirt Alan wore showing above a depression in the thick moss. She crawled over and knelt next to him. She saw his fibula, washed clean of blood, thrusting from his torn trousers. Alan's face was white and Tatau knew he had lost a lot of blood. He looked up at her and attempted a smile.

"Tatau, I hurt, bad."

She realised her medical bag was somewhere overhead outside the cave. She reached down and cradled Alan's head. She felt the sharp edge of a protruding sliver of basalt rock behind Alan's ear where it entered his skull. She held her breath and felt tears form in her eyes. She tried to keep her voice steady.

"Shhh, fella. We will sort something out."

Alan smiled through his agony. "My head is numb."

Tatau watched him watching her. She saw him press his teeth together in some manly effort not to cry out. Unable to move his head he swivelled his gaze, attempting to see through the gloom. His mouth was stretched wide in silent agony. He relaxed a little and coughed up a spurt of blood which sprayed Tatau's face and trickled down from the bridge of her nose and across her cheek. She peered into Alan's eyes, knowing he was so close to going. He looked at her again, seeming to be cross-eyed. He shifted his gaze.

"Tat. I see them. They are…they are…*big*."

Tatau saw Alan's eyes widen. She shuddered.

"No!"

Tatau tried to comfort him in his last moments. She looked at his face and realised Alan was not actually looking at her, he was looking just over her shoulder. She felt a soft breeze behind her, ruffling her hair. A cry from behind made her jump. It was La'akwai. Again the movement, an exhalation puffed against her hair. Then, still cradling Alan's head, Tatau felt something touch the back of her head. Feather-like at first, it became insistent. Tatau felt an encroaching terror. She kept her head still and dropped her gaze to look down at Alan. She saw the loose muscles of his face. The lips had drooped and were pressed up against one of her palms. She knew he was gone. She lowered his head and manoeuvred her hands so she was able to lay his face against the soft moss. She closed her eyes and breathed deeply. The feeling of being rubbed on her head stopped. Tatau lay still for a moment.

A strange smell like herbs burning alerted her to something close, something behind her. She was horrified at her predicament. She felt a pressure—something seemed to be crawling up the outside of her left thigh. She jerked her arm and swept her open palm up the length of her pants. There was nothing there. She clenched her teeth together in an effort not to make a sound. Something again touched her hair. Slowly she turned. There was nothing behind her.

Tatau watched her boots sink a little into the spongy moss. In the gloom she could see growths—etiolated plants, their leaves blanched, growing without light—clinging to the cave walls. Her thoughts centred. At first she wondered what had been missing from the picture. La'akwai was no longer there. For a moment she thought she saw a flickering just in front of her face, as if there was some movement right up against the rock face. She reached out and touched the place. Her fingertips brushed something soft and she jerked her hand away. For some moments she stared at the spot. She felt afraid and moved away.

Where were Renai and Luti? She leant down as if that would aid her in seeing into the gloom of the further recesses of the newly opened cave. She could see nothing back there and was reluctant to venture into that dimness. She looked down at Alan's broken body. There came a whisper from all about her as if voices were trying to get her attention. Tatau turned, but could see nothing tangible. She looked up and saw by the aid of the light that there were handholds where she could climb out of the cave. She wondered if La'akwai had found his way out while she had been tending to Alan. With one look back at Alan's slumped form, Tatau stepped across some fallen rocks and put her hands up against the surface of the chimney of the cave. Then came the awful feeling she was not alone.

La'akwai had been facing towards Tatau when she had cradled Alan's head. His back was against the wall when he felt it ripple against him. He felt strange, as if he was being lifted into the air. Something came down in front of his face. He tried to move and struggle against the descending sheet but found he could not. Again the wall rippled at his back and seemed to recede. La'akwai began to cry out as he sank into the rock. The film thickened around his face. Now he could only vaguely see the outline of Tatau. He called out to her, but the meshy substance covering his face fell into his mouth. He saw Tatau approach the wall where he lay, but he knew by her actions that she could not see him. She reached out and he felt her fingertips touch his throat. She drew her hand back. She appeared confused and frightened. La'akwai felt the wall at his back open. He slid into the gap and the meshy substance tightened, thickened. He screamed, the sound muffled by the ever-tightening gauze of the face covering. The wall opened further.

Tastebuds across the wide expanse of wet rock drank in the flavour of live food. Denticles covering the huge tongue ground against each other, shredding La'akwai's clothes and raking his flesh. The throat opened and the creature swallowed him whole.

Tatau stood on the flat ground outside the circle of stones. Ahead, near the entrance to the narrow ravine, Renai had taken a length of nylon rope from a backpack. He was in the act of returning to the collapsed cave entrance. Tatau turned and looked back down into the aperture and could no longer see Alan. She turned at the sound of Renai approaching. He stopped and looked at her, saw the look on her face and he knew it to be true.

Outside the stone circle, Renai sat heavily on the muddy ground. Tatau knelt and put a hand on his shoulder.

"I'm sorry. There was nothing you could have done, we could have done. I'm sorry, Renai."

Renai found his mouth was too dry to speak. He swallowed and worked up some saliva. "What about the others?"

Tatau shook her head. "La'akwai was down there with me, but he seems to have vanished. Luti? I don't know." She paused and looked at Renai. "I'm sorry about Alan. He was crushed — that huge boulder, you know."

Renai put a hand gently on Tatau's arm. He began to tremble.

He exhaled loudly and tried to keep his emotions in check. "Just the two of us." He began to feel afraid. "We can't manage without Luti and La'akwai. Alan is a big fellow. We're going to have to go back to the coast and get help. We can—we can find this place again with the GPS.

Tatau nodded. "Yes. Yes, that's best."

Renai looked at the surface of a nearby standing stone. As he stared, he thought he saw a ripple glide across the expanse, causing a patch of moss to move. The colouration of the stone's face seemed to darken and then lighten. Variegated mineral veins radiated out to the edge of the stone. Renai blinked and for a moment thought he saw the outlines of a monstrous creature.

"Do you smell that?"

Tatau sniffed the air. She frowned and sniffed again.

"Yes. It smells like…cooking meat."

Renai looked across the natural amphitheatre. Tatau saw he was panicky.

"Let's call Luti, he has to be here somewhere."

Tatau walked towards the entrance of the ravine, calling out for Luti. No answer came. She walked through the twisting passage to the outside entrance. The mud was deep and showed no bootprints. Returning, she called again, but still Luti did not respond. On her way back to meet Renai, Tatau walked past a standing stone with deep-carved petroglyphs. As she glanced at the stone's face, she thought she saw the surface ripple. She stopped and blinked in the sunshine. Lifting her arm, she shaded her eyes and looked again. For a moment she thought she saw movement, reminding her of a wriggling fish burrowing into sand to hide itself, before lying still and waiting. She could not see Renai, but she heard him calling out for Luti. Tatau waited but there was no answering call. She walked past the standing stone and followed the sound of Renai's voice.

Luti was trapped and held immobile. He watched in confusion as Tatau seemed to stare straight at him, her face so close to his. She'd frowned and stepped backward, turned and walked away. Luti tried to call to her but his mouth was covered by something.

He felt something close about his ankles and apply pressure. His vision blurred as if a film had dropped across his eyes. He shouted, but his voice was muffled as something fell into his mouth. He coughed but could not dislodge it. Not able to turn his head, he followed Tatau's passing by swivelling his eyes. She walked from view. The pressure on his ankles tightened and now he felt something slide upward. His lower legs were surrounded by something, and he was held firm. He tried to kick his feet but was unable to budge. He felt heat intensifying about his lower body. He gasped for air and waited a moment. The heat grew and through his clothing he began to feel himself burning. He struggled in panic and felt pressure all over his body as he was held fast. His clothing was being burned from his body and he felt the scorching heat upon his flesh. He tried to cry out but the gauze choked his throat. Luti felt a searing heat burning his ankles; he screamed as his legs became scorched. Flesh peeled off.

Tatau stepped away from the colossal standing stone and made her way into the centre of the circle. She shivered and stopped. There was a shimmering in the air above. She looked up at the tops of the stones. The space appeared to ripple; she saw the change, but only briefly.

All about the stones, between them and even the walls of the amphitheatre began to ripple as if in a heat haze. The shapes of the standing stones bent and formed odd angles. The surrounding cliff walls seemed to Tatau to vanish and then reappear as a different formation. The walls changed back. She looked up in time to see the patch of cloudless sky alter and discolour from azure to green and back. She blinked and the entire area above her head, including the tops of the standing stones, turned over, flipped, like a billboard made from metal panels or pixels all changing in unison to reveal another sign beneath. For the briefest moment Tatau saw a writhing movement, as of something immense overhead, briefly revealed and then once again hidden from view. She gasped at the revelation of that one glimpse: she thought she saw flashing colours streak upward on some vast amorphous creatures towering between the stones, then the stones and the entire surrounds re-flipped and Tatau saw things were as they had been. She gave a shout of terror, desperately wishing to get away from the stones, feeling as if the great weights would topple down upon her, crushing out her life.

She spied Renai and noticed he held a strip of moss in his hand. She watched him raise it to his mouth and start eating it. She saw the look of greed upon his face. Tatau realised it was the same kind of moss the others had licked for their hallucinatory effects. Tatau felt she should try to stop him, but all desire for decisive action had departed. She watched Renai sit on a boulder near the centre of the stone circle and began wolfing down the fat clump of moss. In the space above her head, things seemed to have returned to how they were. She felt the air charged with energy and realised it felt good. She no longer felt afraid standing next to the huge standing stones. She looked at Renai and frowned. Her feelings of lethargy weakened and she decided to stop him eating the clump of moss.

Renai sat on the boulder inside the circle of stones. He held what he thought to be a fat bread roll between his teeth and chomped down. He chewed the bread and swallowed. Noticing Tatau staring strangely at him, Renai grinned and took another mouthful of the roll. He began to feel lightheaded. He saw the stones of the circle appeared to have altered shape and somehow moved closer to where he sat. He glanced again at Tatau and saw she too had moved closer. He stared wide-eyed at his companion and was surprised to see she looked taller and, wider. He blinked and jumped when he felt a touch upon his arm. He looked up and saw Tatau's face far above him. He watched in growing fascination as her face seemed to melt and her smile detached itself from her face. Her mouth was twisted and blue and he thought he saw laughter in the shape of circles coming from between her brown and blue lips. He laughed and took another bite from his bread roll. He felt a flapping near his mouth. He saw an enormous moth with thick legs which seemed to want to steal his bread roll—it kept grasping it and Renai kept jerking his hand away. He heard someone speak to him as the moth scrabbled about his face.

"Grobbin amerong mffitahh. Nnnnnnn-op!"

Renai laughed and tried to take another bite from the bread roll, but the moth had it in its legs and was pulling it from his grasp.

Tatau was finding the entire episode rather frustrating. She pulled the clump of hallucinogenic moss from Renai's grasp.

"Renai, oh, come on. Let go!" She threw the chewed moss across the grass between the stones. "Come on, Renai, get a grip."

Renai stared up at her with his mouth open. Tatau began to feel the change in the space about her. She felt cold. She glanced down and saw the look of growing panic upon Renai's face. She wondered what was happening to his befuddled mind. He was not actually looking at her, but past her, up into the air above their heads. Her thoughts raced. She wanted to curl up on the ground, away from the feeling of tremendous pressure pushing down from above. Her mind shrunk away from the oppressive feeling sapping her life force. She felt she was being psychically drained and she wanted to cry. She looked down with horror at Renai's face and saw the contorted mouth, the crinkled forehead and the eyes staring at something, something above. Then against her will, Tatau moved her body under that weight and turned her head to look up.

Nothing.

She heard Renai move in the mud. He had fallen off the boulder and was now squirming on the ground with his mouth stretched wide. But no sound came from him. He wasn't breathing. She balled her hand into a fist and punched his chest. He gasped and let out a wheezy rush of air. He took a long breath and, still looking past her above their heads, he began screaming and trying to snake away on his back through the sodden grass. Again he ran out of breath with his mouth open, unable to draw breath; again Tatau punched his chest. And he breathed and screamed. Now Renai had flipped over and was on hands and knees, crawling away. Tatau felt something wispy touch her exposed neck. She stopped and let out a sob of terror.

She turned and looked up. The air was somehow moving but she saw nothing. She flicked her gaze towards Renai and saw something on the periphery of her vision—something moving. With terror mounting, she held her gaze on one spot of grass and at the edge of her vision she saw red wetness ebb and flow. She rolled her eyes towards the movement and the moving shapes stayed in place. Tatau turned her head slightly towards the movement and she saw. Appendages, huge and glistening, pierced with stick-like stalks, shifted and scraped together about her, filling the place between the standing stones. Great wide eyes opened on wrinkled hide, blinked, and the mass of red flesh dripped moisture and moved closer, pressing down upon the amphitheatre. The earth beneath Tatau shifted and the sound of rock under the grass crunched and splintered. The standing stones seemed to melt at their edges as the living things altered shape. Tatau closed her eyes and fell to the grass and lay on her side. She listened and felt but did not hear shapes and presences shifting and sliding. Something touched her leg and she was grabbed and tugged a little along the ground. Too horrified to resist, she began sobbing. She was released and lay mute and gasping for air in the suffocating surrounds. Turning her head to one side, it sunk a little into the soft ground. She saw Renai's head close by, pressed up against one of the standing stones. She saw the rock face wobble as would a jelly mould. A rasping sounded, reminding her of something being roughly shaved. Renai's shoulders were heaving and his back arched, then fell; the action was repeated again, then again. He made no sound but the movements continued and seemed to Tatau as if he was a puppet being jerked on its strings. A suspiration sounded close by her head, as if there was something at her throat but just out of view. Something pressed against her body, feeling like soft dough pushing insistently. Tatau saw Renai's head flush against the stele. She felt a pressure on her consciousness and an invasion of her thoughts. She heard someone cry out the word "Mama".

When it was relayed to the Kwaio elders that none of Renai's group had passed by the village gardens, the elders sent their people to find the missing visitors. It was not until late afternoon when Tatau and Renai were found amid the circle of standing stones. With the reverence accorded their sacred place, the elders had Tatau and Renai removed. On hastily-made bamboo litters, the pair was taken by selected warriors back down the twisting trails to the coast. As quietly as they had come, the Kwaio left Renai and Tatau in the care of the Bina Lagoon people and vanished back into the forest.

Renai had not fared well. He lay on his woven mat out on one of the small lagoon islets he had spilled blood to build with coral and earth. Tatau stayed with Renai for three days, calling her hospital for supplies to be delivered by motor boat. She saw as best she was able to Renai's horrific wounds. Under her ministrations, his condition slowly improved. But it was his face that had everybody wondering what had taken place up in the Kwaio highlands of The Beast. The left side of Renai's face was flattened as if it had been brutally scraped back and forth upon some immense grater. His ear was missing and there was no longer any skin upon his lower jaw or upon his cheek. The rounded bone on both areas had been shaved flat and the tatters of fleshy surrounds appeared to have been cauterised, melted as if his face had been dipped in acid. Looking at Renai as she tended him on his woven mat under his thatch roof shelter, Tatau knew something had happened to both of them, but she felt as if there were memories missing from her experience.

Within a week Renai was up and off his bedding. Despite the horrible damage to his face he seemed to suffer no lasting pain and did not complain of any discomfort. Although now physically strengthening, he appeared incapable of answering questions put to him regarding the ordeal.

It was Tatau who began feeling a delayed effect of the encounter up in the mountains. Over those days she vaguely recalled fleeting scenes from her time in the amphitheatre of the standing stones. Try as she might, she could not fit the pieces together. She remembered a whirling of great boulders; she remembered flying things. There might have been voices and rustlings in the air about her face, sighing of things not seen, but she could not be sure. She remembered being touched, an insistent exploration.

On the day of Tatau's departure for Kirakira hospital, Renai stood on the end of the Bina lagoon jetty as she boarded the inter-island ferry. She looked at him and he had smiled that timid smile and stood still like a lost child.

After that Renai was always toiling away raising garden beds in the land plots granted his people by the Upland Kwaio owners; he organised plantings and cultivation and always there was the quiet smile looking out of place on his ruined face. He never spoke again. His timid, faraway look suggested to all who knew, that Renai had seen the frightful gods of the Kwaio.

And He Shall Suffer for His Art

We were two alcohol and drug-fuelled young men renting a semi-detached on the CBD's edge. My friend Mack had lived on the same street as me growing up and we had been best friends since middle school. I had always been into computers and Mack had always been interested in art. I remember him drawing pictures in his school exercise books. He sold colour pencil drawings he did of tigers snarling and copies of panels from action comics to students so he could buy things he wanted.

Mack coasted through high school. He daydreamed in Biology classes and was not interested in anything but his art. Our group thought he was going to drop out, but he somehow made it through and did finish. He was never interested in going to uni. All he wanted was to set up a studio.

I went to uni to get the degree I was told was necessary for a secure future. Mack? Well, he took a job in a home hardware warehouse so he could earn easy money and live his dream. He spent most of his pay on drugs and alcohol and art equipment. His room in our share house was littered with canvasses, brushes, paints and easels.

On the weekends, when we had friends over, we would all gulp vodka and snort powder and end up doing silly things and tell each other sick jokes. We would babble stuff trying to talk over each other. Often Mack would stop halfway through a conversation and walk to his room to work on his art, inviting us in to watch him work on jungle scenes with exotic animals or science fiction paintings of planetary systems with futuristic craft.

Back then Mack was good company and we had great times in that house. He was always eager to show me and our friends his latest project. But something changed him. One day he seemed to close up, to shrink within himself. He stopped joining me or visitors in the lounge. The change in him was first noticeable with his conversation which, over a matter of weeks, became somewhat guarded. Whenever I asked him questions or engaged him in conversation his answers became monosyllabic and his tone was one of growing weariness.

I knew depression when I saw it. I was waiting for Mack to tell me about what was troubling him, but he never did.

One day, after a trying workday I sat in the lounge with my eyes closed, listening to birds outside in the trees and trying to wind down. Mack came in and sat in an armchair next to me. I opened my eyes and looked at him. He leaned over and spoke quietly to me.

"Rennie, there's something wrong with my phone. Every time I answer a call there's no one at the other end, but there's a sound much like a cicada buzzing."

I remember staring at him and not really understanding what he was saying. But now, looking back, I realise it was when the real problem started.

I know Mack continued painting in his room because he would come out in his painting smock to fix coffee or to make a sandwich. During these times he never instigated a conversation. He was polite when I showed interest in hearing what he was doing, but he made me feel as if I was bothersome and this made me feel uncomfortable and hurt.

One day he came home with an electric jug and a toaster, which he took to his bedroom studio. This was the first of his actions which saw him become increasingly detached from me and his other friends. He became secretive. When I did see him about the house his hands and his forehead were smeared with paint. At this time I realised he had stopped using bright colours and had begun to favour dark ones.

In late spring, Mack quit his job. He just stayed in his room and worked at his easels most of the day and into the night. I guessed he had a decent savings account, because he paid the rent and his share of the bills and was always ordering in food.

Eventually Mack stopped showing me his work and that too hurt, because he had always valued my opinion. He looked thinner every time I saw him. He eventually stopped even saying hello to me. Although I tried many times to draw him out so he would talk to me about what was troubling him, I was unable to get him to confide in me.

Mack became a recluse. I would wake at night to the sound of him pounding his fists on his desk. And there was the muttering. Through the walls I couldn't actually hear what he was saying, but I figured he was talking to someone. There were no pauses in what he was saying, so I guessed he could not have been having a conversation on his phone. Some of the words I heard made no sense. His increasing secrecy became intolerable to me. He would wait until I had gone to my room before he would come out. Sometimes when I walked into the lounge past his room I saw his door shut. It was as if he wanted to come out but quickly retreated when he knew I was about. I felt guilty because I know I should have made more of an effort in order to help him with whatever he was going through. Instead I took the easy way out and stopped caring. Then came what I had been dreading, the breakup of the house.

It was such a relief when I approached Mack to tell him I was moving out. He took the news with a mere shrug, then went back to his room. I held my anger in check and went about looking for a cheaper place to live on my own.

It took a while, but eventually we found separate residences. Mack did move, but it wasn't through his own assertiveness, I had to take responsibility for him. I managed to find for him a double garage in the inner west for his art equipment and his clothes and canvasses and I even had to hire a removal van for him. It took a three-month advance payment of rent before Mack's new landlord agreed to allow Mack to use the garage as a live-in workspace.

I stood with Mack outside his new space. I could see his depression was deepening but felt helpless to act. I realised that

I couldn't help him unless I was asked. This made me angry. There was nothing left to say and I simply walked away.

It was a while before I began to feel settled. I put myself into my job in an effort to forget the breakup of the house and Mack's decline. Of course that did not work. So it was only a matter of weeks before my curiosity emerged.

One day after work I caught a cab to Mack's garage studio. I was surprised to find his landlord in the empty garage sweeping the concrete floor. He told me that Mack had moved all his stuff during the night. I realised I should have remained in touch with my friend. It was close to eight months before I saw Mack again.

It was coming on for winter; the last autumn leaves were a rain-sodden mess strewn through the city parks. One day after work I was walking past Central Station on my way home. I heard shouting across the road near the adjoining park. Turning, I saw a crowd gathered next to the bus stop. I crossed to see what was happening. Then I saw Mack. The face had aged and the once fit, upright body was now stooped, but I knew it was him. His appearance shocked me.

I stood watching, not quite knowing what to do. I was torn between wanting to rush over and rescue him from the situation, and with just turning and walking away. It would have been so easy to turn away. But I remembered all that we had once shared and I could not bring myself to abandon him like that.

I pushed aside onlookers and made my way closer to him. I saw that the coat Mack wore had the left sleeve missing and his arm was bare except for a soiled glove he wore on his left hand. As I neared, he drew an old rusted carpenter's blade down his right arm, opening up the flesh beneath. Blood oozed out and I heard some of the gathered crowd gasp. Mack turned sharply behind him and he growled out some words. It sounded something like: "And what would *you* know about creativity?"

I looked at the blood on his arm spilling down to spread across his wrist and in under the dirty glove. I was shocked at this gruesome act. I stepped in and put my hand on his shoulder. He smelled awful and his was hair was matted. He looked much older than I knew him to be and his unkempt state suggested that he had not bathed for some time. Mack looked at me, and slowly recognition came to those haunted eyes. They were the worst things about his appearance. He looked as if he was frightened of something. He blinked and then the tears came. He began to cry. He lifted his bare arm and clutched at my jacket. When he spoke, his voice could hardly be heard.

"Ren? Rennie. Oh, yes. I was hoping you'd come."

Mack used his other hand to wipe away his tears. I felt safe enough to reach up and take the knife from him. He let me, perhaps not even realising that I had done so. He gave a short, sharp laugh, and then abruptly stopped. His breath smelt horrible. Then he turned his head and hissed out a statement as if he was arguing with someone.

"He's a friend. Leave him alone."

I put my arm about Mack's shoulders and pushed our way through the crowd into the park where we could find some privacy. I felt like lashing out at the spectators, but I knew that it would not help matters. I felt ashamed owning to the fact that I knew this broken man. Amid the chatter and nervous laughing of the gathered crowd I led Mack to an unoccupied park bench. All the while he gripped my hand in his dirty bloody glove. I helped him sit. Sitting next to him, I was overcome at the smell of urine coming from him and his raggedy clothes. Mack gave a sob and wiped his runny nose on a lapel of his soiled jacket. I heard his breathing become more stable. Although I wanted him to let go of my hand and wished to get away from his stink I sat there, knowing he would eventually speak. Then he looked down and saw my hand in his. He jumped a little and let go. Then he looked at me, staring with that haunted gaze, attempting a smile with his sun-cracked lips. He stared at the concrete path, and then looked back up at me watching him. He spoke in short bursts, as if not quite knowing what to say first.

"I have wanted to see you. I didn't know how to find anyone. We get confused, you know. I…um…we have been hoping to find you. This confusion is not good for us. We didn't know how to find you—"

I was now almost in tears. I put up with the urine smell and just had to ask.

"What do you mean *we*, Mack? Who else is looking for me?"

Mack looked about, startled, as if he had given away some secret. He was frightened.

"I meant me. I mean me."

I felt a little unnerved and did the only thing I could think of. I patted his shoulder and tried to console him.

'It's okay, Mack. I'm here."

He blinked and sniffed.

"I...*We* have been wondering what become of you. And now you're here."

I tilted my head and looked at the sky. Right then I felt something ever so lightly brush across the back of my neck, just above my collar. Thinking it might be a floating strand of spider web, I rubbed my hand across the area. Turning back to Mack I saw him staring with horror at the back of my neck. When he saw me staring at him he changed his facial expression. Then as if to guide me in a new direction he spoke. This time he appeared more composed.

"Hey I'm sorry for all this. It's just that—you see, I get real involved in my painting and sometimes I forget to eat and, you know, wash." He looked embarrassed. He fumbled for words. "I mean, we were wondering if you might... We have a place a few blocks up the road above a shop. We're halfway through—"

I held up my hand to stop him babbling.

"What is it, Mack? Tell me. Spit it out."

Mack took a breath.

"We're halfway through a series of paintings. We're getting ready for an exhibition."

I found it hard to believe that a man in his deteriorated physical condition could complete a series of paintings, let alone contemplate holding an exhibition. I wondered fleetingly how he could afford painting equipment.

"You said *we're* painting. Who is *we*, Mack?"

He bared his decayed teeth. I was saddened to see this shell of the lively and humorous man I had shared a house with. Mack lowered his voice.

"I'm going to hold an exhibition soon with new works." He looked down at his bloodied arm, the blood looking like red tree branches. Then I guessed what he had been doing. It all came back; all the times he had come from his room in the house with red smeared on his painting smock or on his fingers. Now looking at his arm, I realised that he had all this time been painting with his blood. I felt queasy.

"Mack. Why?"

He became defiant, sitting upright and staring at me, all previous tears and emotional brokenness gone.

"You want to see the stuff or not?"

This assertiveness took me aback. Before I could properly think about what I was doing, I stuttered out an acceptance to his forceful invitation. I had immediate reservations about accompanying him, but I had committed myself. He leaned down and picked up a wet leaf from the footpath. His grimy jacket sleeve rode up his right arm and I saw the white scars crisscrossing his grubby skin, almost a mirror to his left arm, visible under the newly spilled blood. I knew they were old wounds, self-inflicted for his art. I wondered how the rest of his skin looked. Mack straightened and flicked his bloodied arm and I saw drops of blood fall upon the leaf. He held it up.

"That's art, Rennie."

I stared. I felt insulted.

"Mack, that's a leaf."

He glared at me.

I regretted saying that to a person of his sensibilities, but then I realised the man I was talking with was not the man I remembered. The smell of urine wafting from him was now not so overwhelming. I looked at my watch. Realising that might offend him, I tried to hide my action, but he appeared not to have noticed. He placed the leaf gently back onto the concrete and sat up straight.

"It's only a few minutes' walk. I'll show you our new stuff and see what you think. Okay?"

I frowned as I stood and I felt I had to keep him focused.

"There's only you and me, Mack, just us two."

He said nothing as he showed me through the park and along

the path to some traffic lights.

He led me from central station up a long hill to a place several blocks past a semi-industrial district. I was wishing I wasn't there. I wanted to go home and relax. I was in my own world, staring at the path while following reluctantly.

When I next looked up, I realised that I had followed Mack into a crossroad. I let him lead me up past some decaying shops that looked to have been closed for decades. I followed him across the road and he led me past a boarded-up shop, its side wall forming part of a laneway. I looked behind me, seriously contemplating returning to Central Station. Instead I turned back and resigned myself to see Mack's artwork. I followed him into this narrow confine and we walked past sagging iron fences with old nails lolling out of their holes.

At the rear side entrance of the boarded-up shop, Mack pushed through a gate and we crossed a patch of burned grass. Strewn about were bottles and piles of coiled wire. A shopping trolley lay on its side amid weeds. I ducked under a string clothes line as I followed Mack to a flight of wooden steps. As I looked about at the desolation of the place I felt that I too would despair should I have to live amid such a wasteland.

Now feeling anxious and all the more stupid for actually agreeing to follow Mack to his home, I began to wish it was all over. We climbed the stairs and made two turns before we reached a door at the top. I stood behind him as he fumbled for his key. While I waited for him to open the door, bare of paint except for a few flakes of faded green, I glanced above his head. What caught my attention was the symbol smeared on the boards above the door. The symbol had obviously been done some time ago and was a faded rusty colour in the shape of a hand. It was crudely done, as if in a hurry, but it was clear to me that this hand had seven fingers. The hand did not have a thumb, just seven fingers. It looked creepy and I again felt as if I should walk back down the stairs and away from my old friend.

Mack opened the door. A waft of foul-smelling air, a mixture of paint and rotten food, hit my nostrils. He held the door open and offered for me to go first. Right then I felt as if another cobweb had brushed across the back of my neck. I stepped across the threshold and looked about the cluttered space, thinking I had entered some awful hellish realm. From the light of a west-facing window, the only light able to reach the interior, I saw paintings hanging crookedly upon the walls. The smell was sickening; it was as if he had kept farm animals cooped up. Plates containing old food lay on a soiled bed which was shoved under the window. Old pizza boxes and empty Chinese food containers littered the floor. The riotous colour of the canvasses filling the wall space appeared to meld into one giant mural. Looking about at the colours and odd angles of the works gave me a feeling of vertigo. I could not look for long at some of the works because they were horrific images of violence—sharp axe-blades imbedded into people's flesh, their faces contorted into stretched frozen screams. It was then I realised that Mack was insane.

Mack clapped his hands. He smiled a smile I had never seen before. All I wanted to do was leave. He stopped smiling and stared at me, almost as if he had somehow read my mind. Then without warning, he turned and growled out a statement that suggested he may have heard someone insulting him.

"Enough! I will finish! It will be good." He turned back to me.

"Please, Rennie. Don't go yet—look at my new work, okay? Then go, if you must. Oh, you want a drink?"

I nearly choked in my haste to refuse.

"Oh, that's alright, Mack. I'm fine." Then I added, so as not to anger him: "Sure I'd like to see your new work. That would be good."

He clapped his hands again. Then he made me feel more uncomfortable. Although he had not flatted with me for nearly a year, he stripped off his coat and all but had to peel his one-sleeved shirt away. He was there in his pants, and then removed them. Now in his underpants he picked up his painting smock, smeared with crusty layers of dark colours. His body was scarred all over. Scars—some old and faded and pink—criss-crossed his chest and legs and arms, right up across his shoulders. Then there were the recent wounds, some half healed and some angry red open cuts. I could not look away. A gauze pad taped to one of his legs had blood seeping through, showing what looked freakishly like a pain-contorted face. I felt like crying.

Mack turned to a table cluttered with art paraphernalia. I glanced at the mess and saw what I thought was a plastic model of a fingertip, something Mack would collect for show. As he bent I saw the back of his neck fully for the first time that day. The flesh was scaly with raised, purplish welts, as if he was suffering from extreme eczema. He raised his hand and with his dirty fingernails scratched the area. Flakes of skin came free and drifted in the sunlight coming through the window. I covered my mouth and nose with my hand. He turned and I looked down and saw that he had taken a pair of secateurs from the table. My stomach tightened. I felt no fear for myself, only fear for him. With the secateurs, Mack pointed to a couple of paintings on easels which I guessed were works in progress. I really had no desire to look at them.

"This," he said, pointing, "is *The Sharp Smile*." In the centre-piece of the work were old school razor blades, the kind my granddad used, not painted, but real blades, bloodied, which he had somehow glued to the canvass. They were poking out from painted slices of bread—a gruesome three-dimensional razorblade sandwich. I saw teeth-marks on the blades. I looked at the corners of Mack's mouth and I saw the fresh pink scars running from the edges up along his cheeks. I felt ill, knowing he had actually lived the inspiration for this piece.

Flies buzzed and batted against the window. And I stood there in the middle of the room like a man caught in a net. Mack looked about his studio. When he regarded one or other of his hanging works I could not help following his gaze. The place was a nightmare made real. He turned to me baring his teeth in what I guessed he thought was a smile. He raised the secateurs and dragged them back and forth across the nape of his neck. I was shocked to see how scrawny that scaly neck was, set upon his stooped shoulders. He shuddered, grunting and moaning as if with pleasure. He pointed to the other painting, a riotous amalgam of blood and congealed oils.

"This one's called—but wait, let me show you."

I looked behind me at the door, wanting to escape. Instead I turned quickly back to face him, some part of my consciousness warning me that I was in danger. With a creeping feeling of dread, I watched Mack grip the secateurs, fumbling as he removed the stained glove from his left hand. I stared in disbelief when I saw his hand. Clotted blood covered his skin. It was some moments before I realised what I was looking at. *Two of his fingertips were missing.* I couldn't move, instead I stood gaping at that mutilated hand. The next few moments were a blur.

I saw Mack reach down with his good hand and pick up a jar from the cluttered, low table. The room's smell was nauseating me. Mack jiggled the jar in front of me. I saw two tiny spiders, the kind that bounce and jump, running about the bottom. Mack suddenly smacked the stumps of his fingers against the jar's side. He howled. Then he began to laugh. I stepped away. The stumps begin to ooze fresh blood.

I backed away, my mouth dry. Mack upended the jar and the little jumping spiders fell onto one of his finger stumps. He prodded the spiders and they jumped across to the nearest vantage point, his next finger stump; that finger was bleeding more, and the little creatures got stuck.

Mack laughed. He dropped the jar onto the floor and leaned down towards the cluttered table and with his right hand, already holding the secateurs, picked up a paintbrush. He straightened, facing me with a crooked grin. Lifting the brush, he stabbed the horsehair bristles down onto the tiny spiders, mashing them into the blood on the end of the stump. He pulled the paintbrush away and the glued spiders came with it. Mack turned to the second of his canvasses and swept a brushstroke across the bloodwork. Turning back to me, he cackled gleefully. Then what seemed as an afterthought, he punched the bloodied stumps of his left hand onto the canvass, leaving red circles like fat full stops, as if to say that it was now complete. I felt bile rise into my throat. Mack turned to me.

"Rennie, I call this *Spiders on the Stumps.*"

Mack's voice grew louder to my reeling senses. He was shouting, as if he was trying to talk over someone else in the room with us.

"You want another one? Alright, I'll give you another one, you parasitic fuck."

He dropped the paintbrush and gripped the secateurs. Then he closed the blades around one of the remaining fingers of his left hand. I turned my head away and closed my eyes, but I still heard the sickening *snick*. I groaned with fright, not even having the strength to stop him. I saw the spray of blood and the finger stump severed at the first joint sailing up into the air as if in slow motion. I ran for the door. I fumbled with the handle and finally managed to pull it open.

It must have been perversity that made me glance once more back into that terrible studio. That glimpse showed me enough. Crying out, I stumbled out and rushed headlong down the stairs. All the way down and across the yard to the gate leading to the alley, I felt as if someone was scrabbling with their fingers at the back of my neck.

That last glimpse back into Mack's studio is etched into my consciousness. What I heard and what I saw before jumping out onto the top of the stairway will haunt me forever. Mack was screaming.

"I won't listen. Do it. Just do it. Go to him!" Then Mack stuffed what looked to be severed finger stumps into each of his ears like two monstrous earplugs.

I have tried to keep my life in order since my visit to that blood-spattered studio, but it is becoming increasingly difficult. I can't sleep for more than a couple of hours at a time before I wake in fright. I feel weak and now I am unable to get myself out of bed in the mornings. I feel as if I have a weight on my shoulders, as if I am carrying a physical burden. The back of my neck has become very scaly and it itches terribly. The only thing that seems to give me relief is scratching the area with the pointy end of a pair of scissors.

Silent is the River

(This one's for Rick Kennett)

Edward Pellew Islands,
Gulf of Carpentaria, Australia

1

"*Mary Celeste,* Jack? We refurbish an old barge and turn it into a houseboat, and you name it *Mary Celeste*. Man, you might be picking a fight with fate here."

Jack was standing in his friend Jarra's runabout as it bobbed in the light swell of the marina. Brush in hand, he held the side of the houseboat to steady himself as he daubed a flourish on the final letter of the houseboat's name. He looked up. The sun was directly above Jarra, so all Jack could see was a mass of dark skin and a halo about the other man's windswept Afro. "I'm not superstitious, my friend."

Jarra watched an incoming trawler clear the breakwater of the marina. He saw the familiar lines of the fishing trawler *Lady Radcliffe* heading towards the houseboat. A scurry of movement out on the catch end of the deck showed him something was wrong.

"Hey, Jack, Jackie. The *Lady*'s coming alongside. I think we might have a problem."

Jack stood and walked along past where Jarra was descending the inner stairs to the stern. He watched as a couple of familiar faces made ready with the snag ropes to attach the *Lady Radcliffe* to the pier bollards. Jarra joined him on the pier and caught a mooring rope tossed by one of the deckhands. He stepped aboard the familiar trawler, just as the *Lady*'s big diesel was shut off. His old friend Chugger, the mate, sidled down the way from the bow. Looking up, Jarra saw young Notebook, the seasoned deckhand, climbing down from the wheelhouse.

"What's up?" said Jarra.

Chugger scowled up at the bright sun.

"You know this place, Jarra, the tropics never fails to chuck surprises at a man.

"It's Fred", said Chugger. "If him suckin' on that loose tooth of his forever and a day wasn't enough, now he's got some kind of parasite lodged in his goddamned throat. Lucky you're here, fella. You're the man we need to see." Jarra nodded and turned to Jack.

"Jackie, we need the first aid kit. Man I hope you haven't pawned it."

"Shuddup" said Jack. "I still have it." He moved off the pier and into his boat. Jarra turned back to Chugger. "Where's Fred now?"

"In the galley. Say, man, have you planted a tree on your head or is that your mop?"

Jarra laughed.

"It's the real deal, Blondie."

Chugger called down to Fred.

"Hey, you loafer, bring yourself and your passenger up here. Jarra wants a look-see. C'mon man, hurry up, we've got a catch to make."

Jarra knew well that for all his bluster, Chugger was a softie at heart. He waited for Fred to come on deck. Jack arrived with the first aid kit as Fred came up through the hatch. He was pale and seemed scared. Jarra leaned close to the old man and heard his wheezing. Fred was sucking at his loose tooth. He stopped to speak.

"Jarra, I feel I'm suffocating—don't seem I can stay breathing for long." He coughed and gagged, his head jerking forward like a pecking chicken. Jarra put his hand on Fred's shoulder. Fred coughed again.

"Help me out here, J."

Jarra guided Fred up onto the decking of the pier.

"Sit down there, Freddy. We'll sort this out." Jarra grabbed the back of Fred's neck as the old man gagged again.

Jarra looked at Chugger.

"Where's the boss?"

"Asleep in his cabin."

"You got any fish guts left over?"

Chugger turned to the deckhand, Notebook.

"Get the guts bucket."

The young man was gone a moment and returned holding out the bucket. Jarra set it down. He spoke to Fred.

"Matey, I need you to lie down, and no, you're not going to like this."

"Do it Jarra."

Jack, Chugger and Notebook stepped back and formed a semi-circle about Fred as he lay on the pier. Jarra opened the first aid kit and extracted a brand new fishhook. He put the hook between his teeth. Reaching into the bucket of fish guts he pulled out a sliced section of intestine, already warmed in the sloshing liquid by the sun. He held the stinking flesh away from his face and turned to Jack. He shook his head.

"You're no good, you'll just spew on me." He turned to Notebook and his gaze passed on to rest on Chugger.

"You'll do. Lean in here."

Chugger cursed.

"Why me? I know you're going to pull some weird hoodoo right now."

Jarra smiled.

"No hoodoo, practical stuff, Chug. Open your hand." Chugger obliged and Jarra dropped the section of fish intestine down into Chugger's palm.

"Now get ready, Chug. I want you to put that under Fred's nose, I mean right under. And get ready to pull away, fast, okay?"

Chugger seemed uneasy.

"Sure."

Jarra repeated himself to Fred.

"I said before, this is going to be unpleasant. But you gotta try and stay still."

Fred dry retched, eyes watering, and behind him Jack did the same.

Chugger whispered to Jarra.

"What the hell is in his mouth?"

"Nose leech, and its arse spikes are hooked in the back of his throat."

He watched Chugger's eyes narrow.

"A nose—"

Jarra nodded.

"Let's just do this." He stopped whispering. "Hold the guts where I said."

Chugger did as he was asked. Jarra took the fish hook from his mouth, and, holding it between thumb and forefinger, made ready his other hand to grab what he knew would soon slide from Fred's nostril. Jarra spat over the side of the pier. He spoke.

"Hold still Fred, this won't take long. Chug, hold the meat there. Yeah, there."

For long moments no one on the pier breathed. Seconds later a slick, bloated, purple-black parasite slid from Fred's nostril and waved in the air next to the proffered fish intestine. Jarra moved closer to Fred and barked an order to Chugger.

"Pull your hand away, now!" Chugger moved back and Jarra darted forward, one hand grabbing the tip of the leech and his other hand stabbing the creature with the fish hook. Somewhere behind him he heard Jack cursing. Jarra held the fish hook steady, feeling the skewered creature writhing and attempting to pull back into the dark safety of its fleshy burrow. Fred groaned. Jarra shouted at him.

"Don't, man!" Jarra held his breath. "I'm nearly done." Sweat formed at his temples and slid down his cheeks as he twisted the fish hook. Fred cried out as he felt the bloated creature, its spikes tugging at the back of his throat. He gagged and did not stop. Jarra held the back of Fred's neck and with an effort which sickened him, twisted and yanked the fish hook. Amid Fred's cries and Jack and Notebook's groans, Jarra felt the creature's grip inside Fred's throat slacken. He further twisted the hook and finally felt the leech relinquish its hold. He tugged at the creature and felt it come free from where it had been dining. All of the men leaned closer to Fred and as one watched with horror as the blood-engorged thing slid free from Fred's bleeding nostril. Notebook wanted to vomit—instead he dry heaved.

Jarra held the leech up, watching it writhe on the end of the fish hook. The sun highlighted the slimy, blood-coated mass. Fred turned over onto his belly and emptied the contents of his stomach over the side of the pier. He placed a finger up against the unharmed side of his nose and snorted blood and slime from the damaged nostril. He moaned and saw his blood swirl away on the swell. After a moment he felt a little better. He stood. His throat ached from where spikes had been torn away. He wiped his nose on a sleeve, and turned to see what all the chatter was about.

Jarra held the leech up for him to see. The thing was already deflating, Fred's blood seeping from the hook's puncture wound. The length of the creature was shrinking as it dried and emptied under the sun. Jack leaned forward and poked the leech. It did not respond. The men waited until they were sure the thing was dead. Jack was the first to speak. He turned to Fred.

"Where were you?"

Fred shrugged.

"I took a stern wave across me head north of the islands. Thing must have come in on the wave and latched on to me face. Crawled up, I s'pose." Fred turned and spat blood and caressed his sore throat.

"You're a good man, J."

Jarra watched his friend.

"I don't want to have to do this again. You want to keep this?"

Fred waved his hands.

He took the hook from Jarra and tore the leech from the spike. "Piss off!" he said as he tossed the dead sack into the tide.

Chugger regarded Fred.

"How you goin' there?"

"Okay now. Could do with downing a few shots."

"A few shots it is, then", said Chugger. He saw faded, stencilled numbers painted on the metal hull of Jack's houseboat. "Is this a Second World War barge?" He looked at the fresh paint below the bow. "You've named her *Mary Celeste*, Jack? Are you looking for trouble? Let's hope it doesn't bite you where it hurts."

Jack set his mouth tight.

"Jarra's already pulled me up on that."

The group walked out of the marina up a grassy slope to a sprawling, one-storey weatherboard pub nestled under the palms and bougainvillea bushes. Jack chatted with Chugger.

"So, Chug, you and your sleepy captain and the crew here for the night?"

"Nah, off again today. We head north to grab a haul of mud crab off New Guinea."

"Careful up there," said Jack.

"Yeah, we know the pirates and their guns; we're always careful to keep an eye out in international waters."

Chugger clapped Jack on his shoulder. "Your boat looks 'bout finished. Didn't see your motor. What you got to push her?"

"Big old Dodge diesel."

"Yeah that should do it", said Chugger. "What d'you plan to do with her?"

Jack glanced up at the gulls wheeling overhead.

"Might hire out for charter; she can sleep six."

"Sound idea", said Chugger. "Best off working for yourself lad, best way to live."

Jack nodded.

"I'm with you. Pity you're not here for a break. Me an' Jarra an' Flynny are taking a couple of newcomers out across to the McArthur for a couple of days. I'll give her a run to see how she handles with the extra weight. Flynny's taking care of supplies for the trip."

"Who are you taking?" said Chugger.

"A young Kiwi woman, Angie, here to teach middle school, and a bloke from the government."

"Who brought them in? Don't tell me. That lanky gambler, Flynn, flew them here in his old rust-bucket—how is he, anyhow?"

"Yeah, Flynny's good, said Jack. "He's supposed to be helping us out here. He'll be around somewhere."

"Who is the government man?"

Jack moved his head from side to side to stretch his neck muscles.

"Name's Dien, Armanis, a weird little fellow; always fussing with straightening his tie and checking to see if his shoes are polished. Seems decent enough. He's staying up at the rooming house. Says he's from the Department of Immigration, here to check rumours of people trafficking."

Chugger snorted.

"Good luck, he hasn't got a hope in hell of making it work, not up here, by himself."

Jack nodded.

"I did a quick web search on him", said Jack. "Seems our Mr Armanis has a degree in Australian Military History."

Chugger whistled.

"This fellow might be quite a decent bloke—they don't give those away without you working for them."

"True", said Jack. "Still, I think he reckons being up here, he may as well be in Mongolia."

Chugger laughed.

"Let's hit the bar."

2

The next morning, Dien sat in his upstairs room in the island's only boarding house. He held a book on the military history of Northern Australia and the Gulf. A siren sounded from a boat somewhere out in the marina. He jumped a little on the bed when he heard a series of thumps on his door. Grabbing his backpack and coat, he opened the door to see the pilot, Flynn, grinning at him. Flynn was his usual exuberant self.

"Mornin', Mr Armanis, ready for adventure? Me and Angie got you some country clothes from the markets for the trip upriver on the houseboat. Better than all those government man suits and ties, eh? What were you thinking?"

Dien ignored Flynn's question. But he could not help smiling at the man's enthusiasm.

Reaching the beachfront, they entered an old section of the marina. Within a few paces they stepped onto the squeaky boards of a pier and walked along to Jack and Jarra's houseboat. Being familiar with the history of navy vessels, Dien saw the new corrugated iron and wood construction was built upon an old war barge. He could not see any stencilled lettering to tell him of the wartime nature of the barge and figured it was hidden under layers of rust.

Angie and Jarra were unloading the jeep they had taken to the markets. Flynn had to stifle a laugh when Angie presented Dien with his brightly coloured board shorts and nearly matching shirt. Dien felt obliged to say something.

"Thanks. Yes. I'm thirty, hardly part of the younger set. But thank you. I'll wear them."

Flynn spoke with exuberance, ignoring Jarra's quizzical look.

"I couldn't find any boots or such for you. Guess you'll have to make do with your shoes and socks. No bare feet up where we're going, sorry, too dicey with snakes and such."

Jarra and Jack busied themselves with loading provisions for the trip across to the McArthur River. They had left it up to Flynn to give Dien and Angie a tour of the *Mary Celeste*. Jarra went into the lower-level storeroom at the stern, checking the extra canisters of diesel and containers of drinking water were securely tied. Satisfied, he opened a tall, tin cupboard and made sure the rifles were all secure. He stepped into the main section of the lower deck and checked the rods and fish gaffs were all accounted for, lying across their nails above the hammocks.

It was mid-morning and Jack was already moody. Jarra saw Jack holding a broken hammer.

"Yours as well, eh? Guess we're out of hammers."

Jack nodded.

"No mind. I'll get me a dirty great big sledge when we get back. Meantime, a bucket to cover this ought to do the trick, we need to warn the others to be careful. The hammer-breaker was a rusted metal bollard, short and T bar-shaped, broken at the ends. Jack left to find something to cover the bollard. He returned with a child's plastic sand bucket and looped the handle round the bollard.

"We got twenty-seven degrees and fine for two days—means we get a shower."

He climbed the internal stairs to the upper deck and scaled the ladder to the wheelhouse, a narrow room the width of the craft. He started the big diesel motor. Over the sound of the motor, Jack heard Flynn showing the newcomers about the *Mary Celeste*. He chugged out of the marina and within a few moments had rounded the headland leading to the open waters of the Gulf of Carpentaria.

Gulls wheeled low over the water, trying to find fish on the surface near where the propeller was churning up a wake. Jarra's small runabout, tied by a long rope, smacked the waves in the swell beyond the wake. Jack leaned forward out of the wheelhouse window and saw Flynn with Angie and Dien up on the bow, showing them the wooden toilet shed with the long drop to the water. Jack headed a course across the shallow inner gulf towards the mainland river estuary.

Flynn continued his tour.

"Four rooms, two on each deck, walkway between each as you see." He stood in the open doorway between lower bow and stern rooms. "We've got food lockers, water, fuel containers, diesel motor's in the locker over there—and Jarra", he said waving his hand at his friend who was watching the tour with some amusement. "Through here we've got the card table, gaff and fishing rods. Jarra will share with you, Mr Armanis. Mosquito nets are camouflage—army surplus, was all we could find. Least up among the mangroves the bugs will have a hard time finding us."

Dien refrained from looking down at the ugly Hawaiian shirt and coloured shorts he wore. Jarra decided to join the tour. Flynn walked under one of the beams holding up the floor of the upper deck and led the way up the inside stairs.

"Up here we have bow and stern rooms. Angie, your berth is in the bow, I'm in the stern and Jackie has his kit up in the wheelhouse." He led them out onto the upper port walkway and stood on the decking boards. "We only have boards outside to let rain run off through, the deck inside with that metal lip should help things stay dry if it rains." Flynn leaned on the upper railing and looked over the side. "There's a yellow bucket down there covering a rusty bollard. Walk round that." He pointed up the short ladder bracketed to the outside wall. "The wheelhouse holds four standing—just. It's the only place with glass in the window spaces at the moment, but give us time. We can all take turns to pilot upriver when we get across to the mainland. All we have to do is stick close to midstream and watch for log snags. It'll be fun. You two might want to put your packs in the bins next to your kits, keep 'em out of the way of crawlies. We get a few long-legged things climbing on board, but most of 'em don't bite. Oh, and watch out for the spiders, they'll carry your boots and shoes off and make homes in them."

Dien shook his head and smiled.

Jarra sat with Angie on a bench at the stern. Jarra spoke.

"So, Ngai Tahu Maori, eh?

Angie nodded. "Yes. Southland in the South Island—Te Wai Paunamu. And you?" she asked.

"Yanyuwa—saltwater people." He raised an arm and swung about. "This here's my blood land, mother and father."

Angie regarded her companion.

"It's quite shallow through most of the Gulf? What's the average depth? I'll need to know for when I'm with the children."

"It doesn't get more than about eight meters, with some deeper channels."

He ducked as a splash of sea spray caught him unawares. "But I reckon you'll find the kids already know about their back yard. My guess is it's the whitefella's world you're here to teach 'em." He sensed Angie's discomfort and changed the subject. "We can't go swimming upriver or go ashore at night because of crocs."

Angie sat for a few minutes comforted by the sound and the feel of the big diesel motor vibrating along the lower deck. She spoke without looking at Jarra.

"I read somewhere there was a lot of violence here in the early days."

Jarra shrugged.

"It's the same as you guys in New Zealand. Our mobs were

shot and murdered by the British. Blood spilled on both sides. This land is built on blood and greed. I've heard stories told by my elders who were told by their elders about seeing white men for the first time. There's tales regarding whitefellas on horses shooting at the blackfellas for sport. It was a brutal culture." In an effort to lighten the mood, he related a tale of his grandfather.

"Hey, it's not all bad. There's some funny stuff. My grandfather, Jim Crane-Man. He was real funny. Chatty dialogue in place of proper speech. Black as me and some say I got his hair. Jim was a rider on a Kimberly station with a stockman named Harry Peckham. After some time as boundary riders, Harry and Jim teamed up as mail riders for the district. One day there was a major flood along a river way eastward and Harry and his horse were drowned in the crossing. Legend has it Harry had thrown the mailbag to the bank and shouted to Jim 'Save the mail'. The story goes, Grandfather did save the mail and stayed a rider until Redwater tick fever took him in 1951." Jarra paused and thought. "Well I guess the part about the tick is not funny, but you can imagine a guy being so dedicated to his job he would rather drown than lose a sack of mail."

Mid-afternoon, Jack came aft to speak with Jarra and Angie.

"I've left Flynny and our government man up in the wheelhouse. Let's get some lunch together."

Dien came down from the wheelhouse to collect the sandwiches Jack had made for him and Flynn. After he left, Jack sat on the bench and ate with his companions.

"River estuary's ahead. We'll go upstream for a few hours, see some sights and drop anchor for the night." He leaned with his back against the stern rail and chewed on his lunch as he watched the estuary narrow to form the seaward end of the river, the channels dividing sandbanks with stumpy trees and bush clumps giving way to patches of mangrove alternating with small sandy patches of river beach. Thick foliage lined each side of the waterway. Jack stood. "I've got a couple of things to do. I'll catch up with you soon."

Jarra watched some large wading birds. Angie followed his gaze.

"Brolgas", he said. "Lots of birds up here, also fly-ins from Indo and east Papua." He stood. "I better go and take my turn in the wheelhouse for a bit—you okay here?"

"Oh yeah, enjoying the sun and the scenery." Jarra nodded and left her. She watched as the boat chugged past a tree snag poking out of the water. Cormorants perched, wings stretched to dry on branches poking from the river.

Jack returned with bottles of water. Angie saw the sunlight flash across his cheek and she saw the yellowy gold shape of the beer can tattoo. Jack sat on the other end of the bench.

Both felt the boat turning midstream as the person in the wheelhouse manoeuvred the craft round another bend. Jack stepped to the railing. "Here, have a look at this."

Angie stood at the railing.

"See there?" he said, pointing through a break in the trees lining the bank. "That's a Chinese cemetery, lots of 'em in gulf country."

Angie saw the cluster of headstones, partially covered with forest creeper and moss.

"A lot of people have died up here."

Jack looked along the bank.

"The Chinese and Muslims and convicts built this country. Wherever miners, prospectors or cattle drovers went, Chinese followed to sell them food and clothes, followed by the settlers and the sly groggers and the whores. Every little settlement had a Chinese market garden on the outskirts. This is Old Borroloola landing, where the cattle were mustered through to head north. Was a wharf here once, used to take boats and barges ferrying logs and cattle down to the coast."

Angie drank some water.

"I heard somewhere the Chinese were pretty much reviled."

Jack nodded across at the cemetery.

"Well, yeah, they were treated real bad by some who were criminals themselves, thieves and killers. Everyone treated them bad, like they were bottom of the food chain." He finished his water. "I'm gonna get out of the sun and hit my hammock for a bit. I'll catch up with you at dinner."

Angie spoke: "I appreciate you asking me along."
"Hey, good to have you here."

3

It was the long hour before dawn. A three-quarter moon sat in a star-clustered night sky. Jarra leaned on the starboard handrail. He listened to night sounds surrounding the anchored craft. He saw light shining on his hands, the moonlight putting his veins in high relief. Leaving the rail he stooped, his Afro still brushing the underside of the upper deck. He tried to make out the riverbank but cloud cover had hidden the moon. Feeling his way along the narrow walkway he ran one hand along the wall in order to find the opening to the cabin and back to his hammock. He rubbed his tired eyes and cracked his knee against one of the posts holding up the railing. He stumbled and threw out his leg to right himself. He felt his foot kick something in the darkness and he stumbled further. He reached for the rail but missed where he thought it was and in the darkness he found one leg stretched out awkwardly. He heard the sound of a plastic bucket bouncing along the walkway. As he fell he threw his arm out, hoping his hand would find the deck so he could stop himself from crashing face first onto the boards. He felt something snag one of his wrists and pain shot the length of his arm.

He twisted in his confusion and fell against the railing. The post shook and the railing attached to it bent outwards before snapping. Jarra felt a sense of weightlessness as half his body hung out over the river. He felt pain as he twisted and his wrist was yanked around where it was snagged. A warm wetness spread across his wrist. Everything seemed to happen in slow motion. Something close to the deck had hold of his wrist and he was now off the boat and heading for the water. His dangling legs entered and he felt the cold river. His forehead smacked against the metal hull of the craft. Up against the hull, dazed, he hung in agony. The warmness running down his arm began to roll across his shoulder and down his back. Little tinkles sounded in the water, and through the pain Jarra realised his blood was now pouring across his body. He shook his head again to rid himself of his confusion. He felt fear.

Cloud cover left the face of the moon, and the boat and the water and the river bank were visible. Jarra closed his eyes to the terrible pain where his wrist was caught. He realised the horror of his situation. He fought back momentary panic and slapped his free arm against the side of the boat in order to get a handhold atop the flat hull. He knew what had happened. Somehow in the dark he had dislodged the child's bucket from the sharp bollard which Jack had been trying to hammer out. Jarra knew then that the metal shard had sliced through his wrist and he was now dangling from his open wound.

He lifted himself up from the water on his impaled wrist and managed to grab hold of the decking lining the walkway. With his good arm he lifted himself from the water so he was able to rest his chin on the boards. With tears in his eyes he twisted his impaled wrist, trying to ignore the terrible, burning pain. He pulled, the flesh of his wrist tugging at the metal bollard. His arm came free from its impalement. He cried out, this time with the hope someone might wake and hear his plight. He hung gasping, weeping from pain. He knew he was bleeding and needed to stop the flow.

Out on the river he heard something large entering the water and he knew he had unwelcome company. In near panic he ignored the stabbing pain and lifted himself up and over the edge of the rim of the hull and rolled onto his back on the boards next to the broken railing. He knew without doubt what waited for him in the water not one metre from where he lay. Again he became conscious of the warmth flowing from his torn wrist. He managed to stand, and gripped his wrist to stop the blood flow. Under the light of the moon he climbed the inner stairs to the second level and on up to the wheelhouse to wake Jack and to find the first aid kit.

It had taken Jarra a few seconds to rouse Jack. At first his friend was grumpy, but after fumbling about, he lit the lamp. Jack acted quickly.

Sitting with Jarra behind the wheelhouse near the railing on the iron roof of the upper deck, Jack held his friend's wrist. Working by moonlight, he tugged the clean fishing line through the needle puncture and looped it through the previous stitch to tie off. He used the scissors from the kit to cut the line and applied disinfectant to Jarra's wrist. He wrapped the stitched wound with a bandage and clipped it down. Jack was scared for his friend's safety.

"The bollard slipped between your tendons. Y'know, Jarra, it's supposed to be you helping your drunken buddies through their boozy antics and fixin' them up, not t'other way round." Jack took a small bottle of whiskey from the first aid kit. "You want a couple of shots? It'll help you forget your pain."

Jarra shook his head.

"Not for me, just give me a few of those painkillers."

Jack took a long swallow of the whiskey and screwed the top back on. He handed Jarra the bottle of painkillers and watched as his friend used his teeth and one hand to open the bottle. Jack handed Jarra a water container and watched his friend drink. He took the container and placed it next to him.

"You gonna be right? Y'know, for a darkie I swear you're losing your colour. You've lost a lot of blood, it's everywhere. Who the fuck's gonna clean up this mess?"

Jarra laughed.

"Damned croc nearly got me."

Jack held up the whiskey bottle again.

Jarra shook his head.

"You know it's illegal to ply the natives?"

"Jarra, I'm sorry. I should've fixed the bollard 'fore we ever left."

Jarra shook his head.

"You did nothing wrong." He held up his wrist and, in the moonlight, checked Jack's handiwork. "Nice job. You're a good mate."

Jarra wandered downstairs and for a while paced the deck. He rubbed his bandage. As he sat he realised all was not right. He began to feel odd and so walked down the inner stairs and sat cross-legged on the metal hull under his hammock. He listened to Dien breathing. Weary, Jarra let his head drop until his chin rested near his chest.

He was seven years old, rake thin, all arms and legs and frizzy hair. It had taken him quite some time to run from the shanty town where he and his kind were hidden from view by the white folk in Normanton. Even though it was night-time, Jarra knew his way. He was all youthful energy and the run to the beach, where he now lay hidden behind the outboard motor of a runabout, had not even tired him. He wriggled forward until his head was out in the moonlight. He saw the raft out in the water and the people on it, lit by the kerosene lamps they had brought with them. To Jarra they seemed like big demons. Jarra watched; some whitefellas standing with his uncle on the anchored raft in the water, a little way from the beach. He saw the frightening white man, Mr Wakefield, the cattleman from the big station. Jarra saw the cattleman's workers were also standing out on the raft; they had tied his uncle to some bamboo poles which made a frame. Jarra tried to make sense of what was happening. He saw the cattleman lift a stock whip and bring the end down with a great crack across his uncle's back. Jarra had been watching the scene with a sense of detachment, but he jumped a little on the sand at the sound of the whip crack.

He heard voices behind him and the sound of many feet approaching along the sand of the beach. Jarra tried to hide further in the shadow of the outboard motor, but it was of no use because he had already been seen by his elders. He sensed movement by his side and felt his arm gripped. He was pulled to his feet and turned about. He looked up at his father. As if in a dream, young Jarra heard the man speak.

"This is not for the likes of a young one, boy."

"Papa, why are they whipping uncle?"

He felt his father's strong arms hug him.

Before his father could explain what was happening, there was a shout from the cattleman on the raft.

"You folk stay where you are. You know we're in our rights to do this. A stock thief is a stock thief. Y'all know we're in our rights."

There came another crack and Jarra jumped when he heard

his uncle's anguished cry come from the raft. He knew they were punishing his uncle, and Jarra leaned back into his father's arms and he began to cry because he did not understand why this was happening. There came another loud crack from the raft and again Jarra heard the cry of his uncle. He felt his father trembling and Jarra wished he was back in his bed warm and safe near his mother. He dared to look around his father and up into the faces of the other adults present. White and black, he could not see his mother. Jarra heard a loud voice from someone near him. He saw the whitefella fisherman, Mr Lohan, holding a kerosene lamp up near his face. Jarra watched shadows dance across Mr Lohan's face. Another crack and a cry sounded from the raft. He heard Mr Lohan's gruff voice.

"Wakefield, you are an ignorant fool, too afraid blackfella's blood will spill into the earth. You have to whip someone out on water? You men have no right to this frontier justice. This is the last time you are rafting a man for punishment. Now you cut that man down or so help me we're coming out there and we're going to sort you out."

Wakefield shouted from the raft. As if in a waking dream, Jarra heard the cattleman, but this time he heard something different in the man's voice, almost as if the man was scared of Mr Lohan. Jarra stood still in his father's warm arms.

"Lohan, you and that rabble have no right to stop this. We'll see what you got to say when the coppers come tomorrow, eh. Laughing then, eh?"

Jarra heard the big voice of Mr Lohan above the other voices on the beach.

"Fine, we'll see. Meantime, hand him over and go your way."

The man on the raft answered.

"No harm. Can you be sure of what you say?"

Lohan answered.

"You can go on your way tonight, after you take down your whipping rack and clean your damned raft. I promise you and your boys can go on your way. Nothing is gonna happen to you, tonight, my word."

Jarra jerked his head upright. He shuddered in the dawn light. He saw he was still sitting cross-legged under his hammock near the doorway. He heard morning birdlife, and the fleeting images of his dream became a thing a vague unreality. He noticed his wrist was itching. He reached his good hand down to rub his bandage. Feeling a lump and a burning sensation he looked down in the dawn light and blinked, not believing what he was seeing. From under the blood-soaked bandage he saw emerging what seemed like a wet, crimson rope. He gaped, not taking in what he was looking at. His eyes refocused and he stared along the length of the wet ropy thing down to the metal floor. He jumped when he saw the rope move, swell, at floor level. He watched as the crimson cord made a swallowing motion. Jarra began scratching the bandage round his wrist in an effort to stop the itching. He glanced at the wet, red rope and saw it pulsing, each pulse raising and lowering the bandage. A spray of blood spurted from the bandage's lifted opening, spattering the floor at his feet. He saw the bloodspots on the metal hull and to his astonishment he saw them vanish, almost as if they had been sucked up. As if in some awful nightmare from which he could not extract himself, but was merely a passive player, he looked at his bandage. He saw it twist around his forearm. He began to feel weak and found it hard to stay upright in his cross-legged position on the deck. A lump appeared in the red rope at the bandage and he watched as it travelled down the wet length until it reached the floor. He began scratching again and it dawned on him he should rip off the bandage. He felt a tiredness which did not allow him to act upon his thoughts. He tried to gain his feet, but stumbled to land on his knees. He dragged in a huge breath of air. With his free hand, he leaned forward out of the door opening of the cabin and managed to grasp the handrail of the boat. With a supreme effort he pulled himself upright. He felt his bandaged wrist tugging him backwards as the wet, bloody rope became taut. Jarra was horrified and jerked his arm forward. At first he encountered resistance, and he felt a snapping sensation as his arm came free from the rope. He heard a twanging sound, and then a snap as something wet spattered against the metal deck. With a sob of relief, Jarra turned in time to see blood vanish as water would on a hot metal surface. The wet blood rope was nowhere to be seen. He tugged at his bloodied bandage and with a frantic effort pulled it up to look within. He saw nothing but the rough stitches from Jack's sewing job. He blinked and staggered against the railings.

He walked through the cabin, past Dien still asleep in his hammock, and out onto the port walkway. He leaned down. Lifting the walkway boards, he checked the metal hull next to the section where he had broken the railing in his earlier fall. There was no blood to be seen, and he wondered if someone might have cleaned it up. He realised everyone was still asleep. Jarra stood unsteady on his feet, gripping the nearest solid handrail. He was afraid, and felt as if the walls of the craft were now moving, sliding back and forth. Vertigo threatened to topple him. He moaned as he stared out at the dark line of trees on the riverbank, but he could not make sense of what he was looking at. He pressed his teeth together and worked his jaw muscles. He felt ill and afraid he might be going insane.

<h1 style="text-align:center">4</h1>

The day was warming. Angie changed into fresh clothes from her pack and washed her face in water from the storeroom basin. Jack poked his head round the door jamb.

"Hey, there. I've upped anchor. We can stop a ways upriver this morning. There's a high bank further upstream where we can tie up and make landfall from the top deck, away from crocs. We can walk round and stretch our legs.

Angie dried her face.

"Sounds great."

Jack glanced at the diesel locker.

"Feel free to jump up to the wheelhouse. You can have a go steering if you want."

"I'd like that."

Jack passed the bow cabin and glimpsed Dien exiting his hammock. Climbing the inner stairs, Jack made his way forward. He met Flynn on the top deck.

"Flynny, got a smoke for your captain?"

Flynn patted his pockets.

"I'll get some."

Jack thought of Jarra and wanted to find him to see if he was okay.

"Have you seen Jarra?"

Flynn shook his head.

"Nah, but his runabout's gone. Off wandering, I s'pose."

Jack did not mention the accident. He hoped his friend was not feeling too bad and the stitches were holding. Turning away, he climbed the ladder to the wheelhouse.

Dien stretched and yawned. He stood at the rail with Angie on the lower deck. They said nothing for a while, each looking at narrow, sandy stretches of beach. On the low banks of the river, large gums and thickets of tea tree blocked any view of what lay inland. Angie watched a flock of black-and-red-plumed parakeets wheel overhead.

Dien wandered stern and sat on the bench. He heard a voice from above and realised Jack was attempting to sing a song. Dien smiled, realising his companions were not so bad. He decided to visit the wheelhouse.

Jack sat on a raised bench up in the wheelhouse looking out for river snags and signs of sunken logs. Dien climbed the ladder. Jack spoke.

"Rain is comin' soon enough. Still."

Dien noticed Jack's beer can tattoo on his cheek. Jack knew what Dien was looking at, but he decided to play a game.

"What, fella? What? Is there a bug on my head?"

Dien was a little startled and he stammered. Finding composure as best he could under that wild-eyed watchful stare was not easy. He blurted out the last thing he wanted to.

"Ahh, no. I was. I was looking at your tattoo."

Jack pulled his clincher to confuse Dien. With his stare even wilder and his pale eyes seeming more crazed, Jack blurted out:

"What? I have a tattoo? Where?" He lifted one hand up to his face and began running his fingers across his face and neck as if in an effort to let his fingers find the ink. Jack watched Dien's growing discomfort become horror. Jack gave Dien a goggle-eyed look of panic and stopped all movement. Jack stared at Dien and Dien could not look away. As he watched transfixed, Dien saw Jack start to smile.

"Man, you should see your face—if I had a camera right now... Flynn had that done to that to me in a dodgy tatt parlour, in Cairns, when I was pissed outta my head." He stopped smiling. "You might like to get a better sense of humour while you're up here. In your job you're gonna meet folks up here who'll try anything to fool you. Some of them don't take kindly to questions from government people. You wanna make it easy on yourself, get a laugh track into you." Jack called out to Flynn: "Flynny, you tattooing bastard!"

Flynn climbed the ladder and poked his head in the open doorway. He shook his head at Dien's clothes and dress shoes.

"Man, you'd never get lost in the bush. A chopper would spot you miles away."

Dien stared at Flynn.

"You seem to enjoy having fun at my expense" said Dien. "But I *will* take advice from Jack and make you part of my new laugh track."

Jack grinned. Flynn was confused.

"What's that mean?"

Jack laughed.

"Never mind. It's okay. Show Mr Armanis how to move this rig properly. I'll be back later." He turned at the door. "Hey, Dien, relax, enjoy yourself."

Down at the bow Jack sniffed the air. A faint whiff of something sour caught his attention. He took another breath and the sourness became a sickly smell. Jack frowned as he recognised the smell as a familiar one, yet he found it hard to place, almost like an unpleasant odour of maggoty meat, sweet yet sickening. He glanced at the riverbanks to see if he could see a dead bullock or some other carcass, but he saw nothing which could suggest the origins of the smell. He walked down to the diesel motor in the storeroom.

Up in the wheelhouse, Dien spoke.

"You know, you people aren't at all what I expected."

Flynn snorted.

"Not everyone up here wears cork hats and wanders round sayin' *strewth* and *stone the crows* and *bugger me senseless*. You'll find most folk know what's happening out in the rest of the world." He pointed out a rickety jetty jutting from the riverbank out into the water.

"It's another of the rotting Borroloola cattle wharves."

Dien looked along the tree-lined bank.

"Is it a big town, this Borroloola?"

Flynn turned the wheel midstream to avoid the exposed branches of a sunken tree, watchful for little waves on the surface of the river suggesting submerged logs.

"We call it 'The Loo'. It had a big past but it's not much at the moment. It used to be a thriving place for all sorts of thugs and shysters and sly groggers. In the early days it was a shithole full of dangerous sons of bitches. You build things of wood up here and people will put you in a freak house. Wood's no good on account of dry rot and white ants."

Watching the river ahead, Dien listened, fascinated with Flynn's story.

"Before the turn of the twentieth century there were Aboriginals spearing cattle and pastoralists seeking revenge, miners and prospectors murdering each other for a bigger claim, jail escapees, bushrangers, horse thieves. With a belly full of bad alcohol, many miners worked with dynamite blasting wells, blind drunk—heaps of deaths and maiming. Summer 'round the Loo is deadly, it's a dust bowl, rivers dry up—this one's too big. In 1887, the place was going to be the big town of the central gulf, but it up and died with its dust and dry rot. Not much better now. Alfred Searcy, a pioneer stockman, once said: 'The heat is enough to make the eyebrows crawl.'"

The sun was high in the east. Warm rain soaked the river surrounds, turning dust into mud. It moved on within the hour, leaving the air muggy.

Dien wandered on the lower deck and thought of gun runners and murderers and drunken dynamiters.

Flynn called from the wheelhouse ladder.

"People, we're docking, stretching our legs."

Jack stepped onto the walkway to stand next to Dien.

"Been hearing about the murderous bastards?"

Dien smiled.

"Fascinating stuff. It's better those days have gone."

"Not quite yet, Mr Armanis. A lot goes on up here city folk don't know."

Flynn called from above: "C'mon up Jackie, that high bank's ahead."

Jack and Dien felt the boat slow as Flynn switched off the diesel and coasted slowly towards the deep water next to the river's western side. Flynn climbed from the wheelhouse and joined Jack. They watched and gave instructions as Dien stepped ashore onto the bank with the mooring line. Flynn followed and showed Dien how to tie a bowline around the trunk of a tree. It took Dien a few tries to get it right, but when he straightened the men saw him grinning at his accomplishment.

"Nice work", said Jack. "A few more boating skills and you'll make a fine Territorian."

Angie came up to the top deck.

"Our new captain?"

Dien didn't enjoy the attention. He shouldered a small backpack loaded with water, insect repellent and some macadamia nuts. He followed the others across the railing onto the bank. Each went their own way, pushing through the bushes lining the high bank. He had decided to walk at the back of the group so he could get an uninterrupted view of the surroundings. One section of black-watered, cloying swamp went all the way to join the river where there was no bank. Dien wandered about, spying bright-coloured birds, swamp lizards and various weird-looking insects. He kept blundering into big spider webs stretched between odd-looking trees; each time he brushed his hair and clothing. After about forty minutes he heard Jack calling everyone together. Dien was hot and sweaty. He made his way back along the trail he had come and found he was at last back to the houseboat. He watched the others step over the railing onto the top deck. He stepped forward to climb over the railing. The free shoulder strap of his pack caught on something. Dien turned, and in his haste he lost hold of the pack. He felt it rub his shoulder as it dropped. He was in time to see it fall between the boat and the riverbank, only to lodge between the two just above the water. He swore and hurried down the inner stairs to retrieve it. On the lower deck, he came up short when he met Jack.

"Listen, sorry, I dropped the pack down there", he pointed. "I'll get it."

Jack glanced over the edge.

"No problem. Use the gaff on the wall by your hammock. You untie the rope yet?"

"Ahh, no, not yet."

"We have a system. You tie the mooring line, you untie it— everyone takes responsibility. I'll go up to the wheelhouse and wait for you."

Dien felt he was at last an accepted member of the crew.

"Thanks, Jack. I'll be a moment."

He retrieved the gaff and lay along the boards, ducking his head under the railing so he could hook the gaff end through one of the straps of the pack. He stopped when he noticed a strange smell, a sweet sickly odour. He took another breath and began to feel ill. He lifted his head and dry heaved as the smell became intolerable. He glanced down and noticed painted letters and numerals, barely readable, on the metal hull near his face. Craning his head he read the faded, stencilled paintwork and he knew what he was looking at. He calculated the width and length of the vessel. He knew he was right even though he did not like it. As he lay on the boards, head under the railing, Dien felt his scalp tighten. He pulled the pack up with the gaff and dragged it over the side next to him. He exhaled and drew another breath. The sweet, sickly smell was still about him so he quickly sat up. He remained there on the boards thinking. He wondered if Jack knew about this. He doubted it, because if he had, he surely would not have built on this particular hull. He got to his feet and checked the pack. He leaned out over the railing and saw Jack waiting for him. He decided after untying the mooring rope he would approach Jack, although he was not quite sure how to explain to him what kind of craft he had bought.

5

His face was smudged with dirt from where he had been lying on the swampy earth amid the trees. A little way upstream from the houseboat, Jarra squatted barefoot amid a clearing in the mangroves, his toes sinking a little into the mud. Next to him a wide furrow in the sloping mudbank showed the passage of a large saurian into the slow-moving river. Jarra saw no water seepage into the furrow, which meant the croc had been there after the last tidal surge. He guessed the croc had heard him coming and had entered the water within the last fifteen minutes. On a raised branch of a submerged tree near the far bank, Jarra watched a black-and-grey shag, wings open, drying itself in the afternoon sun. Looking around the surface of the water he could find no bubbles or any disturbance which would betray the presence of the croc.

The sun was warm on his bare back. He smiled, knowing the croc was returning, probably now interested in the still form next to the boat. Jarra knew the intelligence of the species. He could not yet see the beast's eyes above the waterline in the shadows upstream, but he knew it was there, regarding him, without doubt waiting for him to enter the water.

Jarra remained alert, his thoughts partly turned to what he was to do and how he could explain things to Jack and Flynn. He knew they could not abandon the craft here, they had to return it to Vanderlin. The return crossing was imperative if the necessary ceremonies were to be performed by his elders, which meant he had to go back on board He knew Jack would understand. He wondered how Jack had managed to find and buy the hulk, how its presence in Vanderlin had escaped everyone's notice. He tried not to think about his dream and what he now knew it signified. He knew he had received the only warning he would be granted, and knew not to act would be fatal for someone of his blood. He shivered again, dreading the thought of climbing back aboard the punishment raft, knowing it was a thing of thirst, now recently reawakened by his foolish accident. For a moment he closed his eyes, still aware of the croc's presence.

He opened his eyes. His racing thoughts had shown him glimpses of the night of the whipping of his uncle, of the blood spilled onto the hungry deck; all the floggings and rope stranglings over the decades of his kind perpetrated for perceived wrongs. Whitefella's frontier justice. Although Jarra was a well-educated man in what he saw as a whitefella's world, he could not deny the power of his people and the secret strength his ancestry provided. He turned his head to look upstream. He saw the croc's eyes above the surface and locked eyes with the beast. This he could understand. While watching the beast watching him, Jarra remembered the night before. He thought of the rope of blooded flesh attaching him to the hungry raft.

He stood watching the approaching croc. And he knew the raft waited for him to take another swallow. He stared at his dirty bandage, now loose and dangling from his wounded wrist. The hidden area itched, maddening him. He thought he could feel the area throb as if something was trying to crawl out from beneath the skin.

Now the croc was within fifteen metres, a mere three of its body lengths; it was primed to move fast. Jarra knew well that from that distance, with a sudden burst of speed, the croc could be upon him within seconds. He stepped through the stinking mud and placed his hand on his runabout and pushed it motor first into the McArthur's silted water. He climbed in. The runabout floated slow out into centre stream. He grabbed the pull cord for the outboard with his sore arm. A mental numbness settled and he tried to concentrate. After a moment he was able to find strength to start the outboard. Looking back he saw the croc was no longer on the surface. He was afraid the beast, now submerged, was waiting for him to make a mistake. He turned the rudder and twisted the throttle and faced downstream.

It was nearing twilight when Jack left Flynn up in the wheelhouse and joined Angie and Dien at the stern on the lower deck. He looked at Dien's rope knotting the metal pole holding Jarra's runabout.

"Nice work, shipmate."

Dien shrugged.

"I'm getting the hang of it."

Angie had earlier helped Jarra with a fresh bandage as she listened to his explanation. She remembered his mood at the time. He had been quite subdued and not at all the talkative and friendly person she had known for but a short time. She had at first wondered if something had been wrong, but thought his sullenness perhaps had something to do with Aboriginal spirituality when out in this fantastic land. Angie had finished dressing his wrist and he had thanked her. Besides glimpses of the man on the upper deck and up in the wheelhouse, Angie had not been able to speak with him since. She sat on the bench listening to Jack speak as he showed Dien another nautical knot. She smiled as she saw Dien frown, concentrating on trying to fit in. Jack spoke to her. Angie watched his face and she could see he was troubled.

"We're heading back tonight", he said. "It will be a good trip, and the weather is more of the same."

Angie nodded.

"Jarra's is alright, isn't he?"

She saw Jack hesitate.

"Jarra? Yeah, he's fine. Misses his family when he's gone too long is all."

Angie knew he was lying.

Jack glanced up at the low roof as if he could see all the way to the wheelhouse.

"I'm going to refuel the motor so we don't have to do it in the dark. Remind me not to forget a generator next time, eh? We can have some light." He kept his face from her as he walked off to the motor locker.

Angie turned on the seat and watched Dien with a piece of rope trying out the new knot. For a reason she could not yet understand, she knew Dien too had something on his mind and all his banter and concentration of getting a simple scouting knot right was a cover-up for something. Angie thought of Jarra and Jack. She knew there was something going on.

"I'm a little hungry," said Dien. "Would you like some food?"

Angie smiled.

"Sure. A chocolate bar and some water would be good."

Dien walked off in the direction of the storage room.

Stars were showing and more were winking into view as if someone was switching on the power. Angie heard voices and tried to make out individuals but could not. She felt the diesel engine start, and a moment later the craft shuddered as whoever was up in the wheelhouse turned the boat midstream to face north and home. She smiled as she caught herself thinking of the islands as her new home.

She heard Jarra's runabout strike against the metal hull as the big houseboat turned midstream, tugging the dinghy behind. Night had closed and Angie saw the riverbanks and lines of trees only as dark silhouettes against the sky. Stars shone as rippling specks upon the surface of the black water. She breathed the night air and wrinkled her nose at a strong, sour odour. A breeze blew across the stern, washing away the smell, and she was able to breathe fresh country air. She put her hand up and laid her wrist upon the stern rail. Her fingers found the rope tying the runabout to the metal pole. She gripped the rope and felt the tautness. Closing her hand tighter about the rope, she flicked it and heard it twang. It took her a moment to realise something was not right. She gave the rope another flick and again heard the twang. She realised, judging by the sound and the feel, the rope appeared to be dragging something much heavier than a little runabout floating along in the water. She stood and looked out into the darkness, not able to see more than a few metres. She could not see Jarra's boat. This puzzled her because she knew the dinghy was aluminium and she should be able to see the light shining off the metal. She twanged the rope a third time and felt, to her sudden discomfort, something of great weight was being dragged. The taut rope shivered and pinged in her loose grip. She started and held her hand in position, again tightening her grip. The rope shivered again and smacked against her palm, pulling her a little forward. There came a sudden jerk as if something on the other end was mimicking her actions. Something had flicked the rope from the other end. Angie tried to rein her thoughts in order to control the direction they were headed. Try as she might to dispel the thought, though, she could not dislodge it. She felt sure something out at the other end had tugged her towards the railing.

Dien squeezed into the wheelhouse with Jack and Flynn. He closed the door. Jack leaned forward and pressed his face up against the glass and sat down on the bow in the dark, the lighted end of a cigarette glowing next to the starboard rail. He knew it was Jarra perched on the wooden anchor housing. He had spoken with Jarra earlier and could only begin to understand the anguish his friend must be suffering. He frowned and felt his own fear rising at the other news he had been told by Dien. He had already told Flynn and Dien what Jarra had related to him. Flynn was fearful for Jarra, and he was now feeling as if the houseboat had become a malevolent thing. He thought of the metal hull below. He wiped his mouth with one hand.

"You had to go and name it *Mary Celeste,* a fucking death ship."

Jack whispered to himself: "You don't know the half of it."

Flynn glared at him.

"What's that?"

Jack sighed. With one hand on the wheel he watched the river ahead. He used his free hand to turn down the flame on the kerosene lamp hanging from the wall. He lowered his voice, prompting the others to do the same.

"Mr Armanis, tell Flynn what you know."

Flynn turned to Dien and raised his eyebrows.

"Ah, what now?"

Dien spoke in low tones.

"I saw the faded stencilling on the side of the hull this afternoon. I studied military history and I know what it means."

Jack growled at Dien.

"We don't want a history lesson, man. Tell him."

Dien took a deep breath and spoke in a rush.

"The hull of this houseboat was used in the Second World War to collect the dead, decomposing Australian soldiers from the Pacific island beaches."

Mouth half open, Flynn stared at Dien, their faces lit by the flickering lamp flame.

"Oh give me a fucking break! First I'm told it was a punishment raft for the Aboriginals and now you're telling me it's—"

Dien finished for him.

"We're standing on a corpse barge."

Flynn turned in the cramped space to glare at Jack.

"Where the hell did you buy this thing, you fucking fool? I hope Jarra only knows his part, not the war history."

Jack shook his head.

"Shit no. Not with all he has on his mind—it's a wonder he's even on board."

Dien spoke.

"Can't we leave and make our way to the coast in the run-about?"

"No we can't", said Jack. "That little thing can't hold five people, we'll end up as croc fodder. And we're not walking forty clicks through this place. Jarra needs to get back to Vanderlin to put this Jonah to proper rest with his elders' help, with ceremonies and stuff. I'm not leaving my friend alone here on this thing. Our only option is to head home and get the hell off." He turned to Flynn. "Mate, I'm sorry. I didn't know. How could I? What was I going to do, demand a history of the thing from the scrapyard in Normanton before I bought it?"

Flynn shook his head.

"Nah, guess not. Let's keep this quiet from Jarra." He checked his watch. "If we go all night, take shifts at the wheel, we should reach home by dawn."

Flynn saw Jack point out the window, down towards the bow. Flynn saw the burning end of Jarra's cigarette down next to the anchor housing. Flynn left the wheelhouse. At the bottom of the ladder he met Angie walking along the boards of the upper deck.

"Hey", she said. "Have you seen Dien?"

Flynn pointed up to the wheelhouse.

"You'd better go up. Jack and Mr Armanis have something to tell you."

In the wheelhouse, Dien stood in the light of the flickering lamp. He had enough military knowledge to picture what it must have been like for the unfortunate men commandeered for war barge duty. He could see them in overalls and gas masks, on body-clearing duty after fighting had moved to another beach. He imagined the screaming shells in the distance, the big robber crabs feasting on the bodies, and he could imagine the horror of the soldiers loading rotting corpses and shovelling limbs and heads into piles aboard the fetid barge. The sorting by badge number and uniform and flesh colour would come later at makeshift morgues. Dien felt ill. He heard someone climb the ladder and turned to find Angie looking in the door.

6

The moon, fat and near full, had risen high. Dien woke. He checked his watch, the luminous dial showing just after 3:00am. He yawned and climbed from his hammock and sat on a fruit crate at the cable spool, his feet on the cool metal. He heard a swishing sound, at first quiet in the night air, but getting louder as if something was drawing near. Sitting upright he became fully awake. He stayed still, not even moving his head while he listened. He heard a soft thud as something unseen struck the outside wall. There was a moment when the night seemed to hold its breath. There came swishing sounds and more soft, padded thuds as things hit the wall.

The moonlight lit the inside of the downstairs room. In the gloom Dien listened and soon became aware of a kind of shuffling drawing closer along the boards outside. He stiffened. The shuffling stopped, seeming to Dien to halt outside the doorway. He leaned forward trying to see through the gloom, but he was unable. He held his straight-backed position, now alert and apprehensive. The shuffling started again, a kind of wet swish, pud, swish, pud, this time seeming to enter the room near the floor. Dien jumped a little and drew his bare feet along the metal floor towards his crate. He waited and listened, but the sound had stopped. He became aware of another sensation. He gathered his bare feet close to his fruit crate seat. He waited a moment and realised he was feeling something touch his feet.

The pressure was applied again, this time with insistence.

Without warning there came the sounds of some swishing, whistling sounds and several metal objects hitting the hull. A familiar smell entered the confines of the darkened room. There came more sounds of pinging as metal objects hit the deck of the boat. Daring to move, Dien reached down to the floor and picked up a hard object. By the dim light of the moon, he studied what he held. Astonished, he realised he was holding a hot, crumpled bullet casing. Looking closer, Dien saw the casing was not a modern one. He studied it further and even in the bad light he knew without doubt what he held was a Second World War Enfield rifle bullet casing. He drew his arm into the room and gagged at the smell filling the space. He sniffed the casing and dry heaved; it smelled like rotting flesh. He dropped the casing and wiped his fingers on his shorts.

He heard a thump against the wall near him and he saw a lengthening shadow deeper than the semi-gloom of the cabin, suggestive of something with many arms, inch down the wall opposite. He spun about but saw nothing there. Something big splashed out in the river. Dien watched with growing horror the many-armed shadow moving up towards the darkness of the ceiling, where he felt something best not seen waited for him to move.

Flynn was upstairs sitting up in his hammock, his legs dangling over the side. Something had woken him; he was not sure what kind of noise it had been but he thought in his half-sleep it had been a kind of swishing sound from somewhere on his level. He reached over to a nail on the inside wall of his room and found the spare kerosene lamp he had hung there. With his matches, he lit the lamp and turned the flame up. There came a suggestion of another swishing sound, but it was quite faint and Flynn was not sure if it was real or fancied. He sat still, legs dangling and listened to the nightlife stirring along the riverbank. A faint scratching sounded from across the walkway near the head of the stairs.

Now fully awake, he noticed a terrible smell had entered his space. There came a faint fumbling tug on the lower part of his jeans. His shirt was grabbed and tugged. He became afraid at not being able to see anything. He felt his face touched ever so gently, as if someone was caressing him. He jerked his legs up and with one hand wiped the spot on his face where he was touched. Another tugging came on his jeans, this time feeling more insistent. Flynn pulled his legs into the hammock.

A plopping sounded on the floor as if something wet and heavy had been dropped. The smell became intolerable. A horror came over Flynn as he sat, not able to move or even think coherently. With sudden resolve he jumped off the hammock and rushed towards the stairs. He stepped on something wet and soft, almost slipping over in the gloom of the central walkway. Managing to hold his balance, he rushed down the stairs. With the sole thought of getting away from the room, he ran from the downstairs walkway out onto the lower deck and hurried to the stern. He stopped by the bench seat and gasped for breath. For some moments he stood sucking in air and exhaling heavily.

Something warm pressed against his bare feet and he lifted first one then the other in confusion. One foot seemed to be held. He jumped up onto the bench seat. Something black and frothy bubbled up from under the hatch cover in front of the bench seat. Flynn ran back to the room where the gaff was kept. He did not see Dien crouching in the dark on the cable spool. Snatching the gaff, Flynn ran back to the stern. He thought he heard someone call his name, a plaintive cry, but in his haste did not stop to check it out. Rounding the corner to the stern, Flynn got back up onto the bench. He leaned over, staring at the froth. Using the gaffe, he levered up the hatch cover. The metal groaned as he pulled the lid up against the bench seat where he crouched.

He squatted, staring down into a shadowed, roiling mass of corruption. An enveloping stench filled the air. His throat filled with his previous meal and he gagged. He tried to swallow but the reflex was shut off. Instead, a rush of stinking food sprayed out from his mouth across the boards and down towards what was rising from the hold of the barge. By the moonlight Flynn could see what looked and smelled like chunks of rotten meat rising, and extended pseudopodia spilled forth and thrashed, spraying blackened blood.

In the wheelhouse, Jack kept a steady three knots. He yawned and realised he should hand the wheel over to one of the others. From the corner of his eye he saw something white out in the darkness ahead. He leaned forward, keeping the speed steady. Squinting, he watched the dark water, and by the light of the moon saw the way was clear of sunken trees. From below, audible above the thrum of the motor, he heard a clanging sound as if someone was bashing a hammer against the hull. He listened, all the while keeping his gaze on the river. He heard the sound again—above, he heard a man's voice calling. He was about to slow and stop to see what was going on below. He saw the flash of white ahead. He leaned forward again, staring, trying to make sense of what he was looking at.

Jack felt a kind of giddiness settle on his thoughts, almost as if his consciousness had tilted. The feeling sickened him and he swallowed. His eyes caught movement outside the window. Something smashed against the side of the wheelhouse with such force it knocked him sideways. He fell and caught the doorframe in time to stop himself falling out over the side. He put his hand on the floor and pushed himself up. Jack saw he was alone in the wheelhouse. Before he could steady himself he felt a blow to his face. He shook his head and blinked several times, trying to focus. He knew he had to stand and grab the wheel before he crashed into the riverbank. With some effort he gained his feet and as he managed to grab the wheel he saw the enormous white thing rear up against the glass. He gaped, open-mouthed, as if mimicking the mouth he saw pressed up against the front window. The mouth grew as it opened to stretch wide across the entire window. Jack saw big teeth. He let go of the wheel and backed up. He twisted in an effort to escape the thing pressing against the window. He heard the sound of glass splintering. He tripped and landed on his knees. Now in a panic, he scrabbled across the floor to the open doorway. A crunching sounded above his head. Jack reached the doorway and clambered out, not daring to look up. A stench washed over him and he gagged, not able to breathe. The air about his face was being sucked away.

Angie sat up in her hammock. She lifted her mosquito net and listened. From under her she heard a kind of slithering. She pulled her legs towards her bottom and sat still, listening. The sound came again directly beneath her. She grabbed the edge of her hammock and leaned forward to look over. Under her bottom she felt something push against the seat of her jeans. She jerked away as best as she was able to in the restricted confines. Her bottom was touched again. For a moment she wondered if it was one of the men playing a prank on her. She realised none of them would even think of behaving in such a way. She felt the back of her t-shirt tugged. As she spun about in the hammock, she heard a loud splash out in the water. She heard a man shout, voice quite high-pitched as if he was scared. She sat still, becoming afraid to move. There sounded under her a loud banging as if someone was hitting metal.

A crunching sound, like wood and glass splintering, sounded from above. Angie heard a man's voice upstairs shout; the cry was repeated several times. She heard fear in that cry. She leaned over the side of the hammock, but in the gloom of the cabin she was unable to properly see the floor. Again she heard a kind of slithering in the darkness. To her horror she saw a shadow seem to slide down the wall opposite. She twisted, not able to stop her encroaching fear. A large shape loomed above her. Angie flung her arms up. She heard the familiar voice above her face and she knew it was Jarra.

"Angie, you have to move, *now*. We've hit something, up in the wheelhouse, maybe an overhanging branch." He helped her off the hammock and waited as she stepped onto the floor. "This way", he said leading her out onto the upper deck walkway. She followed him along to the ladder. The light from the kerosene lamp was flashing as if the lantern was being jerked. Jarra looked up the ladder and thought he saw something white above the roof of the wheelhouse. He heard a cry sound from above and did not recognise the voice. He called out.

"Jack. Jackie!" He began to climb the ladder.

Angie heard a man shouting from below.

"Help, somebody help me. Please."

Angie glanced up at Jarra climbing the ladder. She ran along the walkway for the internal stairs. On the metal of the lower deck a rotten smell made her choke and gasp for air. She breathed through her mouth and stopped. The man's cry sounded from the lower walkway outside the storeroom. Behind her she heard heavy hammer blows striking the hull.

Dien felt someone running their fingers through his hair. There came a rasping whisper next to his face. He felt a rush of warm air play against his cheek. A blow was delivered to his chest and he staggered, the air punched from his lungs. He grabbed the outside railing. Reeling, he ran his hand against the railing as he moved along. Then there was no railing. His hand was grabbing at air. He fell and landed belly first onto the deck. Agony rushed like fire across his stomach and he felt sudden exhaustion. He felt his arms go out over the edge of the boat where the railing had been torn away by Jarra's previous fall. With momentary clarity amid the stabbing pain in his stomach, Dien realised he had landed on the broken bollard. His hands grasped at the air and slapped backwards against the hull and he cried out as his head and upper half hung in the air above the water, his fall stopped by the rusted bollard now slicing into his stomach. He could not help screaming with pain. In his terror and confusion he called out to a woman, to Angie.

He lay there and gritted his teeth, trying to regain calm and fight his way out of his position. He felt a warm wetness spread across his stomach and as the growing pool spread under him he began to bellow his agony. He was aware, through the pain, of a sucking sensation against his stomach, almost as if a greedy thing had pushed stretched lips up through the gaps in the boards to gulp at the spillage. A slight pressure was applied to his belly and he vomited. In the water below, Dien thought he saw red lights blinking on and off. A loud splash sounded from below him and something heavy thudded against the hull, inches from his face. He heard the hiss from below and realised there was a large animal near his head. From somewhere far away he heard his name called. The voice seemed to recede and then grow nearer.

Dien felt weak and began to feel strange. He heard a voice above and he sobbed out a quiet word.

"Angie?"

He smiled when he heard her voice.

"I'm here, sweetie. Hold still. Oh, my God."

Dien felt his legs grabbed and he was pulled. He cried out.

"No. No. No. Oh, please no. Stop."

He felt his legs released. What felt like a hand was placed onto his back. Again he heard Angie's voice close to his face.

"Sweetie. Oh shit! Jarra. Jarra! Help. Help me!"

Dien felt water splash his face, giving him thought other than the sucking at his belly, where already the blood was slaking the awful thirst of the barge. There came a rush of hot fetid air and he gaped down at the dark water, his eyes wide. He felt his head grabbed. His neck twisted and he felt something wet snap shut across his face.

Angie was leaning down close to him when she saw the crocodile rise from the black water and close its jaws, engulfing Dien's head. She cried out and fell on the walkway, her back against the wall. Under the light of the moon she saw her companion's body twist on the deck and there came a snapping of splintering bones. She reached out to grab her friend as the great reptile used is massive body weight to twist and tear Dien free from the bollard and drag him screaming over the edge into the river. Angie snatched her hand back and drew her legs away from the edge.

Under her the deck of The Beast dried as Dien's blood was sucked and ingested by the parasite. Metal pushed up through the gaps between the boards to ripple under her bottom, tasting her. She slithered along the walkway until she was well away from the broken railing. From somewhere above she heard men shouting and the sound of glass splintering. She stood with her back against the wall. She moved towards the stern. With one arm she reached behind her and her hand found the corner of the wall. She moved her fingers insect-like around the corner and turned to face the stern and the bench seat she knew to be there. At first she was not able to comprehend what was happening. She blinked at the sight before her. There, kneeling on the bench seat, was a stinking, slime-covered man—she guessed it was Flynn—grunting and screaming as he hacked at something thick and writhing on the deck. She stood, not able to move as Flynn brought the gaff hook slashing down again and again.

At the wheelhouse door Jack felt something pressed against his throat. He could see nothing but the sensation sickened him, feeling as if a wet mouth, cold, insistent, was pressed against his flesh. In his terror he grabbed the doorway and pulled himself up onto the corrugated iron of the roof of the upper deck. He was too afraid to look behind him. He felt something sticky wrap round his chest. With a frantic effort he grabbed at the appendage and ripped it away. He gained his feet and ran towards the stern. He looked over the low railing at the edge down two levels to the bench seat. For a moment he was confused as to what was happening there. There were two people and something else which writhed in a frothy sea of black. Before he could turn away, a dark column like black rope snaked up towards his face. Jack staggered backwards and turned. Now not knowing what direction he faced, he ran, his onrushing terror speeding him back towards the wheelhouse. Behind, he heard something slap the metal roof at his heels. Ahead he heard a cracking as something white snapped off against the remaining section of the wheelhouse. With a moment of clear sight Jack saw the familiar, frizzy shape of Jarra's hair silhouetted in the swinging light of the smashed wheelhouse. Jack managed a low moaning call for help, but he had no strength in that plea. He heard a swishing sound and felt the boat rock sideways. He took a running leap towards the wheelhouse in an attempt to reach his friend and find safety in his company.

He was stopped mid-leap with both his feet off the roof. There came a sudden pressure behind his eyes and a stabbing fire flashed about his face. He cried out and felt himself thrust backward, his legs dragging out in front of him. He jerked his arms up, his hands scrabbling at the terrible pain in his face. He felt his legs dragged until they slid over the edge of the roof and the railing at the stern, above what was happening on the lower deck. Jack sobbed out a scream as he felt his legs kick into the air. The snapped-off tree branch held him in place through his eye socket, leaving him dangling high above the black water of the nighted river. He gurgled his agony and clawed at the imbedded branch. Blood squeezed from round the edges of the tight fit. Jack writhed as the branch end lay impaled into his brain and his legs jerked in agonising spasms. A trickle of blood ran down across one of his cheeks and flowed over the tattoo, looking like a red trickle of liquid spilling out of the can. With dimming senses, Jack saw but made no sense of the houseboat motoring away downriver to be engulfed by darkness. A bubble of snot and blood popped as he let out his final breath.

Jarra thought he heard someone scream out on the roof behind the wheelhouse. He pulled the handle of the throttle back to stop the houseboat. He pushed the red rubber pad and switched off the engine. Peering out of the shattered windows of the wheelhouse, he guided the boat to the river bank. He glanced down the ladder and could not see Angie. Looking back along the upper roof into the darkness he thought he could see a long, dark shape upriver but he could not be sure. Puzzled and frightened, he called out.

"Jack? Jackie?" He waited and called again. "Jackie?" He began to feel afraid for his friend. He thought of the others. "Angie?" No answer. "Flynny?" He heard clanging and muffled screams from the stern. He heard riverside bushes scraping along the walls of the houseboat. Fearing that the craft would get stuck on an underwater branch, Jarra had no choice but to restart the diesel and head back midstream. He wanted to call for Jack again, but knew in his heart something terrible had overcome his friend. Still he insisted on calling to Jack.

flynn stood by the open hatch cover and heard a sound on the roof two levels above him but did not dare look up. Instead he watched as shadows spilled out from the interior of the barge. A geyser of blood and meat, black under the moon, sprayed out over the stern. Purple-black ropes snaked from the aperture, blood and accompanying chunks of rotting flesh thudded down onto the deck. Froth bubbled up to the lip of the hatchway, thickening by the second to a dense, stinking porridge. The hull of the floor began to bubble. As if in a dream, Flynn heard a roar as of some great prehistoric beast. The barge rocked in the water and Flynn slipped amid the black porridge. On his knees he held the gaff and leaned over the hatchway. With a frenzied cry he bent down and began to hack with the hook and end spike the shapes which oozed and flopped below the lip. Still the putrid masses of ropey intestines poured from the hole, covering Flynn nearly to his waist. He heard a voice screaming from behind him, but did not turn, instead continuing to hack at the engorged ropes. Flynn felt a blow to the side of his head and he fell to one shoulder. He lay there stunned. He tried to rise but could not find the strength. The stinking porridge flowed into his opened mouth while he tried to scream. He felt the viscous mass enter his nose and flow up the passages, his eyes covered by the ooze.

Angie stood aghast at the scene before her. She saw Flynn lying on his side, struggling and screaming in a sea of bubbling froth and squirming ropes. She felt the soles of her feet being sucked at. She heard groans of twisting metal as old, rusted rivets popped their holes. Her heart went out to Flynn and she quickly stepped forward to help him. She slipped on the thick slime and fell face down, her nose sinking into the mass. She thrashed for a moment and managed to lift her face. Something black shot forward and with a rudimentary maw covered her nose and mouth. She tried to cry out but her breath was cut short. She felt a sucking at her throat and felt the bile being drawn up from her stomach, the hot liquid, sour and biting filling her throat.

Flynn tore at his eyes, removing some of the black thickness. Through his horror he was sane enough to realise Angie was lying next to him. He fought to try and help. He managed to rise up onto one elbow. With a shout of rage he let go the gaff and grabbed the thing suffocating Angie. He struggled to gain purchase on the stinking, wet horror. After some attempts he dug his fingers into the soft mass and ripped it from her face. Angie gasped for breath and got to her knees and staggered backwards away from the open hatchway.

Flynn tried to stand but slipped and Angie saw him fall head first into the open hatch. Scrambling forward nearly waist deep in putrid flopping masses, and ignoring the things grabbing at her, Angie looked over the lip of the hatch. She saw Flynn's eyes widen with terror at his predicament.

The hatch closed with a metallic crash, cutting off any escape for Flynn.

Angie felt her legs gripped. Looking down, she saw a thick ropy thing coil around her thighs. She was lifted from the deck and thrown with brutal force against the outer wall of the storeroom. She heard a crack, and numbness settled over her as a trail of blood from her split skull traced her slow passage down the wall into the engulfing mass. Cut off from its parent body, the thing began to shrivel.

Jarra kicked splintered wood away from the wheelhouse doorway. In a final decision he felt he had no recourse other than to let the craft free-float downstream. He managed to turn, and, holding a lit lantern, climbed down the ladder. He knew he had to go down to the lower deck to find what had happened to the others. For a few seconds he stood listening to sounds other than the familiar night noises. He dared to call out again.

"Jackie? Angie?" All was quiet. He stepped forward into the upper walkway and moved over to the inner stairs. He desperately wanted to hear another voice. He made his way down to stand on the step above the metal hull, not wanting to stand upon it. Steeling himself, he stood on the metal floor and waited. He shivered and thought of the awful fate awaiting him. After a moment he stepped out onto the boards and walked to the stern, now ready to face what he was sure would come.

He rounded the wall and with a trembling hand, held up the

lantern. He stood looking down at the crumpled form lying by the bench seat. He stared at the blood smear on the storeroom wall and saw it was already fading, as if the wall was drinking it. Carefully putting one foot before the other, Jarra stepped across the dry metal and knelt next to Angie. He breathed deeply the fresh night air. He leaned closer to her, putting two fingers against one of her wrists and holding his ear across her nostrils. He placed the lantern onto the dry deck near the hatchway. Angie coughed.

He gave a sob of relief. Cupping her head, he gently moved her shoulders and laid her on the deck. Angie coughed again and her eyelids fluttered open. She gave a small smile and coughed again. Jarra grinned down and smoothed damp hair from her face.

Angie spoke first.

"Hey there, bro, what's happening?" She sat and drew her knees up against her chest. She glanced at the now closed hatch cover and moved up against the wall. "What's happening? Oh, my fucking head! Where's—" She stopped, remembering Flynn. A tear formed in each of her eyes.

Jarra felt himself begin to weep. He made an effort to control his emotions.

"The others are not here. I think—"

Angie reached out and put her hand on his wrist.

"Sweetie, they've gone."

Jarra felt hollow. He clenched his teeth together and looked up at the moon and the familiar constellations, looking for bright new ones. He felt small and weak.

"It's under us. We have to leave."

He watched Angie use her back to slide up the wall. She spoke, her voice regaining strength: "I'm okay. Let's get you home."

Jarra nodded weakly. He left her and walked without strength towards the anchor housing. He pulled the metal crank handle. The anchor dropped into the dark water and the barge slapped against the bank. He breathed the night air and stood looking at his feet as if in an effort to see through the hull into the belly. The beast had slaked its thirst for now and was waiting. He knew this and was now not afraid.

He walked back to the stern. He grabbed the long rope attaching his runabout to the corpse barge. Pulling it in, he tied the rope off. Turning, he wiped tears from his eyes. Angie stepped forward and winced in pain. She climbed over the railing and stepped down into the runabout and sat at the stern by the outboard. Jarra climbed past her and sat at the bow. Angie pulled the cord of the outboard, bringing the small motor to life. She grabbed the throttle handle and revved it once. Standing, she untied the rope and felt the runabout float free. She felt the looming presence of the barge grow smaller behind her, but she did not look back.

Jarra sat. He knew there would be time to think and to grieve when he found his elders. He would bring them back and they would do what was right. He did not know how he was going to explain things to the white authorities. Jarra realised how thirsty the land was, a land built upon blood and suffering. In silence he watched Angie watching him as she steered a course towards the Gulf.

The Absurd Quest of Thomas Wu

1

South Island, New Zealand

Tom couldn't remember a sadder day since he had lost his parents. Granddad Hector's funeral had been a sombre affair, with only business and museum associates attending. Tom barely recognised anyone, hunched under umbrellas in the Christchurch autumn afternoon. The two weeks since, he'd organised the sale of Hector's rambling, five-bedroomed Californian. He'd grieved while negotiating with Canterbury University, the removal of the contents of Hector's museum rooms, relics from the South Pacific from Hector's numerous 1950s expeditions to Melanesia and beyond.

Tom sat in his midtown bookshop, his eyes closed as he remembered the funeral. He wiped a tear from his cheek and sat thinking of his granddad, Hector, and of the circumstances leading to his present predicament.

At his bookshop, Tom reached under the counter and extracted the cash box. He unlocked the register and sorted out the money. He switched on the front desk computer and looked out the shop window.

Then he heard a voice. Looking about, he saw the customer. Tom forced a smile.

"Hey, yes. How can I help you?"

The fellow in front of Tom appeared anxious.

"Would you have a copy of *Return to Arcturus*?"

Tom looked at Angus's cat. Spud was still dozing. Tom spoke to the man.

"I've heard of *A Voyage to Arcturus*, but I have never heard of a sequel. Are you sure about the title?"

The customer sighed.

"It says so on the net. So it must be available somewhere."

Tom stared at the man.

"Sir, you don't necessarily have to believe everything you read there. I'm pretty sure that there is no such book."

The customer seemed put out. He rubbed his fingers onto his palms. Turning about, he spoke.

"What's in those boxes on the floor up the end there?"

Tom looked to where the man pointed.

"Them? Don't know. We'll get to sorting them eventually."

"Can't you sort them now?" the man asked.

Tom shook his head.

"No can do, like I said, when we get to them and not before."

"But surely—"

"Listen", said Tom. "You know how long it would take me to sort through that lot for one book for you?"

The man leaned over the counter.

"Can you get it in?"

Tom stared at the computer screen.

"Get it in? I'm pretty sure that the book doesn't exist. Besides, where would I get it? This is a second-hand bookshop. We don't order directly from reps. Oh, wait. I know. I'll put an ad in the paper for you. No wait. Give me a while to search the Internet. When I find a copy I'll go and pick it up for you. Will you mind the shop, just until I get back?"

The man wrinkled his nose.

"No need to get sarcastic." With that he turned about and walked back down the central aisle of the shop to his area of interest. Tom watched him select a fat paperback from the science fiction section. The man glanced at Tom. Then ignoring him, he opened the book.

Tom called out.

"Hey, are you gonna buy anything or just finish that trilogy here before the weekend?"

Tom walked outside onto the pavement to get away from the smell of unwashed customers. He looked down the shopping strip. He rubbed the side of his nose with a finger, blinked and looked along the row of shops. He sniffed the air and found it sour. He felt the skin about his stomach tighten. He looked up and down the street. He swallowed and hurried back inside.

00:3 minutes

The shop phone rang. It was Tom's estate agent calling to say she had finalised the sale of Hector's house. *Hector's house.* Tom sighed, not really wanting to deal with the situation. He calmed his breathing and answered the woman.

"Oh, of course, I'll have the place emptied and the keys to you by Monday morning. The transaction went into my account early this morning. Thank you for all you've done for me these past few weeks. It's been hard, but—what? Oh, of course, the garage as well. The museum people are to empty Grandfather's relic rooms. Yes, I'll remember to cancel the mail." Tom nodded and worked the fingers of one hand like the pincer of a crab. "Yes. Okay, yes, I'll take care of that. Thank you again."

He had also gone through the tedious process of arranging for a curator of the Oceanic Anthropology Department of Antiquities from the Museum of Canterbury to visit the house and assess whether the collected items in Pop's two museum rooms were worth preserving. Tom had realised it was the best he could do to keep the old man's memory alive.

00:2 minutes

Tom sat fidgeting behind his cluttered desk. Half a dozen browsers were wiling away their time flicking through books before heading back to their workplaces. He used a pale finger to rub the fine hair thinning on the back of his head. He tucked his stick legs to one side under his work desk, something he was always forced to do to comfortably seat his skinny, 2-metre frame. He scraped his bottom lip back and forth across his teeth and watched the customers browsing the shelves. He sighed and rubbed his balding spot. He glanced at the antique maps lining the walls above the rows of shelves. He knew he should be selling modern products, such as self-help books, retina readers and immersion games; the ET channel had called them *IGs*, but Tom had found it all gibberish.

At thirty-five, he felt he was wasting away, gathering dust, a forgotten thing, like those dusty items Hector so cherished in his relic rooms. He had seen the irony in selling travel books, when he had only ever been to Australia on book-buying trips. He picked up his phone and keyed the number for the Canterbury Museum. He waited while someone put him through to the curator of Oceanic Anthropology.

00:1 minute

Tom recognised the cultured tone of the woman's voice. He realised that it was how he had always expected someone with such a title would sound.

"Hello, Mr Wu. It's Helen Campbell, I was just thinking about you. Thank you for your call yesterday. I must say I am pleased that you thought of us here at the museum."

Tom chose his words carefully, hoping to sound refined and worldly.

"Thank you for your interest, Dr Campbell. I was wondering what day would be good for you—I mean your department—to view my granddad's private collection."

"Thursday would be good for us, Mr Wu. You mentioned the other day your having to hand the keys over to your real estate agent early next week. Perhaps my department could be finished relocating the collection by then. We can take care of cataloguing at a later date."

Tom nodded to himself.

"Yes, yes, that would be great, thank you so much."

The curator spoke quickly, almost as if she wished to end the conversation before Tom could voice any queries.

"Well, that's settled then. I thank you again. So, we will see you Thursday morning then."

00:30 seconds

Tom felt a little put out. He frowned.

"Um, okay, see you then."

He put his phone onto the desk and rubbed his bald spot. Then he lifted one hand and tapped his thumb and forefinger together like a crab's pincer. He looked about his shop, then out to the street. He was about to go outside again, but remained seated, unable to move. He found himself holding his hands as fists.

00:10 seconds.

Tom cocked his head and blinked. He felt the floorboards under his feet begin to vibrate. He sat upright and looked at the windows giving a view of the city street. Then the room began to violently shake. The book cases tipped and the books began to fly off the shelves.

00:00

The shop windows shattered.

It was a couple of minutes to one in the afternoon when the earthquake toppled Christchurch Cathedral and devastated the central business district. The ground had tilted and a roaring sounded overhead, like a giant airliner skimming the roof of the city block that housed Tom's shop. It had been five months since the first major quake and the ensuing aftershocks had struck the city. People were fully aware what was happening. Weakened single towers and rows of shops still standing after the first event now toppled. This time, a large part of the central business district was reduced to rubble. The chaos in the first hour had seen thousands of shoppers and many shop owners standing dazed in the centre of the streets, some screaming from terror, others simply numb, as they lost balance repeatedly during the aftershocks. The air above the city was a pall of dust and smoke as many fires threw a blanket of suffocating, swirling ash across the city. The wails of the sirens from emergency units could be heard above the rumble and crashes as already tottering buildings finally succumbed to gravity and added to the devastation. Cars and trucks lay cemented in liquified soils, many with only their back bumpers visible above ground level.

Within hours, hospitals up and down the coast of the South Island were at capacity. Rescuers were themselves being rescued from underneath still-falling masonry in the central business district. It was some hours later that emergency services pulled their ground staff from the city centre to regroup and assess the situation. And everyone knew and dreaded the weeks to come when the bodies of those trapped beneath fallen buildings would start to be found, rotting where they lay, at work desks or in cafes, their smashed coffee cups and their computers lying beside their broken bodies.

Tom had been lucky to have escaped with his life. During that first hour, he had stood outside the ruins of the block in the middle of Cashel Street, where his shop had stood. He was shaken and very afraid. An emergency worker, also frightened, had asked Tom and others of the little group he had huddled with, if they could remember how many customers had been in their shops when the quake struck; none of them could remember. The terrified group had been in shock when the two policewomen had led them through the rubble and away from the fires, to a designated marshalling area. Tom remembered being asked many questions by police, themselves looking frightened. But Tom had been unable to be helpful.

During the chaos of the direct aftermath, Tom had fled from the marshalling area. He had met others running, but they had office fire extinguishers and first aid kits in their hands. Some stared at him as he jumped empty-handed over fallen rubble, while already-weakened brick walls crashed down around him. He felt guilt as he left the CBD and made his way to the inner suburbs. He had still the presence of mind to fear that they might wonder if he was running away. He wondered if some of them might think he was rushing to another office block, maybe to help an injured loved one. He thought many things and felt guilt growing as he made his way to the suburbs north of the park at the city's periphery.

It felt as if hours had passed when he found himself wandering the outskirts of the city centre, up a familiar road to Granddad Hector's home. An aftershock growled deep in the earth under his feet, rocking the entire street. Tom stood on the footpath, scared for his life. He closed his eyes for a moment until the ground was still. The neighbourhood was quiet for a moment, as if it was holding its breath. He opened his eyes and turned toward a cracking sound. On a neighbour's house he saw several bricks fall away from the top of a chimney. He waited for the crash. It came as the bricks hit the steel roof and with a horrible grating, sliding sound, toppled over the edge onto a garden bed. Looking about, Tom saw a tree stop shaking as its leaves became still once more. With fear remaining, he hurried past the houses to Granddad Hector's. He looked up at the three chimneys of the old home and was relieved to see that no bricks had fallen.

Dogs were barking across the neighbourhood. Tom vaguely remembered hurrying past people out on the street. He had ignored groups talking wildly, panicked at the unfolding events. In the driveway to Hector's, Tom saw that his old Transit van seemed to be alright. He saw that the carport roof had not fallen down. He scrabbled about in his jacket pocket for his house keys, all the while wondering if there was any internal damage. Inside, Tom stuck his head into the kitchen sink and turned on the cold tap. There was no water. Instead, he opened the fridge and found a half-full bottle of water. He looked about and thought of Hector, wishing the old man was there to comfort him. He regained some composure and sat on the old-fashioned couch in the lounge.

Old family photos lined the walls, with scenes of his father and his mother and him now hanging crooked upon their nails. Another, smaller aftershock rocked him on the couch. He was terrified at the deep rumbling from inside the earth. He saw a small rain of dust dislodge from the ceiling and looked up. In a corner, he saw a large crack in the wall that had not been there that morning. He gazed about the room and his thoughts turned to his granddad Hector, dead these three weeks. He wondered how the old man would have felt about his beloved city being reduced to rubble. Tom felt exhausted and he began to tremble.

His shock was lessening and he felt his emotions coming back.

It was then, as he sat alone and afraid on the couch that he began to cry, for his grandfather and for his city. He sat for some time. He wiped his eyes and then guilt came. He remembered just standing in the middle of the street, the road buckling and heaving beneath his feet. He had been afraid, as had the others. But he had sometimes wondered, before this, just how he would react in a crisis. During those moments of reflection and self-delusion, Tom had always pictured himself as a hero. He had always thought that in times of peril he would put aside feelings of fear and go to the rescue of others. Reality had shown him who he really was. He felt emotionally ugly and he gave a final sob and heave of his shoulders as he sat forlorn on the old couch.

He got up and switched on a light and just stood by the wall, remembering and remembering. He had helped no one, had not braved the choking dust covering the rubble of his city block. He had not stayed to hear the cries of the trapped and the dying. Tom had stared about in disbelief and had allowed himself to be led away to a marshalling area to answer questions. He had not volunteered as a rescuer as so many of those in his position did. He had simply crept away from the carnage and had slunk back to Hector's, afraid and ashamed. In a fit of anger he slammed his fist against the wall. How had he fooled himself into thinking he was different to the coward he was? He went back to the couch and lay down.

It was dark outside when he woke. He rubbed his eyes and saw the thick wooden paling holding the *For Sale* sign leaning against the side of the old television. He blinked and stared at the bright red lettering. He looked back at the large crack near the ceiling. Turning to look at the other walls, Tom saw two more cracks, one gaping wide, a thumb's breadth, reaching from ceiling to floor. He gave a short, snarling laugh. He stopped and looked about. Then he stood and retrieved his water bottle. Outside, he heard the persistence of the sirens. Shouts came from across the tree-lined street, as neighbours assessed the damage to their suburban houses. He heard children crying.

Standing in the middle of the lounge he looked about at the

familiar objects, now seeming strange, not quite real. He remembered Granddad Hector living here, when they were as a family. Tom turned to the brick archway leading from the lounge to the long hallway down to the bedrooms—and Hector's private study museum. Tom realised that the people from the museum would now be having their own problems and no longer be coming. He walked across the carpet, and for a moment he stood under the brick arch. He looked down the darkened corridor and started off down the length. Stopping at the third door, he reached out and closed his fingers round the handle of Hector's private museum. Then he opened the door.

Tom remembered when he was a boy, back to when he would have fascinating conversations with Hector in the big study research room where relics lined the walls or sat stuffed into boxes which would never be emptied and catalogued. Thoughts returned of those adventures his grandfather related about the vast sand wastes in Arabia's Empty Quarter; of the blistering cold navigation of the Sacred Mountain Kanchenjunga in the Himalayas and other fabulous journeys. He realised now that some had been Hector's tall stories, told to a spellbound boy for the benefit of his education in geographical matters.

Hector had imparted within young Tom a spirit of adventure and a desire for knowledge of the mysterious and unreachable. The spark had diminished during Tom's teen years. Somehow life had seemed to get in the way, until the spark died. Instead of travelling the world, Tom settled for a life in a book shop, surrounded by globes and maps.

If Hector had ever been disappointed in Tom's decisions, he had never shown it.

He had not set foot in the space for nearly two decades and he wondered if the room would seem smaller because of the intervening years; and there came a realisation that perhaps the remembered collection would be nothing more than a few spears hanging from the walls, an old shield perhaps and a dozen crumbling cardboard cartons with old tatty Pacific Island relics spilling onto the floor. Already he was dreading that even the old wooden world globe would be nothing more than a little spinning ball amid old fountain pens and note books and chipped rock paperweights on top of an old, child-sized desk. He breathed the dust of decades and the mustiness made him cough. He felt for the light switch and flicked it on. He readied himself for disappointment. Then he sucked in his breath and blinked. It was all there, unchanged and so familiar.

His first thought was how big things were. The desk was a great walnut director's desk with forward-facing shelves and doors with big cast iron handles. A second desk, darker in colour, sat alongside, forming an L-shape. The main desk was at least two metres long and there on top, covered in dust, was the globe, not a small ball on a pedestal but a great wooden orb a metre in diameter. Tom gave a short laugh of amazement. He looked around the walls. Hanging from every part of the space were spears and shields and robes made from feathers. Tall shelves which he did not remember stood flush with the wall, hiding faded wallpaper, old even in the seventies. A low cabinet sat in front of the high, west-facing stained-glass window. Tom stared at this for some moments. In the long, flat drawers he knew he would find a fantastic array of insects, all pinned to yellowed paper. He laughed, realising that he just needed his re-entry into this room to have all the names come flooding back to him. He turned and shut the door. Then, stepping across the faded carpet, he sat in Hector's leather chair. He rubbed his hands along the worn armrests and looked about. Ahead, in his direct line of vision, he saw the large chief's cloak from Auckland. He remembered back when he was a little boy, frightened that there were giant Samoans walking the streets of Auckland in the 1950s, with war paint and exotic feathers hidden under their western clothes, just waiting to pounce and to drive spears through anyone who dared to cross their paths. He smiled at the thought. As he looked at the various items, his thoughts took a less nostalgic turn. During the last year of his life, Hector too had forsaken the collection and had abandoned it to dust and grime.

Tom glanced at each of the items in turn, spears, headdresses, cloaks and shields; small carved stone idols on low tables, all draped in spider webs and cloaked in dust. Without anyone left to share the relics with, Tom now realised that he was looking at objects that had no place in a private home. These items were, no doubt, bought and sold many times by white men during and after the nineteenth century. They belonged in a proper museum. Then Tom realised that he was probably wrong there as well. He found himself reappraising what he had been taught by Hector. And Tom knew that these relics did not even belong in a museum in New Zealand; they belonged in a room somewhere at the place of origin. Looking about he began to feel guilty about the objects. Then for the first time in his life, he began to feel distaste for the collection. He realised then that neither he nor Hector were good people. And it hurt.

For the first time in twenty years he touched the globe.

Tom spun it as he did as a child and watched the countries, just discernible under the dust, reel by. When the globe slowed, Tom stuck his palm upon it to stop its movement. The globe spun under his pressed palm for half a rotation, leaving a line of its dust-covered surface swept clean. He poked his index finger down hard. The globe stood still under his finger. He leaned down and looked at the island chain sitting northeast of Papua New Guinea. He remembered Grandfather Hector's tales of discovery near the New Guinean border with the old Dutch territory of Irian Jaya. Tom picked up a piece of paper from the dusty desk and found a pencil. He looked at the map again and copied the words from the globe where he had stopped it with his finger: Runakau, Tokonu Islands. Then he put the scrap of paper into his shirt pocket.

Walking back to the doorway, he switched off the light and turned to face the darkened hallway. At one end, the light from the lounge guided his steps past the bedrooms. He walked into the lounge and stood looking at the old television. Hector had never been one for modern appliances and so garnered all his information from what he called "the old idiot box". Hearing sirens wail along the main road two streets over, Tom found the remote and switched on the television, flicking through the channels, realising that all were showing the news.

The city centre had already been cordoned off. Floodlights had been erected at the safest periphery. Tom watched emergency workers scurrying about in an attempt to keep the ghoulish spectators from venturing too close. He found it hard to believe he was looking at the city which, hours before, had been a vibrant centre of streets and shops full of people. He heard the voiceover of some breathless reporter.

"Christchurch CBD no longer exists. Emergency services have just reported that an entire 10-block square of the inner city is being cordoned off into what is already being labelled *The Red Zone—*"

Tom slouched where he sat, already beginning to loathe himself for the coward he had realised he was. He growled at the television, at the rescuers running about, at the voiceover, and he growled at the big yellow excavator machines which were being filmed arriving outside the Red Zone. It was then that he made up his mind to just up and leave Hector's house, to not clean or to move anything, just leave the country. He would do what he always did best—run from trouble. He cursed himself.

"You scum arsehole bastard. You prick."

He sat for some time, wondering how he was going to organise things. He thought about contacting his friends in the book trade in Sydney, but decided instead to text them that he was safe. He checked his messages and found he had several that had come in during the afternoon. He bulk-sent and dropped his hand onto the couch, his thoughts turning to the city in ruins. The television was playing the devastation second by second, and journalists and camerapersons were held back by lines of police, all trying to appear to be in control. Tom thought about his shop and wondered again about the several people he knew for sure had been browsing. He did not recall seeing them out on Cashel Street with him. He cursed again. There was nothing left for him. He had nothing left here. The house was no longer his and he had to vacate. He looked across at the archway and thought of the relic room—a place for the dead, holding things pilfered and now unimportant. Then he remembered the note he had written himself. Reaching up, he took the scrap of folded paper from his shirt pocket. Then, opening it, he again read what he had written. Runakau: Tokonu Islands.

He stared at the patch of carpet with the little pile of plaster dust than lay under the crack in the wall. He used the remote to switch off the television. He realised that the airport would be a seething mass of commuters, but he decided it was better to sleep the night in a departure lounge and wait the many hours for an available flight to Australia, than to risk staying in the house and having a wall fall on top of him. He stood and turned off his phone. Then, with a plan forming, he used a flannel and the water from his electric jug to have a cold body wash. He changed his clothes.

At Christchurch airport, Tom had expected to be turned away due to outgoing flights being cancelled. To his surprise, flights out of the city were ongoing but incoming flights had doubled due to rescue units of police, firefighters and army personnel arriving from Auckland, Wellington and Dunedin. Seven hours after arriving amid the crowds at the airport, Tom provided his passport at the departure counter and put a single suitcase through the baggage counter. He had watched the rows of relief workers leaving the airport to board shuttle buses to the devastated city. Again he felt a coward for not staying and helping. He knew what he was and hung his head. He wandered through to the departure lounge and an hour later boarded a flight to Australia.

Sydney's Kingsford-Smith Airport was abuzz with the news of the devastation. Even here rescue workers were boarding flights to cross the Tasman. Tom watched people talking and he felt shame.

Some hours later, Tom boarded a flight to Rabaul out on the Papuan Island of New Britain. Rabaul Airfield had recently been haphazardly resealed, and cut a swathe through a forest of sago palms. The arrivals-departures lounge was abuzz with people from many backgrounds. He overheard the conversations of geologists and oil people, surfers and biologists and even Mormon missionaries all using Rabaul as a jump-off into to the Solomon

Islands, or Manus or the Caroline Islands up in Micronesia.

After walking to the town across the isthmus, and checking out the local food vendors, Tom had escaped the heat and returned to the busy airport. Here a new crowd were awaiting their flights on the ageing *Air Niugini* planes. Tom looked about; part of him felt as if he was actually doing something with his life, instead of just reading about others' travels, another part felt disgust at what he had proved himself to be.

In the small terminal, he began the long wait for the flight out to Runakau. It was 7:00pm when he settled back in a rattan chair to read as he waited the ten hours for his flight out to the Tokonu group. During this time he found himself not reading, but just sitting watching people come and go. He overheard snippets of conversations as they passed and wondered what they might be doing with their lives. He slept with his book open on his chest. At one point he woke with a start, mistaking the roar of a propeller aircraft outside for the sound of an approaching earthquake. He glanced about and stretched and checked his watch, and saw that it was 6:00am. He felt sore and rubbed his aching legs. It was with mixed feelings of excitement and regret when he answered the call to board the flight for the haul out to Runakau.

Tom knew the plane would be old, but when he saw it from down on the runway, he was surprised to find it was a 1950s propeller-driven antique. He wondered if it would get him safely out past New Ireland's Latangal Island to the edge of the Pacific Ocean without ditching into the deep. The aircraft sat low at the back with nose pointed at about 30 degrees. Twin propellers front of each wing looked ungainly and the window ports were of the old-fashioned, rounded style. He thought it looked like something out of an old *Indiana Jones* movie. He pictured the cabin would have space for goats and chickens and there would be crates of bootleg liquor. Upon entering the ancient aircraft he gaped and blinked, not believing what he was seeing. He had guessed correctly. Lining each side of the forward part of the cabin in crude luggage racks, were cases of beer from all parts of the Pacific. He laughed, not even bothering to count how many. Looking into the passenger section he counted six people strung out among the thirty or so berths. He found a window seat halfway down the sloping aisle and sat his suitcase on the seat next to him. With his long skinny legs pressed close to the seat in front he sat uncomfortably for some moments, turning sideways across both seats and relaxing. He felt the aircraft shudder as the propellers were started. The old craft rattled against its bolts.

Tom felt excited and nervous. He reached into a side pocket of his luggage and took out a folded map of Latangal Island, which he'd found in Port Moresby. Sitting amid the noise of the cabin, he studied the map, tracing his finger out past the long isthmus. There he saw the word: Tokonu. He smiled, thinking it rather humorous at how island groups got their names. He recalled the time when he questioned Hector about The Three Kings Islands north of New Zealand, wondering why they were called that when in fact there were more than thirty. From that day on, he'd often wondered just how many islands and islets and wave-breaking reefs there were on the planet; just how many remote places that had merely been seen from a ship and had not actually been explored. He wondered whether such were the case where he was about to land. He wondered if there could be more stacks and reefs below than accounted for even on his enlargement map. He studied the island chain, holding it not quite open against the seat in front. His phone would have given him better a view of the island terrain, but it was turned off and packed away in his bag. He kept turning back and forth across the seats trying to get comfortable. He slept for a while.

A stomach-sinking patch of turbulence buffeted the ancient plane. Tom sat up, in a panic. The craft seemed to drop for some seconds before the pilot steadied it. He looked at his watch and judged the time it had taken since leaving Rabaul. He looked out of the window of the plane. Below he saw a green forest canopy blanketing steep hillsides and realised he had arrived and the plane was descending. He saw three coastlines of the large main island of Runakau. The shape reminded him of a T-bone steak. A row of lagoons, sandy-bottomed and shallow with light blue water, stretched away along the middle and out of sight into the low mist shrouding that part of Runakau. When the plane banked in preparation to land, Tom caught a glimpse of two other much smaller islands sitting inside surrounding reefs. These three, along with several tiny islets, made up the Tokonu group, sitting parallel to Latangal on a ridge bordering a deep oceanic trench separating the Bismarck Sea from the Pacific. Tom figured that if people thought that Papua was remote, then they should try being all the way out across the Bismarck Archipelago.

It was just before 9:00am when the plane taxied up to the bamboo and thatch-roofed terminal at the end of the earthen runway. Tom stood and picked up his suitcase and waited to leave the aircraft.

2

A rickety minibus met the few passengers at the tiny terminal. The driver, a hulking Tokonu islander, introduced himself as Eel.

"Welcome to Runi. I hope you're used to one-star accommodation, my friend."

He laughed — a big hearty sound. Eel continued chatting.

"If you're not used to running rough and ready, you're not gonna like the locals. Oops, too late, you're already here, aren't you?" He gave another booming laugh, which made Tom smile. Tom sat in the seat behind Eel as the big man scrunched in his seat and started to belt out a tune in what Tom guessed was Tokanuan. Eel manoeuvred the rattling bus around potholes. To Tom's consternation, Eel turned to face him.

"No money here for decent roads, so watch your head." Tom was relieved when Eel turned back to look where he was going. Eel laughed and bounced the bus along the single-lane gravel road. Tom looked out the window of the bus and noticed how lush and green the island was. Eel drove the bus along the edge of a large lagoon. He shouted back.

"We got prehistoric shark teeth all along the shores of these lakes. We ship 'em and sell them in the touristy places in New Zealand and Australia. Great big black teeth; must've pretty sizeable fish, eh?"

Tom nodded. He stared out at the green wall of jungle sitting close to the road.

The main island's only hotel was a ramshackle timber and brick affair. With a rusted corrugated iron roof, sloped to allow rain to run off, it sat some ten metres from the long, curving sandy beach of a bay. Sculptures of beached driftwood erected by someone were placed at intervals along the foreshore. Protecting the sides of the hotel from the winds were lines of tall palms with small ones planted between. Fishing boats bobbed in the shallow water offshore; more were on slipways and dry docks next to the hotel. At the front of the hotel near the beach, a pier with maintenance sheds jutted out into the bay.

Tom watched some of the passengers from the minibus walk off in different directions. He gathered they were locals and not staying in the hotel. He walked into the front door and found himself in a small lobby. A big fan, dust-covered and rocking on its revolutions, hung from the yellowed ceiling. Bamboo chairs and tables sat by the big windows facing the bay. Tom heard many voices coming from an adjoining room. He walked across and looked through a square window set in the middle of the door. He opened it and stepped into the public bar. The smell of sweat and tobacco smoke washed over him. He stood there looking round at the crowd gathered at tables, all chattering as some watched a big television bolted high up on the wall above the bar. The place was full of women and men of many races. Those not watching the television were playing cards, while others were filling in betting forms or rolling cigarettes. A few stopped what they were doing and turned to stare.

Tom turned towards the bar when he heard the publican shout out.

"Hey, you guys! Papua New Guinea selection for the Pacific Rugby Cup's come through." The bar went quiet. The publican grinned. "I've got some paper and pens for you lot. If any of you can give me a full list of who has been selected, I'll waive your bar tabs. You people owe me plenty, so none of you better get it right, okay?"

Tom stared as the crowd in the bar leaped towards the counter. He walked through to the lobby to check into is room, to the raucous sounds of "PNG, PNG, go the Pukpuks."

Tom walked up to a window which he supposed was the

booking office. A slim, tanned woman with hair piled high on her head turned from a computer.

"Oh, hello there, I'm Joyce. "She looked at a register she had opened on a desk. "You're…Tom?" Tom noticed she had a slight French accent; he thought of French Polynesia, but realised he was in fact in Melanesia. "I trust the flight wasn't too bumpy for you."

Tom shook his head and felt sticky in the heat being moved round by the big fan.

"No. It was okay, really. Better than I expected."

"You mentioned over the phone you're here for a holiday. I'm afraid we don't get many people holidaying here. It's mostly repair staff and professional fisher folk." Joyce turned the register round to face him. "Still, if it's a holiday you want, I'll do my best to scrounge up one of the locals to show you around. We don't have any posh rooms I'm afraid, but what we have should make you feel comfortable. There's a fridge and a fan."

Tom was happy with this.

"I couldn't ask for more, Mrs—"

"Joyce."

She watched Tom sign in and date the page.

"Oh, there's one thing, Tom. Don't touch the bugs. If you get certain caterpillar hairs anywhere near your eyes, you will wish you were dead. I don't mean to scare you, but it's the little things you have to be wary of. Oh, don't look so worried. They are not going to be in your room. They're out there", she said, pointing at the rear window of the office. She walked through the office door into the lobby. "Here, let's get you to your room."

He followed her along a passageway.

"Oh," she said. "There is a wake tomorrow for one of the local lads. Poor boy got drunk and crashed his motorbike. They're having the service down the coast at Owenga. There will be a mass of vehicles lining the road during the afternoon. You'll have to put up with a bit of noise tomorrow night when they all come back here. I won't be closing until 2:00am. I have to say that you look the quiet type, so perhaps you'd better not spend any time in the public bar. That lot will have you whisked off to all manner of drunken parties."

Behind them came a loud cheer from the public bar. Tom stopped behind Joyce as she unlocked a door. She turned to him

"Here's your room key." Tom had a quick look.

"It's good, yeah, thanks."

A single bed sat against one wall. A hand basin and a towel on a rack sat flush with the opposite wall. The room's only window was covered with fine mosquito netting. Tom switched on the room's fan and watched it wobble up to speed. Joyce waited in the hall.

"One of the local farmers is taking a diesel mechanic up the coast to his property tomorrow. They are going to working on his fishing boat. "What say I organise him to drive you up to Kiangarapa tomorrow? The locals will want to finish the wake and he wants to be part of it. They'll all sleep it off and he'll drive you up. You'll enjoy Kiangarapa. Full of shacks made of corrugated iron and tree stumps. Nice people, but it's a shantytown. Rugged, but it has good fishing. Only twenty clicks past the lagoons and take you no time at all."

"Yeah, great, thanks. I noticed in the public bar, there are so many nationalities here." He wondered if he was coming across as racist. Joyce either did not notice or she simply did not care.

"Well, the world is a smaller place than it was. But there are still some places, here for instance, which provide a haven for those seeking to get away from things — the rat race, the smell of the cities, their past."

Tom looked steadily at Joyce. She continued. "Some people are running from debt and things, I guess. And some end up here of all places.

He saw her studying him.

"What do you mean 'here of all places'?"

Joyce looked at the palms of her hands.

"Oh, I guess nature made some places kind of weird.

Tom wondered what she meant. Joyce veered into another conversation.

"We have an artist's colony down the coast a little ways at Owenga. All kinds come and go and take their paintings with them. I'm not sure if it's the air or the tricks of light, but they come and they go, you know?"

Tom decided on a day trip by himself. With a map provided by Joyce, he left his room with a bottle of water and some sandwiches which he had asked the chef to make for him. He walked from the pub out onto the main road leading south to Owenga. The day was fine and he enjoyed the walk. He looked about at the small paddocks bordering the road, seeming to hold the rainforest at bay. He breathed deep the smell of the ocean to the left. As he walked he listened to the birdlife hidden among the canopy of the forest. The occasional old and battered car passed him on the road. An hour into his walk he caught a ride with a couple of locals. The trip was awkward because neither offered up conversation the entire way. At Owenga Beach Tom was relieved to exit the vehicle.

He wandered along the beach and watched the incoming tide. Weatherboard houses sat amid the bracken and gorse thistles on the slopes bordering the beach. A stone monument near the beach had a plaque dedicated to shipwrecked sailors. Tom sat and watched the waves while eating his sandwiches. He brushed off his pants and walked up the length of the beach. Turning back, he retraced his steps the distance along the sand to the road. He felt it odd that since being dropped off, he had seen no one. He decided to make his way back to the hotel.

The distance seemed longer than he remembered. After several hours walking, with only the occasional car passing him in the opposite direction, Tom looked about the landscape. He felt as if he had somehow walked down through the hollows and along a piece of the winding road several times. Dusk was approaching. As he walked north, he saw cars and trucks heading past him into Owenga and he realised they were going to the wake. He walked on. Night closed on the island. The rising, dipping, single-lane road taxed his patience. For forty minutes he trudged up and down. He saw headlights coming towards him in the darkness. Tom heard animal sounds from the woods and noticed a curious buzzing sound. He found himself feeling dizzy. He teetered and forced himself to stay upright. The feeling left him when he walked out onto the middle of the road. He waited for the vehicle to pass. He was surprised when the car stopped next to him. Not used to this situation in a big city, Tom hesitated to approach the vehicle. He looked at the person driving, easily visible with the interior lights on. It was a woman. She exited the vehicle.

"You're not from round here, are you? You lost?" She stepped backward. "By the direction you're going I'd say you are staying at the hotel."

Tom nodded in the darkness.

"Yes, I am. How far back is it?"

"If you're walking it will take you a few hours. I'm sorry, I can't take you back, but I'm sure you will get a lift before too long."

She looked to her left towards the island's interior.

She stepped back to her car and climbed up into the driver's seat, closing the door.

"You should hurry along, this is not a place to be walking alone at night."

Tom thought about this.

"You know," he said, "in most places a woman would not stop for a man on a country road, they would consider it dangerous. Thank you for stopping to help."

She smiled.

"It's my pleasure. Again, sorry I can't drive you back to the hotel." She paused and again looked over Tom's shoulder towards the forested surrounds.

"Do stay on the road though, won't you?" She put the vehicle into gear and drove off towards Owenga. With the woman's vague warning still fresh, Tom began to feel uneasy.

He was glad to be wearing his bush shirt about his waist; he unknotted it and put it on. The moon had risen above the black wall of forest. He walked along the centre of the road, listening to the wind rustling through the trees. He trudged along, guessing he had walked close to ten kilometres. Cloud cover hid the moon and he found it difficult to see the road as it turned and dipped into a gully. He stopped and rotated his arms and breathed heavily. Looking ahead he saw two dim lights. Standing still, Tom saw the lights belonged to a stationary vehicle. As he approached he saw a shape leaning against trees bordering the side of the road. Wind whistled amongst the foliage, deadening his footfalls on the road. Tom hesitated near the front of the old Ford pickup. He looked behind him before venturing to speak.

"'Scuse me, do you know how far it is back to the hotel?"

Tom saw the man jump and curse as he turned about.

"What the hell! Hey!"

High clouds moved and uncovered the moon. The man stepped forward and Tom saw he seemed to be a local islander. The man bent down and appeared to be wiping his hands onto the grass at the side of the road and wiping them on his clothes.

"Man! You scared the daylights out of me. What you doing here, my man?"

"I'm walking back to the pub. I got to Owenga and couldn't get a ride back. So how far have I got to go?"

The man stared at Tom and looked past him, as had the woman outside of her van. Tom also turned and looked. All he saw was darkness as the clouds again covered the moon.

The driver introduced himself: "Hey, my man, I'm Sammy, Sammy T. Who the hell are you and what you doing way out here, fella?"

Tom felt a little better now he had company.

"Tom, Sammy. I'm Tom, here for a visit to your island."

Again Sammy looked out into the darkness.

"You could get real lost out here if you strayed off the road. Not good. I was going down the coast to visit my friends, but I think we should get you back to your digs." Sammy stepped forward into the glare of the vehicle's headlights. "C'mon, jump in, I'll take you back."

Tom walked round the vehicle and opened the passenger door, which squawked on rusty hinges. Sammy climbed in behind the steering wheel and slammed his door several times to get it to shut properly. He leaned over the seat and rummaged in the back. Turning and settling himself, he handed Tom a six-pack of beer.

"Have one and crack one for me too." He started the car and turned to Tom and stared, then laughed.

"C'mon lad, you gonna nurse that beer?"

Tom found the man's good nature reassuring.

"Oh, yeah, sorry. I hate to say it, but I don't usually drink and drive." He pulled a bottle from the pack and unscrewed the top, handed it to Sammy.

"Thanks. I don't usually either, lad. But tonight we'll be lucky to meet another vehicle, and besides, you're not driving." Sammy drained half the contents and drove off along the narrow, winding road towards the pub.

After a couple of kilometres sitting in silence, Tom turned to his rescuer.

"Can I give you some money for petrol?"

Sammy laughed at this. With one hand he steered his pickup and with the other upended his bottle and drained the contents. "Chuck me another of those beers, lad."

Tom repeated the task and looked out his window. All he could see was the huge black wall of nighted forest. Sammy sniffed and cleared his throat.

"Y'know, Tom, you shouldn't be out here at night, alone. There're wild boars on these islands—Captain Cookers, big, vicious and territorial. They catch you on their night turf without a weapon, you're history. By the way, boyo, there's places round here you wouldn't want to fall into. For your safety."

Tom drank more of his beer and wondered what the man was alluding to.

"Safety, what, like mine shafts and things?"

"As I said boyo, pigs and such."

"And such?"

"Gravity here is weird," said Sammy. "Can't quite explain it but things turn upside down. Could be magnetic minerals lying under the ground in these parts, damned if I know."

"What d'you mean about gravity and...and minerals?"

"Some places round this neck of the woods turn a person sideways. Roads here were made to stay away from these places. I mean a man can get sent sideways. Y'know? Forget the boars, boyo, there's more to worry 'bout out here than a few wild pigs. There are places where—" He shut his mouth and looked straight ahead.

Tom had no idea what Sammy meant, but he did know with his companion's penchant for drunk driving, he might well be raving about nothing.

Several kilometres later Tom felt relief when he saw the fork in the road he had walked past on the way to Owenga. Sammy steered the old Ford left and a few minutes later Tom saw the lights of the pub. He took a deep breath, happy to have made it back. Sammy steered his pickup past the little general store and down the gravel slope to the foreshore at the front of the hotel.

Tom turned to Sammy.

"Hey, thanks, I really appreciate it."

Sammy ducked his head to look out the passenger window.

"Hey, no problem. Say, are you that fella Joyce has be talking about, needing a little sightseeing?"

Tom laughed.

"Yeah, that's me."

Sammy nodded. "Surprised I didn't guess sooner. How 'bout I meet you outside here at ten tomorrow morning?"

Tom laughed again.

"Sure, I'll be ready."

"Bring some grub and plenty of water, when I drop you off up at Kiangarapa you'll be left to your own devices for more than two hours."

Tom nodded and waited for Sammy to drive off.

3

Sammy pulled up to the hotel car park in his pickup, which looked more battered in the light of day. The paint job was a patchwork of colours and dabs of rust preventer. There were two missing fenders and bashed-in back tray.

"So where's the mechanic you're supposed to pick up?" Tom asked.

Sammy pointed a finger to his own head and pretended to fire a gun.

"Idiot went up to my place with Matt, the pig hunter. He's gonna be doing some culling round the area. I'll meet them there. Jump in."

In the light of day, Sammy's face showed the life of a hard-working island man, a face lined and leathery from years of hand-to-mouth existence, exposed to rain and the lashing salt water, the creased and leathern face of a man with stories to tell. And yet his voice was soft, his manner kind, not surprising for someone who had seen real hardship.

Sammy drove out of town north, up into the wild hill country. Here, rain forest met the beaches. A clay road had been cut decades before, to run alongside the shoreline. Sammy steered as best he could, holding tight to the steering wheel as the vehicle bounced up and down the hills along the rugged island road towards the coastal town of Kiangarapa. During half an hour of bouncing across potholes and looking out at the interminable green fastness of the jungle, Tom jerked up and down in his seat, holding one hand against the cab roof to stop from bashing his head against the rusted metal. He looked out and realised if he had not left the map before, he had now.

Sammy skidded to a stop opposite a big signpost. Tom looked up at its many plank arrows. He was relieved to be out of the vehicle. Turning, he leaned into the cab.

"Thanks, Sammy. I guess it doesn't get any more remote than this, eh? We're off the map, so to speak."

Sammy stared at Tom, as if trying to figure an answer. He set his lips in a straight line.

"Oh, no, boyo, this isn't remote. Listen to me, lad, there are some treacherous patches of ground round these parts. Stay to the paths." Before Tom could question him, Sammy continued: "I'll be back in an hour; you can walk around town. There's not much to see but—" He looked ahead over the steering wheel. Putting the pickup back into first gear, he drove off.

Tom stopped under the signpost and looked up. He was puzzled when he saw there was nothing whatsoever written on the planks. He had expected one of those novelty signs, giving the distance in kilometres to London or to Auckland, or Timbuktu. They were blank. He shook his head.

"Shit, of all the crazy—" He looked along the side road. Ahead he saw a couple of makeshift buildings sitting on the curve of the road. He guessed this to be the start of the town, with the main lot of buildings out of sight around the bend. He turned and looked at the arc of the beach ahead and decided to see that before he went into the town. Near the high water mark he picked up a piece of driftwood and poked the sand as he went. After some minutes he found himself nearing the open waters of the Pacific. Green-grey waves smashed against jagged rocks.

He breathed deep the smell of the sea. He clambered over sharp boulders. He stood and saw a rock pool below. He felt a tingling in his right arm and lifted a hand to rub the spot. He felt as if he was going to pass out. He sat on the rocks in an attempt to steady himself. He felt as if the landscape was closing round him. After a few moments he felt a little better. He stood and meandered back along the beach. Back at the signpost he turned down the side road and walked along the sandy track into town. Every few steps a dizziness halted his progress. He felt as if the earth was lower than it was, and as he walked he felt like a drunk who had misjudged the ground under his feet. With each step, his foot came down heavily to jar his leg. He blinked and felt his surroundings seemed somehow wrong. He stopped and rotated his head. The dizziness stopped and he felt normal again.

He rounded the curve in the sandy track and walked past the first of the buildings. Across the small hill hiding the town he could hear the screeching of the rainforest birds. Divided by the soft sand tract were two rows of what looked to be private houses. He came to a wide gap between the buildings and looked down at a beach. There was a boat riding in the swell. Tom had expected to see a fleet of fishing vessels. There were no people in the town and he wondered if everyone was out on the boats. He continued along what he guessed to be the main street. The town itself was not what he had expected.

Everywhere he looked he saw makeshift homes constructed from paint-faded planks, rusted sheet metal and bottle glass. Some dwellings even had door and window frames made from driftwood. One small home had the front facing the sandy street made entirely of beer bottles held together with concrete. Old oil drums, piles of rope and discarded fishing nets cluttered the areas between the makeshift homes. The smell of drying kelp thrown up onto jagged rocks was pervasive.

He turned and walked back to the wide gap between the houses. There was a sandy track leading between two low hills. He turned up this and began to climb the slope. He could hear the screech of many birds, closer now. He stopped and rested on his hands and knees halfway up the trail of soft, shifting sand. For some moments he had realised something was not right. He zoned into the sounds of the birds again. He knew what was troubling him. Although not knowing how exotic birds sounded in the wild, he knew now these unseen creatures were sounding somehow wrong. He clambered upon his hands and reached the space between the two hills. Standing, he looked down a slope at a marshy tract set in a small valley dotted with weirdly shaped palm trees.

He looked back down the way he had come. Above the roofs of the shanty town

he saw the horseshoe bay stretch towards the headlands bordering the Pacific. He studied the rows of shanties and noticed somehow the town seemed a lot further away than it should have. He blinked, but the distance remained the same.

He blinked again, and it appeared as if the town had leapt, or jerked, towards him. He jumped backwards, crying out in fright. He looked once more and saw the town had not moved closer. He frowned and turned back to look down at the marsh in the little valley. Purple sedge grew from the wet pools and beyond he could see the wall of green jungle fringing the open area. He saw mosquitoes which seemed to have too many legs. Leaving the sandy track of the marram grass-covered dunes, he started down into the valley.

Rain started in from the south. It grew heavier by the minute. The area had many hummocks rising at intervals above the level of the algae-covered water. Tom used these to cross the space. He lifted his face to let the cool water run down his throat and in under his shirt. He felt lightheaded. Ahead through the downpour he saw a wooden footbridge on a stretch of flat, higher ground amid the swamp. He made for it. As he approached, he thought he heard his name whispered somewhere close by. Turning, he could see no one. He felt so good he disregarded it and kept stepping to each piece of higher ground. He walked past a lone tree, bulbous at the trunk with branches splayed. In the centre at the top of the trunk he saw a big piece of knotted wood, crinkled like a prune. He heard a swishing sound. Turning to the tree he saw a long rope of whitish gristle flick out from the prune head, and as quickly vanish back to its hiding place. For some moments he stared at the prune growth, but the gristle never re-emerged. He walked with hurried steps past the tree and continued his slow way across the expanse towards the bridge.

Tom saw it was a short construction, spanning a narrow gorge, the bridge itself made from planks set apart and tied with twisted fibres like home-made rope. He stepped up to the poles holding the rope and noticed a hand-painted sign nailed to one of the uprights.

"This structure is unsafe, please do not use."

He looked along the length, noting it extended for over fifteen metres. It looked well-made and sturdy. He did not think it was in any way unsafe. Ignoring the sign, he leaned forward and looked over the edge of the gap into the deep fissure. Ten metres down, a stream flowed across various-sized boulders lining the length of the gorge. The rain lessened a little, but Tom saw the stream below was rushing with more strength and rising up the walls towards him. In the strengthening downpour he saw someone had left a cardboard box in the middle. The rain was draining from the hillside and from several streams and was now creating a river down in the gorge. Tom heard the rush of water loud from the narrow walls. For the second time he thought he heard the whisper of his name.

He looked at the cardboard box, now soaking and bulging at the middle, threatening to spill out its contents. Tom had a sudden urge to step out onto the bridge and look into the box to see what it contained. He thought he felt a soft touch on his arm. He reached down and stroked the area with his hand. For the briefest of moments he felt his fingers caressed. He pulled his hand away and looked at it. Turning, he saw he was alone. The downpour had momentarily eased. Tom wiped the rain from his face. He flicked his hand and stared at the cardboard box. He remembered something about unattended boxes concealing unpleasant surprises. He wondered if it was a trap, something to entice the unwary. Ignoring his feelings he stepped further out onto the boards, gripping the rope holds. He felt a sudden rush of nausea and he leaned over the rope and vomited down into the rising, rushing water. He slipped a little on the wet planks, but he felt somehow compelled to step further out over the river. He heard a musical laugh. He turned to face the way he had come.

She was very small, and was wearing a strange looking one piece swimsuit. He leaned forward a little and realised she was a tiny adult. Looking again through the rain, he thought she looked very strange. Although he could not be sure because of his limited vision, Tom thought her small frame was somehow shaped wrong. He thought he could see folds of skin, all crinkled tight across her throat, and there were purple birthmarks across her tiny face. Her cheeks tapered, resulting in a long, pointed chin. The rain was once again strengthening. Tom felt the water running across his eyes and down his face. He shook his head but it did no good. Through the rain he looked and saw the little woman standing under the sign, watching him. Tom blinked and again shook the water from his face. He thought she was somehow attached to the very bridge itself, her feet seeming to meld with the boards. He felt the nausea returning. One glance at the surrounding swamp showed him something was very wrong. The entire landscape appeared to be shifting, sliding. He saw the small woman had stepped onto the structure. Without warning she gripped the rope-holds either side and began jerking them back and forth. The entire structure began to rock. Tom tried to stay on his feet. He felt the dizziness grow stronger and the last of his food burped out of his mouth and down the front of his shirt. He spat the sour contents away. In his encroaching panic he found his voice.

"Hey lady, this isn't safe."

She stared at Tom. He heard a whispering near his face.

"Oh, child, so lost and helpless—how sweet for the palate."

The tiny woman renewed her efforts and continued shaking the structure.

Tom raised his voice, spitting rain and the last of the vomit. He wiped his face and looked again at the little woman. She was now standing still, regarding him. Her mouth parted in a smile; the smile widened and he saw teeth which reminded him of a shark's. He noticed her eyes were set far apart. Thorns were sticking out of her hair. He had the thought that the thorns were part of her. He blinked and wiped his face against the driving rain. When he opened his eyes he saw she was no longer there.

He heard a voice at his side. Looking down near his elbow he saw a bird had alighted on the rope. Tom shook more water from his face and stared. The creature appeared to be deformed. It had its beak, hooked and sharp, growing from the side of its face and it had only one eye. Gripping the rope and now fearful for his life, Tom stepped further out onto the bridge, away from the bird. He stared at it. He checked to see if the woman had returned. She had not. Turning back to the bird, Tom was shocked to see it had tilted its head and was staring up at him with the one eye fixed on his own. He found himself unable to look away. He heard the rush of the rising waters below his feet. He felt the bridge move. The bird spoke to him. The voice was like a sad child's, alone and affrighted.

"My, you are a very long way from home and so near the borderland."

Tom looked on in horror. He felt his legs buckle beneath him. He fell onto the wet boards. Before he could get a handhold, he slipped under the rope. He felt himself floating. He twisted mid-air with nothing under him but the savage roaring of the clay-washed river. He heard a crash sounding in the air above him. A sharp pain lanced along the length of his body. He closed his eyes and in terror he waited to die. Above the thunderous rushing of the water he heard a loud growling voice next to his face issue a warning: "Get out!"

The churning water engulfed him.

4

Tom opened his eyes, spat dirty water from his mouth. He remembered something the tiny woman had said; something about being in the wrong place. He looked down, saw he was seated on a metal bench in a white-walled room devoid of furniture. It reminded him of the waiting room of a hospital, only this place smelled rank, like beached seaweed. And the place was big. He remembered dreaming that a bird had mentioned a border or borderland. He shook his head and a spray of water saturated the area about the metal seat. The place was odd in the fact that joins where walls, ceilings and floors should be were not visible. He shivered and brushed river water from his face and arms. He hugged himself to stay warm, happy to be alive after taking the plunge into the cataract. He looked for medical staff, but the place was empty. After a moment of uncertainty, he began to pat the fingers of both hands in a drum roll on the bench. He spat more gritty water.

"I need a beer."

As he lifted his hand to rub his balding spot, he grew aware the bench felt hot. He looked up and down the length of the room and was disconcerted to find there was no reception counter. He found the silence of the place unnerving. Turning, he noticed a door next to his bench. He stood. Through the doorway stepped a small, narrow-faced, very wrinkly man in a cheap, crumpled red suit. Tom saw the man's ears. He stifled a laugh. At first he was not quite able to believe the ears were not prosthetic; he looked for the joins, could find none. They were elephantine and brushed with a swishing sound against his cheap suit when he turned his head. The newcomer scowled at him.

"They're real enough, boy. Stop staring."

Before Tom could utter an apology, the man began to bark out a series of terse statements.

"I am Stenching. That is my name. I am in charge."

The metal bench had heated considerably. Tom's trousers began to hiss and steam rose from the cloth. He jumped away from the bench.

"What the hell!"

Stenching laughed—a glutinous sound.

"Good call, my friend," he said, his ears flapping against his head, his stinking body giving an odour of decomposing meat. "But speaking of hot seats," said Stenching in frustration, "you should try wearing this suit, it's rayon and man, my bum crack is sweaty."

Tom stared at Stenching, watching the elephant ears flap and drag across his shoulders. He was not sure whether to laugh or whether to challenge the creature. Stenching said some words which sounded French. In a booming voice he shouted next to Tom. A section of the wall opened and a demonic creature of biblical proportions stepped from the aperture. Being a child of the movies where effects were substitutes for story, Tom was more surprised than fearful. At first he could not understand the situation he now found himself in. He looked closer at the startling thing towering over him. It grinned down at Tom from on high, its body posture and facial expression suggesting mischief. Tom glanced at the crazy-eared thing calling itself Stenching. His gaze flicked back to the giant before him. He straightened and swallowed. He thought of drugs, and that some elaborate hoax was being played on him. He looked again, but was halted in his scrutiny. He saw something hairy unfurl and flick out from one of the giant creature's ears. The hairy thing darted back to its cover. Tom shrank back against the metal bench. The demon-thing moved closer. Tom stepped away, up against the wall, using his back to slide along. He watched the thing for any signs of threatening movement. During this, Tom was able to see the thing for what it appeared to be. It was some kind of nightmare creature; it was corpse grey and exuding a rank sweat. At each side of its throat, gills corrugated the flesh. The demon was naked and Tom saw it did not have any genitals. He tried to wish himself small. The creature leaned in close to Tom and spoke.

"You were on the bridge. I thought I told you to get out!"

Tom remembered having heard a voice during his fall. He gained courage under the terrible stare of the monster, realising again these were actors and this one was on stilts under his costume. He braved a reply.

"I would get out if you showed me the bloody door to this madhouse. Anyway, where is this place?"

Stenching intervened.

"That's quite enough of this." He turned to face the newcomer in the monster suit. "You, minion," he growled.

The man in the monster suit spoke.

"Yes, Master Stenching?"

Stenching looked up at the demon. Under his baleful glare the demon's double-lidded eyes filmed over. It cringed. Stenching spoke, indicating Tom.

"You, servant, take hold of this loathsome cretin." The creature reached out for Tom, who was sliding down the wall, trying to make himself a small target. Tom held up his hands as if it would be enough protection.

"Now wait. Am I on some crazy movie set? Wait, don't man-handle me—"

Stenching ignored his plea. A huge hand closed about Tom's shoulder. The man in the monster suit hauled Tom to his feet and stood him in front of Stenching. Tom shut his eyes, shrank from the creature at his back.

Stenching growled.

"There's been a mistake, Sapien. You shouldn't be here. You had no right to be up on the bridge." He turned to the demon. It watched, waiting for instructions. Stenching spat onto the floor of the waiting room; the phlegm wriggled and began crawling away. Stenching watched it. He chuckled.

"Right, young Tom Wu, I wonder what version of Purgatoria I should sentence you to. Let's see. Should you be sewn into the mouth of a mummified hippopotamus, for a period of, oh, let's say, forever? I can do that, you know. No, wait! I have a better one."

Tom began to protest.

"Hey. Before you go any further—"

Stenching cut him off by raising his voice.

"What say I have this servant truss you up in wet pig intestines and hang you by your feet, upside down in a drop latrine until you drown in defecation? When you have drowned in excretion you can be duly revived."

Tom looked at the flap-eared man-thing. He stifled a laugh. Stenching would not shut up.

"And after you drown you will be revived and spend eternity in the passenger seat of a *Volvo* with the worst driver in the world. Believe me, I can do that as well."

Tom started to protest at the ridiculous absurdities coming from the elephant guy's mouth.

"No. You've got the wrong person. It's not my time."

Stenching roared.

"Quiet!" He turned to the servant.

"Make this thing be quiet."

Tom cringed. Stenching hooted with mirth at the human's terror.

"Oh, oh, I am pleased." He laughed and patted his own back.

The demon looked perplexed. It dared to question Stenching.

"Where is this one's odorous pit to be?'

Stenching thought.

"It has no pit; this thing shouldn't be here. I'll take it to the *Dark One*, to see what's to become of it."

Tom began to suspect he was hallucinating. He felt the place was real enough and there were really people with him saying things, but nothing else was real. He had a suspicion this was more than likely of Sammy's doing. Some of the locals had decided to play a prank on the new arrival. He remembered the scene on the bridge. He remembered falling into the savage rush of the river. That had been real enough. Tom felt the wetness of his clothes. He felt the pain in his arm from where the giant had him gripped. Turning his head, Tom looked up at the creature, trying to find the latex joins amid the makeup. His fear left him. He stood up to his full height, but was still dwarfed by the crazy bastard holding him. Sensing this change in attitude, Stenching barked with displeasure. His ears flapped in fury. He turned to the man in the monster suit.

"Right, you smoking mutant! Let's get this sorted out." He stared at Tom.

"Maybe you'll end up with a sentence of seven thousand years in the *Pits of Tar*." He spat again, and the viscid mass tried to crawl away. He squashed the phlegm underfoot.

"I have to create an appropriate punishment for this thing. Wait here until I get back." The demon let go of Tom. Stenching turned to whoever it was on the stilts under the suit.

"Alright, you go, get out of my sight." The giant moved quickly for one so large. Stenching leaned close to Tom, who was forced to step back from the waft of rotting flesh.

"You, this way, hurry." Stenching approached the door he had entered. "You are a mistake. Have I said that before?"

Emboldened by the ridiculous nature of his predicament, Tom hazarded an answer.

"You stink something awful. And yes, as a matter of fact—"

"Shut up! I have to take you to the boss to see what we're to do with you."

"You already said that, as well. You said *boss*."

"Shut up!"

"Who've you got dressed for this part as boss?"

"Azray, *Foul Grey One* it's all one. Stay close, there are dangers."

Tom acquiesced and followed his stinking guide through the door and into a vast chamber. He was sure the charade would end as soon as he straightened out from whatever drug he had been slipped.

The only item of furniture in the place was a lectern and a high, three-legged stool. On the stool behind the lectern, another demon squatted like a grotesque records clerk. Smaller than the servant, this creature was even oilier. It watched Tom and it mouthed whispers with fish lips. Tom went with the hallucination. The clerk on the stool moved its lips as it read a passage from an old book laying open on the lectern. Stenching was losing patience.

"Why are you sitting up there using a pen, what's wrong with your desk computer?"

The little records clerk farted nervously and dared to speak.

"Master Stenching, the computers are down, have been for… for hours." It closed its eyes, expecting to be struck. When it felt nothing it opened its eyes and looked. Stenching glared at the clerk.

"Very well, minion, make a note, this Sapien is a mistake. I have to take it to Agarthi to ask the *Foul One* what to do."

At the sound of one of the *Grey* 's many names the clerk wet itself and its pupils rolled up into its head. It dared to speak.

"Fer, Master Stenching."

Stenching looked at the records clerk.

"What?"

"It is Fer, Master. My name is Fer."

"Yes I know, minion. As I said, there has been a mistake."

The clerk looked from Stenching to Tom and back.

"A mistake, Master Stenching?" Its voice gurgled and it peered at Tom, who stared back defiantly. Fer shifted on its stool and dropped its gaze.

Stenching growled.

"Make a note of what's happening. We have to start on the trip at once."

Fer wrote something into the book it held. Tom had been thinking about the way Fer seemed uncomfortable when looking at him. He wondered if it was afraid. He spoke.

"I'm not happy with all this."

Fer gave a weak roar and snapped its jaws shut. With Stenching in the room, it felt less frightened of Tom and so it dared a rebuttal.

"I can't believe it speaks. Do I take away its mouth, Master Stenching?"

"No. Not yet." He turned to Tom. "Don't do it again, I don't like it when you things utter stuff, it grates."

"Whatever you say", said Tom, waiting to see what would happen.

Fer began to whine.

"Sir, my writing implement doesn't work properly."

Stenching regarded Fer, who was by now tittering. It continued hesitantly, its whine servile.

"I mean, it smudges."

Stenching took a deep breath.

"Smudges, you say?"

Taking heart, Fer nodded.

"It leaves ink all over the page."

Tom was listening to this exchange with great amusement. As usual, he said the first thing he thought of.

"You could always blow through the pen to clear it; or you could save up for a brand-new computer, a great big stinking demonic computer. What about that, eh?"

The frightened demon gazed at the ceiling.

"Master Stenching, it's talking again."

Stenching intervened.

"You, Tom, ah, thing, don't talk to the servants. It makes them uneasy."

Turning back to Fer, Stenching tried to be patient.

"I'll get you another pen." He shook his head with frustration. "Oh, I do hate computers."

Fer gave what it thought was a smile, its eyes bright buttons.

"You will? Oh, thank you, sir."

Stenching frowned.

"Shut up. Just…shut up and make your report. I'll take responsibility for the smudges, alright?"

Fer nodded. Stenching looked at Tom.

"Don't you smile, if I see you grinning—"

He pushed Tom ahead and spoke.

"I don't want you here as much as you don't want to be here."

"I doubt it", said Tom. "I don't want to be here so much more than you don't want me here."

Fer wrung its hands, the talons clacking together.

"It's talking again, sir."

Stenching spat a reply.

"You want a pen?"

"Oh, yes. Yes please."

"Then open a damned portal so I can see the boss and get rid of this thing."

Fer blinked and whimpered. Stenching groaned.

"Oh, now what is it?"

"Sir, the computers—"

Stenching sighed.

"Yes. Yes, I know. Well, we'll have to go by foot. Damn, what a long and dangerous route. Why now, of all times?"

Tom decided he had taken enough idiocy. He rounded on Stenching.

"Hey, you fool. Where's the door? I've had enough of your malarkey—"

Across the room stalked an enormous demon-like form, which according to Tom's calculations was nearly three metres tall. Tom was sick of it all.

"Hey, you there, yes, you, the basketball player in the stupid suit. What's your game?" He was infuriated when he was ignored.

"Hey, stop, you ignorant arsehole!"

The clerk, Fer, ducked down behind its lectern. Tom turned to face the one who had entered. He saw the suit had some kind of growth swinging from its throat. He looked harder and realised the appendage was a tumour sac. Stenching saw the striding creature.

"You there, hey, stop! Smug, I said stop! Smug, stop, come back here and take care of this complaining—" But it proved too late. The one called Smug exited the room and was gone. Stenching stamped the floor and flapped his great ears.

"Smug, Smug!" He sighed. "You hulking crap bag. Doesn't anyone listen?"

Fer whimpered and chanced a peek above the lectern to be sure Smug had gone. Stenching half-turned, then decided he wouldn't play the game. He snapped at Fer.

"If anything happens to me outside, I'm holding you responsible." Again Fer ducked out of sight. Stenching turned on him.

"Well, there's nothing for it but to leg the distance. You Tom thing, we have to go. Follow me and stay in sight."

Tom felt a chill blast as Stenching reached a door and opened it. He was confused, but he dutifully followed the elephant-eared man out into a thick red haze.

"Finally, there's a door out of loopyville."

He was standing on the edge of a low cliff. Below, a flat plain stretched away. All round, a red haze restricted visibility. He saw fires dotting the plain. Tom directed his gaze to a small area ahead.

He saw many capering things with too many limbs dancing within the flames. From various places out on the plain could be heard the wails and screams of what sounded as if somebody was being tortured. Tom was confused.

"What the hell?"

Stenching laughed and it sounded as if mucous was lodged in his throat. He flapped his ears and grinned, showing the stumps of broken teeth.

"You've already said that." He reached the stairs leading down to the plain. Tom trudged behind. After some time, he wondered when the stairs would end. Distance and height seemed somehow out of whack and his thoughts were chaotic.

The pair descended the steps, finally reaching the plain. The temperature had risen. Stenching propelled Tom through the thickening mist. Tom complained.

"Why are we walking? Can we take a cab or something?

Stenching laughed.

"This is your lot. No rides for you, no transport—nothing. Get a move on."

"Do you even have transport here?"

"It is elsewhere, and as I said, not for you. Hurry up."

Without warning, Tom was jerked to one side.

"Careful there", said Stenching, "This is Tir n Aill. Don't want you falling down a shaft. There are some pissed-off people down those things,"

Tom pulled his hand out of Stenching's grasp.

"I said I'd follow. Stop mauling." He paused. "A tir what?"

"A tir," said Stenching, "Tir n Aill, a plain." He saw the look of bewilderment. "Tir, a plain. Okay, a treeless flat place. Oh, really! Just stay close."

Tom pressed his teeth together. He spoke at the elephant-eared man.

"Nice suit. Now I know, I dropped a trip and ended up in a horror story. Yeah. I'm used to it. I sit in bookshops being accosted with idiotic queries by whale huggers, sci-fi nutters and gaming freaks. Well, ain't this a normal ol' day for Tom?" A chill came over him. He stopped. His thoughts tumbled. Had he been injured in a crash in Sammy T's truck? Was he in a coma in the hospital, only now coming up out of anaesthetic? He had heard that coming out of sleep from surgery gave people crazy dreams. He wondered if he was lying in bed in a ward somewhere.

Tom turned to his travelling companion.

"I'm in hospital, right?"

Without turning, Stenching answered him. Tom cringed at the phlegmy sound.

"No, you are not."

"So how are we going to get to this place you're taking me?"

"We walk. I have already explained this."

"That's not very sophisticated. Don't you have a Harley?"

Stenching clamped his teeth together.

"The walking is part of the process."

"What process?"

"It's a test of endurance."

"For what?"

Stenching sighed with growing frustration.

"You know, you're like a child." He started to whine. "*Why? How? What for?*"

Tom looked at the wrinkled monstrosity walking beside him.

"Haven't you got a bus? A number thirteen would be appropriate."

Stenching refused to be baited.

They tramped across the tir. Tom felt the air was too thick to breathe.

The mist thickened and the temperature rose. Stenching shook his head, the movement dislodging loose flakes of dried facial skin. The odd companions skirted the metal grilles of numerous narrow shafts. Stenching braved a conversation.

"In these shafts we keep the damned. No such thing as a soul in torment."

Tom decided to go along with the farce.

"No souls? But I thought—"

"Don't think. Shut up. Anyway, the boss was forbidden dealing with souls after the *Glowing One* kicked his arse in Eden.

Now we only take people themselves. We got screwed if you ask me."

Tom looked sceptical.

"And the world is hollow with holes at the poles. Make a bit of sense, would you?"

"It's true", said Stenching, "all true."

Tom felt as if he was being made a fool of.

"Glowing One?"

"Used to be, gone now, no more glowing one; belief does not ensure existence", said Stenching with no show of humour.

Tom frowned.

"What used to be?"

"Shut up, now." Stenching grabbed Tom and stopped him taking another step.

"Watch the pit, I can't have you falling in."

Tom looked down at his feet. He saw to his surprise he was standing at the lip of another shaft, this one with no grille-covering. Tom stepped back from the edge and leaned out over the drop.

"Damn. How'd I miss that?"

Stenching peered down into blackness.

"This pit's a beauty. I had no help making this one, my first solo effort. You want to know what's down there with the human?"

Tom felt his nerve faltering "

"No! Look, I've seen enough. Let's go back?"

Stenching gave a sly grin. "Back to where, your hospital ward? There is no ward, you complete fool. You have crossed over. Do you understand? You have crossed. There was no accident; you walked where you should not have. You strayed from the paths. You were warned on the island not to stray."

Tom turned and stared at Stenching. He felt cold in the warming air.

"They knew?"

"You mean your island friends? Of course they know. They live there."

Tom thought for a moment.

"I'm dead."

Stenching coughed up mucus and spat. Tom heard it thud to the earth. He refused to look, in case it was crawling away somewhere. Stenching chuckled.

"No, you're not dead, you're here."

Tom was baffled.

"So where is here?"

"It's where you are.

"Here?"

"Here, in my world."

"I crossed over?"

"Yes, you breached, through the borderland.

"Borderland."

"Oh, you idiot. Two worlds meet and you crossed. Don't you know anything regarding frontier physics? You're not very well read, are you?"

Tom tried to peer through the thickening red haze.

"But I thought…ahh, never mind, whatever."

Stenching sighed.

"Try not to think, it's bad for you. Follow me and we'll try to sort this mess out." He leered at Tom. "When I'm done with you, I can get back to my pit designs."

The heat increased. Underfoot, cries could be heard from the bottom of scattered shafts. Tom felt hot.

"What do you call this place?"

"Here doesn't have a name. It's just here."

"Where, though?"

"Here, where you are."

Tom growled.

"Oh let's not start again."

"Yes, let's not, shall we?"

Tom licked his parched lips.

"You got anything to drink? I'd like something with alcohol in it."

Stenching giggled, his pachyderm ears flapping in delight.

"No drinks. It is now thirty-nine Celsius, and counting; and no, no alcohol here."

Tom glared at his guide.

"Bloody idiot, show me the front door, will you?" But already he was beginning to believe at least some parts of what he was experiencing were real, he was just not yet sure which parts. He looked at Stenching.

"So that isn't a costume?"

Stenching kept walking as he answered.

"Look at yourself. You're two meters tall and a shoe-size wide and your skin looks like a pale twig. So tell me, is *that* a costume you are wearing?"

Tom nodded, impressed.

"Okay, point taken. And those others, with the goblin shark heads, don't tell me they're real."

Stenching spun to face Tom.

"Would you rather be in a room with them or a sabre-tooth?"

"You have them here?"

"Of course not, they're extinct, you offal sack. You and your kind don't see most of what's happening around you—too busy with the important stuff. And yes, I'm being sarcastic, fool."

Tom looked behind to see if there was anything following. Satisfied there was not, he trudged, silent, after the stinking man. He watched the ears flap back and forth, but he felt no amusement at the sight. He knew he was going through some kind of psychosis and he wondered how he was going to extricate himself from the predicament.

5

A huge form reared up amid the red haze. Huge and partly covered in offal, the creature snapped her jaws together, incisors clacking behind her lips. She barked an order to her servants. She strode through the haze and peered down into a pit. A cry sounded from below, low and muffled as if it had something stuffed into its mouth. Through the haze she was satisfied to hear her minions tormenting the imprisoned victims. Wails and pleas for mercy came from wretches in the shafts. This gigantic creature was an overseer, one of the most feared denizens in all Purgatoria. She was known as *Nil*, and she smelled ripe.

Nil had a suffering man gripped by his ankle and was dragging him shrieking across the plain—a male by the name of Ruben Goldstein. The unfortunate new denizen of Purgatoria whined and sniffled in his terror. One of Nil's minions cringed before her. Nil had caught the unfortunate female servant between the shafts out on the tir. The servant squirmed under Nil's ministrations.

"Please, mistress, pity my fragile body."

Nil gripped her servant round its throat, her massive hand encircling the neck.

"Pity is for others less worthy of me. You were skulking out on your own trying to forage for food without someone there to protect you. Be still and maybe I won't strip your stinking flesh."

The servant began to match Ruben Goldstein's cries of indignation.

Nil flicked out her tongue and tasted both her captives. The servant began to whimper. Nil began to moisten, her abdomen rippling, as if something was trying to push its way out. She ground her fangs together. She licked the sweat from her victims' faces.

"Sorry, little ones, I can't help myself." Guiding her servant to a small depression on the tir she gave an order.

"Stay. I'll come for you." Obediently, the demon crouched.

Nil had only to complete the incarceration of Ruben Goldstein and her shift would end. She dangled the writhing man above the shaft delegated him. She let him go. There came a thud and a cry from far below ground. Nil peered down into the shaft. She growled once and looked through the red haze and sniffed the air out on the tir.

"Mr Goldstein, soon I'm going put someone special in your filth pit."

Goldstein's tremulous voice echoed up the pit shaft.

"What? Who? Oh, no, not my mother. You're not sending in my mother!"

Nil laughed, her voice sounding like the dry shaving of a man's testicles.

"Yes, your mother. You'd better get used to her because you'll be pit-mates for *aaaaaalll* eternity."

Goldstein wailed.

"But...but I'm Jewish, I don't even believe in Hell."

Nil heard footsteps approaching through the haze. She raised her snout, sniffed and licked her wet face, her tongue leaving a slick film across her forehead.

"Stenching", she whispered, "and a Sapien." A smile stretched her fishy lips.

Stenching was also sniffing the air.

"We've got company."

Tom turned.

"What is it?"

"Not good news. Stay still."

Tom needed no coaxing. From out of the haze he saw a big body striding towards him. The mist momentarily thinned. Nil towered up. Tom gaped at her. He saw a face that could have been the model for the Greek *Gorgon* of legend. Her face was a mass of fleshy knobs and creases, yet she did not look old. Looking up, higher than his head, Tom saw the breasts, nipples like fingers. Then, at chin level, was the largest vagina he'd ever seen. In the swirling haze, he believed he saw a dark something flash from between her legs.

Nil leaned down.

"So, Stenching, my floppy-eared minion." She glanced hungrily at Tom. "Stenching, what's that you have? Why haven't you de-boned it and drop-kicked it down a shaft?"

Stenching held his ground.

"It's not meant to be here, majestic one. I'm going to seek instructions from the *Foulness*."

Nil looked from one to the other.

By now Tom had had enough of the situation. He knew this could not be real.

"Hey! Show me the way out and I'm gone."

Nil stared at him.

"Well, so it is a talking one?" She moved fast, her arm reaching for Tom. Stenching shouted a warning.

"No!"

Nil drew back, incredulous at Stenching's insubordination. He rushed into an explanation.

"Forgive me, but the Sapien is a live one."

Nil stepped backwards.

"Alive? Not reanimated? I almost touched it." From her lofty height she regarded Stenching. "You've saved me a painful rash on my beautiful flesh."

Stenching bowed to hide his pleased look. Nil scowled.

"Don't pretend with me!" She took another step back from Tom, eyeing him with new respect. She turned back to Stenching. "To reward your loyalty I'll escort you part way."

Stenching protested.

"It won't be necessary, glutinous one."

Nil shook her head, hair sticking to her throat.

"You're not safe abroad on the tir this day, minion. Someone left the cages open."

Stenching sucked in breath.

"The cages, open?"

"Precisely, so we will detour through the *Fissures of Myen*."

Tom dared to speak.

"*Fishers of Men*, I don't like the sound of that. What say we backtrack to the waiting room and hang about for your…ah… boss to come back. Good idea?"

Nil looked down at Tom and Stenching.

"Does this meat sack have to talk?"

Tom yelled at her.

"Hey, enough." He stepped towards her.

She shrieked and leaped backwards.

"No! It stings." Her eyes narrowed and she licked her face. She snarled. "Come near me and I'll slow-burn your danglies."

Tom retreated.

Stenching intervened.

"Please, mistress, we should get started."

Nil turned and walked a few paces. She skirted a vertical shaft, her heel sending a shower of earth into the pit. A moment later a cry echoed up from below.

"Is that you, Mother? Mother Goldstein, that's not you, is it?"

Nil strode into the haze.

"Come with me this way and no lagging. Remember the open cages."

He and Tom quickened their steps to trot beside Nil. Tom listened to the doomed man's wails recede into the distance.

Tom kept a close watch on his companions. He was intrigued about the mention of the open cages.

"So, what's escaped?"

Stenching sighed.

"They're the *Capybaras of Woe*."

Tom gave a short laugh. He sobered.

"Oh, please, *Capybaras of Woe!*"

Stenching seemed insulted.

"What do you mean?"

Tom found the question stupid.

"Well, it's like saying the *Caterpillars of Abomination*."

Stenching shrugged.

"We'll see."

Howling sounded from the surrounding haze and was answered from several directions. Nil stopped. Stenching and Tom bumped into the back of her thighs. Without thinking, Tom put his hand on the obstruction. Nil yelped and leaped into the air, landed and ran in circles.

"It touched me! I didn't do anything!"

Tom spoke in his own defence.

"I'm sorry. It was an accident."

Nil stopped running and began rubbing the back of her leg.

"I'll give *you* an accident."

Howling sounded again, this time much closer from several directions. Nil tilted her head.

"Get to the *Fissures!* Now!" They raced after her. Close behind, hunters pursued.

The flight to safety remained a vague happening for Tom, a nightmare with frantic leaps over the pits on the tir. After a while, he sensed a change in the air; it was some time before he realised his group had entered a cave system. He did not hear the footsteps of the others, so he stopped. There came a flash as if someone was trying to flick a lighter. He walked towards it. A big open hand was thrust near his face. Another flickering light flashed. There came a third spark and the flame held. Tom found himself staring at Nil's hand. She held a large, oil-tipped taper. Tom looked beyond the hand. The flame lit Nil's face. Her frightful features struck a momentary fear into him. She was a horror. He became caught in her gaze and felt as a mouse would looking down a snake's throat. He raised his own hand and moved it towards Nil's. Nil moved her hand away from Tom's. She spoke.

"There's an urgency I must attend to. I can lead you both through to the hanging valley at the end of the *Fissures*. Once there, you're on your own."

Guided by the taper's flame, the trio moved through the *Fissures*. A pathway had led down from a cleft in the limestone. The trail ended at a sheer wall. Tom saw Nil lean down. He leaned closer to the light. Below was a flat floor covered in loose earth. Nil raised the flaming taper. Tom could see the flat floor continued on into the darkness down an old lave tube. Stenching checked the height of the drop to the floor.

"Not far," he said, leaping off the path at the lip of the drop. Nil and Tom heard him hit the bottom. Stenching gave a grunt and cursed. "Higher than I thought."

Nil stepped off the edge. Tom heard her land.

"Yes", she said, "it's a long way down."

Tom knew they were flexing their muscles. He realised things weren't all going to go his way. It occurred to him if he had a certain physical effect on the demon, he must have an even greater effect on Stenching; all he had to do was figure out what effect it might be. He heard his guides talking as he let himself over the edge of the drop and hung by his hands. He was about to let go when a huge head appeared from the gloom. Nil leaned close, as close as she dared. She held her flaming taper above his head. She wheezed out a throaty chuckle.

"We're up more than twice human height and I'm not even standing on tiptoes."

Tom stared defiantly back.

"We'll get on better if you'd bathe occasionally." He dropped to the ground.

Nil clacked her teeth.

"Enough. We have to be careful. You, human, get between us, but not too close. Stenching, give it room to walk." Tom ignored the jibe.

The trek down the lava tube went without mishap for the first half-hour. Out of the surrounding blackness came the sound of heavy breathing. Tom was still between Nil and Stenching. Something black jumped back out of the light of the dimming flame of the taper. From the cave sounded a rising murmur of voices, growing in volume, an amalgamation of several Germanic inflections. Nil hissed at the men.

"You two, stay still. It's the *Nuns of Discord.*"

But Tom made the mistake of moving. Something reached for him. A sticky sheet brushed his face and he cried in alarm. The voices stopped and things in swishing robes groped forward. He felt his arms seized, talons ripping his grimy shirt, breaking the skin on his arms. He was dragged into a night-black side passage. A wet cloth, sour from something, was scrunched roughly into his mouth. Tom gagged and felt himself propelled forward, all but lifted from his feet, as he was hurried away from Stenching's frightened voice. Tom heard a huffing sound close at his heels. He heard a snuffling come from something large rearing above him. One of the things gripping his right arm was struck in the darkness. In his terror, Tom felt the talons snatched away from his arm, further ripping his skin. He heard a sickening, tearing sound and wetness showered over his head. There were cries and hisses as the other things in the swishing robes responded to the attack. He knew Nil had arrived.

Something began to roar. Tom was flung to the packed earth in the darkness. He was knocked onto his side as something fleshy kicked him aside. He curled up on the dirt and covered his head with his bleeding arms. There came amid the bellows and the hissing, a great thud, as if something hard was striking flesh. Something very heavy dropped to the earth next to him. Again he was snatched at and the cruel talons pierced his shoulders. He was hurried through the dark. He heard the swishes of robes. In a moment of clarity, Tom realised what had fallen next to him back along the passage.

They descended flights of stone stairs, all about sounded the constant dripping of water. Flashes of blue light and odours of dampened moss and rotting things stung his nostrils. Laughter sounded from the surrounding darkness. Things dropped on his head and he felt many tiny legs scuttle across his face. Something crawled into his open mouth. Onward and downward he was dragged. Tom shook his head to rid himself of the crawling thing. The nightmare journey continued. A heavy blow to his head sent a flashing light through his consciousness. He fell.

He dreamed he was in a slaughterhouse. Smells of blood and entrails spurred him back to consciousness. He tensed, waiting for the rough touch of his captors. Bile rose and acid tastes constricted the involuntary muscles of his oesophagus. His stomach knotted as he squirmed in the darkness. Screaming and sobbing pierced the blackness. More sounds of water could be heard dripping from above. Metal clashed against metal. Somewhere a door slammed, cutting off some wretch's scream with a terrifying finality.

He woke. After a few moments Tom was able to see small red glows in the blackness where he lay. With weakened arms he managed to raise his chest from the ground. He shifted his legs. He felt something tugging at one of his ankles. He pulled with his leg and again found he was stopped short. With pain shooting across his chest, he turned. He reached down and found one of his ankles had been manacled to a short chain attached to a wall. He spat out a curse and rubbed his aching arms. He realised he was naked except for his shoes and socks.

Close by, someone screamed. Tom jumped at the suddenness of the cry. He heard the familiar swish of robes. Another scream sounded from further down the space. The cry was cut short and followed by a low moan of despair. Tom stopped moving. He muttered: "Too freaky for me."

As his eyes grew accustomed to his prison within a short time he was able to see the fires burning inside braziers set upon tall tripods. The sobbing from the unseen person had stopped. Peering through the semi-darkness, Tom saw long rods poking up from the red braziers. His stomach constricted and his sphincter snapped shut. He knew what those rods were and he now knew what kind of place he'd been brought to.

A shriek rent the air. Tom shuffled backward on his arse, manacle and chain rattling against the foul dirt under him. He tugged, wanting to distance himself from the inherent agony of the voice. He began to babble to himself. Another cry sounded, muffled, as if from through a closed door close by. Tom backed further away. His chain tightened, restricting retreat.

He heard the sound of a key turning in a lock. He saw the place behind him lighten. He heard a tread, and the light intensified until it bathed him. He dared to turn, at once wishing he hadn't. The creature was dressed as a nun, but there was no face, just smooth skin with a mouth, thick-lipped and green-tinged. He looked away. His chain was grabbed and the manacle bit into his ankle. He was freed and yanked toward the bearer of the light. Tom cursed and struggled. Again he was yanked and he landed on his stomach. His face was scraped across the earth, and dirt entered his eyes. He blinked and realised he was temporarily blinded. As he struggled with the pain of the foreign matter in his eyes, he heard the light bearer speak.

"Take it to the kitchens. This time I want the meat tenderised."

Two shapes swished from the gloom and grabbed Tom. He was pulled to his feet and hurried across towards the door. Behind him he heard the pitiful captive shriek; the sobs started, but were cut off when the door through which he was propelled slammed shut. Tom remembered what Nil had said. He knew he was in the hands of the *Nuns of Discord*.

He was dragged down a passage, well-lit from the lighting set into the rock walls. He studied the lights as he was dragged. He blinked hard against the dirt flakes irritating his eyes. Through tears, he could not be sure if the glare was artificially created. He concentrated on the mystery of the lighting, anything so he would not have to look at the faces of his captors. He closed his eyes and let himself be hurried along the passageway. Tom shook his head and blinked the remainder of the dirt from one of his eyes. Tears flowed, giving surface protection. He was manhandled down another side passage. The cooking smells grew stronger.

He was pulled through a doorway into a huge room. Along the walls were lights similar to those of the hallways, bathing the great room in brightness.

Tom was jerked backwards and felt an obstacle come up against the back of his knees. Weak and scared, he could not resist the strength of his captors. He closed his eyes when one of the devil nuns turned to face him. But he had not been quick enough. He had seen the mouth on the smooth oval of head smile and had seen the tongue dart out, as if to taste the air. He was pushed backwards. He cried out as he fell. He found himself lying on his back on some scratchy substance. He kept his eyes shut while he grabbed some of the scratchy material. He realised it was some kind of straw.

The faceless nuns turned from him. He heard their swishing departure, heard their rasping voices as they communicated. He opened his eyes and saw the nuns approach a big, metal box-like construction. Tom was exhausted. He lay in the straw and watched. Two more nuns came into view. Each was hooded so the heads were in shadow. Tom was thankful. Each nun pushed a trolley set on castors before her. But it was what was on those trolleys which set Tom's heart thumping. He tried to rise, but only fell back. The newly arrived nuns stopped their trolleys next to Tom's captors. He saw their animated movements and realised they were discussing what lay on the trolleys. In pain, Tom sat up on the straw. He got a better look at the condition of the things on the trolleys.

One was a man, swollen and discoloured. The other was a woman. The man was moaning. His chest and legs were bruised. His hands were tied to his ankles and he sat naked and weeping on the trolley. Behind him on the trolley was a metal rack, and in this lay the implement Tom guessed had caused the bruising and swelling. It was a stumpy club, rough-hewn from dark wood, like a shortened, unfinished baseball bat. Tom swallowed when he saw parts of the club were stained. He looked at the other trolley where the woman lay trussed. She lay on her side facing in his direction. Some type of twine was tied about her wrists and this was attached to her legs, joining her knees to her wrists.

From his position, Tom was able to see the big metal box behind the trolleys was a huge oven. His mouth slackened as thoughts came.

The nuns began conversing. Tom wanted to escape. He was beyond caring how anything worked. One of his captors turned to the nun pushing the man's trolley. Pointing down at the cowering man, she spoke.

"Give me the axe, Sister. Just its limbs, the rest can slide down the offal shoot."

The man began to scream and struggle upon the trolley. Two nuns held him while the third went to find the instrument of slaughter. The nun who had spoken turned on the terrified woman. The two nuns holding the struggling man pushed his trolley so they faced their superior. She lowered her head as if able to see the woman and the man. She turned and opened the oven door. Inside, a light flicked on. Turning back, she placed a hand on the head of the trussed woman.

"Set the temperature and baste this thing. We will eat well tonight."

Tom began to tremble. Through his terror he saw one nun arrive back with an axe. He turned in a daze and saw the trussed woman lifted from the trolley. One of the nuns slid out an oven tray and the others placed the woman onto this. The first nun reached up and brought a jar down from the top of the oven. The trussed woman lay squirming on the tray. She uttered low sobs. The nun shook the jar in her hand. Tom saw a dark oil swirl inside. The nun removed the lid from the jar and extracted a brush from the oil. Wiping a little excess from the brush, she began to baste the woman. The captive began to cry. She lifted her head and saw Tom. He tried to move, but his fear had frozen his desire to rise. From the corner of his eye he saw the other nuns cut the bonds of the man on the trolley and place him on the floor. The man lay there staring up, too afraid to move. Tom turned his head and saw the other nun finish brushing oil across the woman's stomach. The nun replaced the oil jar on top of the oven. She switched the oven on and slid the tray holding the trussed woman back into the belly of the great cooker. Tom saw the woman's mouth contort, and he heard her utter a single word before the oven door was shut: "Please." With terror in her eyes as she looked at him, that was all she'd said.

This was enough to prompt him into motion. He crouched on the straw, one leg under him ready to leap off the bench. A heavy hand was applied to each shoulder. He was thrown onto his back and he looked up. Two faceless nuns bent over him; their smirks told they did indeed have some type of sight. One reached and picked up the bloodied club from the trolley, the other reminding the first: "Mother Superior specifically said to tenderise this one properly."

All at once, Tom saw his own end; after the bruising he would be oiled and would follow the woman into the oven, alive. He saw the axe raised above the man, whose limbs, only, were sought for the pot. He mentally saw the woman on the oven tray, basted and roasting in her torment, her organs bubbling. Again he pictured her face and heard her one word: "Please."

The axe rose. Tom saw the club poised above his own head. He struggled under the grip of the nuns. Shouting, he began to fight back. He was able to rise a little from the straw. With all his strength he turned to reach up for the club. He saw the club begin to descend. There were gasps behind him. A commotion sounded at the entrance to the kitchen. Tom heard a roaring, as from some very large animal. Even as he threw himself away from the club, he dared to turn to the kitchen doorway. The club above him faltered and was dropped to the floor. Again, Tom stared at the entrance to the kitchen. He saw her.

Nil filled the doorway, bending to enter the kitchen. Tom braved a glance across the room and saw the axe fall, but not on the helpless man. It dropped with a dull thud to the kitchen floor. Tom cried out.

"The oven, get the oven!" He began to laugh and felt the tears come unbidden. Nil moved, fast. The nuns scattered, but not fast enough. Nil lifted a leg to place her foot onto the back of one of the fleeing women. She pressed down and pinned the nun to the kitchen floor. Moving her foot to the nun's behind, Nil gave a flick and propelled the eyeless woman across the floor, sending the unfortunate's head into a wall. There came a sharp crack. A second nun bashed Nil across her head with the bloodied tenderising bat. Nil snorted air from her nostrils. She turned and grabbed her attacker by the arm and yanked hard. Something popped and the head came off the shoulders.

Through his tears Tom saw Nil's jaws stretch wide. He saw her great taloned hand rise with the severed head. She leaned forward for a bite. The head was placed between the incisors and crushed. Nil spat the contents out, spraying bone and blood. She snarled and snatched at another, missed and turned to look behind her. Turning back she saw Tom, naked and bleeding in the straw. Nil walked across the kitchen and looked at the oven. She squatted over the man's broken body. Tom watched with apprehension. Nil looked with compassion at the man.

"Gone", she said. She turned and walked to Tom, squatted and peered into his eyes.

"You're weak-willed. Nevertheless, I have to deliver you to Stenching. I'll lead you from the *Fissures of Myen*, after which you are both on your own." Nil set Tom free.

Tom tried to croak out a warning about the roasting woman. He couldn't talk. Nil stood and stepped across to the oven. She turned it off, opened the door and reaching inside pulled out the tray. The woman was unconscious. She looked tiny with Nil's hands either side of her waist. Tom held his breath. Nil stood and turned.

"I'll come back for this little one after I deposit you outside the fissures."

Tom spoke.

"What's to happen to her? Can you save her?"

Nil flicked out her tongue to lick her eyelids. She stepped over to Tom.

"You have forgotten where you are. This one is here for a purpose. It's to the sulphur mines for it now. It's going to regret it was rescued from the oven and the bellies of the nuns. Oh, it will regret you having saved it, Sapien. And it will have eternity to thank you for your intervention." She stooped, undressed the headless nun and threw the habit to Tom.

"Here. Wear this."

Tom glared at her, but one look from the Gorgon saw him hurriedly don the dead nun's habit. Nil stepped forward and snatched him up. In another moment he found himself speeding down the passage and up the flights of stairs. She ran with him through the cavern passageways. She reached a fork in the passageways and ran on, half crouching to avoid hitting her head on the ceilings. She dumped him onto the dusty floor of the lava tube. She kept right on running down the tube, her voice growing smaller as she wailed her agony.

"He hurts, it huuurrrrrts!"

Tom lay on the ground of the lava tube. He heard Stenching's voice. Something approached. Nil had another taper and it caught flame at the tip, although Tom was not sure how Nil had managed to light it this time. She leaned down to Tom. She stretched open her mouth and snapped it shut with a clack of teeth.

"If you weren't so important, I'd shred you. Come. We leave. Move."

Still dazed from his terrifying ordeal, Tom got to his feet.

"Alright, I'm walking. See?" He stared at the back of the Gorgon. He wanted to beat her over the head with something.

I'd probably only make her angrier—screw that. He wiped dirt from his face and scraped his fingers into his ears. He gritted his teeth.

Will somebody give me goddamned beer!

6

Tom and Stenching trudged along the lava tube, with Nil close behind guarding the passage. Tom saw a pinpoint of red light ahead. As they progressed the red light grew larger, finally showing the narrow fissure opening to the redness beyond. Nil blew out the flame from her finger. Tom blinked, trying to adjust his eyes to the red haze. He could not see more than about ten paces ahead. A wind, like the breath of some large animal, blew across his face. The haze receded, allowing the open space before him to enlarge so he was able to see for some distance.

He found himself standing with Nil and Stenching on the lip of the hanging valley. The haze retreated further. Tom glanced at Stenching, then at Nil. It was the first time he had seen this Gorgon in near-daylight. He looked away, appalled. He took a deep breath and ran his teeth over his bottom lip. Venturing another glance at Nil, he was surprised to find her regarding him. He blinked and held her gaze. Nil widened her eyes and curled her lips into a smirk. During this, Tom attempted to appear unconcerned. He turned his gaze out over the terrain. He was thinking fast.

"Oh, maaan! What are these things?

He focused and refocused. He saw the landscape below was bare of trees. Stones and boulders lay scattered across the slopes and upon the valley floor. With the breeze dispersing much of the haze, the entire valley was visible. Down the nearest slope Tom saw two figures, men running side by side along the valley floor. Both had metal bands around their ankles, with adjoining chains a metre long. Their run was awkward, a swift shuffle as they fled from some unseen pursuer.

Stenching and Nil watched the men. Stenching ignored Tom. He spoke to Nil.

"Mistress, it's the prey. The quicksand gets them today."

Nil nodded and watched the distant men. After a moment she spoke.

"It means little to me. You are going to Agarthi, right?"

Stenching replied: "Yes."

Nil snaked out her tongue and licked her eyelids.

"Give the *Foul Flower* my regards."

Stenching was startled. This was a reminder that it was to be the first time he would find himself in the presence of the *Flower*. He'd heard stories about certain atrocities and tales of minions being roasted alive. With nerves aflutter, he swallowed. For a reason he could not understand, he thought of walking barefoot in grass and feeling his instep sliding down the edge of a broken bottle. He did not know where the thought came from. He felt as if his skin was shrinking in an effort to suffocate his body. Nil sensed Stenching's discomfort. She looked down at the man's ears flapping. She smiled and spoke.

"Try not to end up on someone's menu."

Stenching glanced up at her.

"You be careful too."

Nil snorted.

"Not likely, is it? Behave yourself."

Stenching looked back down at the men escaping along the valley floor.

Nil turned to Tom.

"I might see you again, hmm?"

Tom studied her face, watched her tongue-comb her hair. He looked up into the haze which filled the upper sky. He sighed, deciding to go along with the hallucination.

"I...um...thank you for back there. I mean it. Thank you for getting me out. I...ahh...guess this is the part where the demonic bargains happen. You do something for me and now I owe you. I'm in debt, right?"

Nil pursed her lips. She lowered her eyelids, allowing Tom to see the starfish tattoos there. He saw a movement and glanced at Nil's crotch. A small tentacle, white as a lily, slid a little from her. Tom watched as the tentacle waggled as would an admonishing finger. It folded back into its nest. Tom looked into Nil's eyes. She winked, and without a word turned and loped back into the cavern.

Tom smiled. He felt good with this fantasy. He had invented an imaginary demonic bargain from which he could not extract himself. He'd read stories and he knew the imaginary pitfalls. He was excited. Turning to Stenching, Tom spoke with sincerity.

"I still don't know how I got here. Am I really in a psychiatric unit?"

Stenching chuckled.

"Space folds, Tom thing."

Tom laughed.

"An old chestnut, I've mixed with science fiction readers and writers for years. Drugs, alcohol and imagination can have an odd effect on a person prone to psychotic episodes. It's just my turn."

Stenching showed patience.

"True. Look, assume that due to the shape of Earth, your world has a peculiar interface between third and fourth dimensional physics—"

"Is this going to take long?" Tom interrupted.

Stenching remained unperturbed.

"Okay. Let's say occasionally, at certain places, lodes of minerals with high magnetic content are found; these minerals possess varying gravitational pulls. At certain places space folds or cracks; these cracks allow physical forms to enter an alternate space—no negative effects. Are you getting this?"

Tom lifted his arms and revolved his hands in the air.

"Go on and info dump, if you feel you must."

Stenching looked down at his crumpled suit coat. After a moment he continued.

"These cracks are breaches, between spaces. Your situation was unfortunate. You dropped from a condemned bridge and here you are."

Tom watched Stenching watching him. Tom spoke.

"Sounds very shaky to me."

Stenching answered.

"So it should, like the bridge. But hey, I might be making all this up."

Tom grinned.

"That could be true."

Stenching smiled.

"Whatever you say."

Tom exhaled. He began to doubt his senses. He turned to see Stenching regarding him. Tom didn't care for the look.

"What?"

"She's after you, she is." Stenching laughed and walked down the slope of the valley towards the two men running. They were now a considerable way down the valley.

Tom glanced behind him, turned and ran to catch up with Stenching.

"Who's after me, that tentacled giantess?"

"The very one."

Tom did not care for the glee in his guide's tone.

"I'm not sexing with that!"

Stenching scoffed at him.

"Well you don't get much else, do you? Might as well grab what comes along."

Tom laughed derisively.

"I suppose you get lots, pong boy."

"Be careful there. Anyway, she usually gets her way."

Tom spoke.

"What's with all the muscles in her wrong places?"

Stenching scanned the landscape.

"A lack of myostatin—it's a balancer, keeps muscle structure from getting too big and causing mutation.

"I didn't ask for a science lesson."

Stenching scraped muck from under his nails. Tom looked down at the two manacled convicts.

"What's the go with them?"

"Them?" They're going to spend eternity here being pursued, trapped and killed."

Tom raised his eyebrows.

"What did they do to deserve this?'

Stenching was aghast at Tom's ignorance.

"None of your business."

Tom stared at a darker patch of terrain towards which the men were running.

"And the quicksand?"

Stenching watched the men.

"Every ninth day the fugitives get sucked down by quicksand. Every fourth day soldiers of the damned run them down and bayonet them; every second day the dogs are let loose and the convicts are eaten by the starving pack. On other days, rocks and things fall on their heads. There're lightning burns, flash floods, earthquakes and the ground opening up. There's spontaneous combustion—always a good one."

"I think I get it", said Tom.

"Also, there are wolves and overseers, capybaras—"

"I said I get it."

"Oh, and we can't forget the new one. We must have the new one, those *Caterpillars of Abomination* you mentioned."

Tom narrowed his gaze.

"You're insane, all of you."

Stenching sighed and turned his back to Tom.

Tom decided to throw the conversation off-balance. He stooped and picked up a small rock from the packed earth. Talking aim, he threw the rock at Stenching, striking him in the middle of his back. Stenching cried out.

"What was that for?"

"I don't like you. I'm only sticking with you because I'll get lost by myself."

Tom looked down the slope and watched the fleeing men.

"Quicksand, you say? We have to help them!"

"You can't help them."

Tom looked at the men and saw they were caught and slowly sinking into a patch of watery ooze. Tom raised his voice.

"Yes we can help."

Stenching remained patient.

"No, we can't."

Tom squatted on the ground and rocked back and forth. Stenching admonished him.

"Get up. Face things, man!"

"I didn't ask to be here."

"I didn't ask for you to be here. Look, I have to regain my status—"

Tom turned.

"Oh. So you're on show here. Is that it?"

"It's you, Sapien. I belong here, but you? You are going—" He chuckled. "Never mind. You'll see."

Stenching looked at the fleeing men.

"They die every day. This is their Hell. They're going to be dying horribly in this valley, in various ways, for eternity."

Tom swallowed.

"A little harsh, don't you think?"

"Harsh? This is Hell!"

"You got that right", said Tom ruefully. "This place is shonky.

And what's with the face-licking giantess?"

"Don't mess with her."

Stenching looked down the valley towards the convicts in the quicksand. Tom followed his gaze. Now only the heads of the screaming men were above the ooze. Stenching approached the quicksand. The screams turned to gurgles. Tom averted his eyes so he wouldn't have to see the men sink.

"Cheer up", said Stenching, "Those fellows will be up tomorrow, scrambling over the edge of that high ridge behind us."

7

Angels prefer enthusiasm to perfection—those enthused have dropped their guard.

High up on a slope above the mountain scree, Nil squatted on a flat outcrop of limestone below her lair. She waited to again catch sight of the shapes moving among the boulders below. Soon, a pack of shaggy hunters came out into the open. A couple of them looked up in Nil's direction. She stood and soon all eyes of the pack were centred squarely on her. One of the pack began a familiar coughing, the sound a prelude to an attack. The rest of the hunters began to cough with excitement. As a group they moved up the slope towards their intended quarry. They chose their footing carefully on the slope. Nil stood and waited. She looked out across the plains below to where the haze distorted the landscape. She heard the pack snuffling as they neared.

She sniffed the air again and at this, her senses fully awakened. Her excitement rose at the thought of the immediate future she had planned. On her scalp, coin-sized circular patches of surface skin bubbled. The circles sloughed across her face and down behind her neck and throat. She smiled and delighted in the warm, fluid feeling tickling her flesh. The circular holes growing in her scalp deepened as more liquefying flesh bubbled up and over the raw red edges of the flesh wells. Out of the pits flicked ropes of muscle, lengthening as they swished and smacked together with anxious life. Sprays of blood misted the air. Nil felt giddy and laughed as she had often done as a child.

The pack leader stared up at Nil. She smiled and rotated her head and shrugged her shoulders in order to limber up. The hunters below hesitated. Several raised their snouts and sniffed the air. The leader coughed and backed away. It bumped into one standing behind. In its fright, it turned and snapped at its unfortunate companion. The second hunter shrank back with a yelp. The pack halted and, as one, realised what it was it had been hunting. The pack turned and with a sliding, stumbling rush ran down the slope, away from the massive predator waiting above.

Nil smelt the air. She watched the hunters as they made their escape. She looked up the mountain. With another glance downwards she resumed her upward climb.

The haze swept across the plain and began to fill the lower slopes of the mountain. Smoke wafted across the upper reaches. From far away could be heard a dry cracking. Nil felt the exertion of the long, upward climb. Gripping tight a grass handhold jutting from the slope, she used her other hand to rub the swelling rounding her abdomen. She knew she was with young, but she did not know for how long. There had been four miscarriages from as many attempts. The last of her kind, Nil had to mate with others not of her species. She realised with a crushing sense of futility that at most, all she could conceive would be a hybrid. There was still one, untried, not of her kind, which was a last possibility; this one, she felt, with its innate sense of hostility and ruthlessness, might turn out to be adequate male material for her needs.

Nil pressed her teeth together and reached above her head to gain a handhold in the rock face. The way grew cluttered with stunted bushes. Thick-stemmed branches of thorn hung down over the lips of shallow ledges. Nil placed one foot on a groove chipped from the cliff-face by her own hand. She gripped a ledge above with both hands. She thrust up and vaulted over the ledge. With intimate knowledge of the terrain, she rolled down into a large depression in front of two limestone boulders. She lay on her back surveying her immediate surroundings. She lay still and sniffed the air, satisfied she was alone. Despite her great size, she gained her feet. She turned towards a short natural corridor leading between the boulders. Following the corridor she came to a narrow space. Ahead a flat rock spanned the outcrops, making a large dolmen. A short way under the cover, she saw the familiar thick drape of thorns filling the space between the limestone outcrops. She stepped forward and listened. There had been no intrusion; she reached forward and parted the spiked branches. She lifted up a large portion of the thorny curtain and snagged it to one side, letting in light. Ducking her head she stepped into her space.

Inside was dry. The sprinkled sand across the floor in front of her space remained undisturbed. Pleased, she strode across the room and entered a smaller space leading further between the limestone buttresses. At one wall of rock she stuck her head into a fissure and saw ahead the second drape of thorn covering the exit from the dolmen. Here too the sand had not been disturbed.

She turned from the fissure. Reaching up she took a crude earthen bowl down from a shelf cut from the face of a boulder wall. She lifted the bowl to her nostrils and sniffed the contents. She looked at the drying truffles, thick and bulbous. From another bowl she poured a sticky black fluid over the truffles. She replaced the bowl and used a finger to stir the food. Raising the bowl, she smiled and opened her mouth. She ate with her hand and licked her lips, ignoring a dribble of food sliding down her chin. She ate, finishing the contents of the bowl, before returning it to the shelf. She returned to the main room. Walking across to one of the boulders, which formed one wall, Nil flipped up a curtain of moss and tucked it into a small crack in the limestone. There, revealed, was a set of bound papers. She leaned closer to view the print-outs, counted them. She let down the moss covering and patted it against the limestone to make it seem a natural growth.

Nil wondered if she would be seeing her dolmen again. She took a deep breath, her chest rising, then relaxing. She glanced up at the rock slab of the ceiling, looked at the petroglyph sigils which were the sign of protection. Tilting her great head, she squinted at the sigils. It occurred to her she no longer believed in things she could not explain. She looked down amid the semi-gloom and saw her feet. She wriggled her toes and bared her teeth with what might have been mistaken as a smile. She stepped down the rock corridor.

She reached the basin and looked down into it. Kneeling, she peered over the lip to stare down the cliff. From her ledge up on the rock-strewn mountain she looked out across the terrain. She had seen to providing herself with a store of food within her protected living space, had duplicated official documents, enough of them to provide her with a powerful bargaining tool. She turned her head to look along the length of the ledge. Her thoughts turned to Stenching and the other accompanying him. She wondered where the pair was. She stared out at the vista. Letting herself down over the lip of the basin, she began a precarious descent.

The water from the underground stream was warm. Nil strode along the tube, ankle-deep. The subterranean darkness was full of splashing and squeaks, and many-limbed white things shuffled and skittered in and out of crevasses. Nil bared her teeth with a smile. Her cavern servants had given her the information she'd needed. Now the white things fell upon each other with lust. As an added reward for their information, Nil had relieved several servants of their outer flesh. These lucky ones had shrieked with delight at her pleasantries; other cavern dwellers not fortunate enough to be rewarded, sniffed and licked the raw epidermis of the lucky ones, their sandpaper tongues rasping across bleeding rawness. Snorts and sounds of gulping were heard back along the tube. Nil spat a piece of skin into the stream and some white gangling thing rushed for it. She grunted as she leaped up onto an uneven ledge. She shook the water from her massive legs and turned her head in the darkness. She smelled her surrounds. Along the uneven ledge she saw a thin rectangle of light suggesting the door she sought would lead her out of the lava tube. She strode towards the door leading to a northern provincial administration building.

In the Hall of Records section of administration, the end of another shift was approaching. At the lectern, with its current ledger in front of it, Fer was back at its post.

Next to Fer stood Smug, a grim, grey figure of ill temper. The tumour sac dangling from his throat swung to and fro as Smug turned to view his workers at their various stations. He growled displeasure at a piece of news regarding Stenching and his charge.

"There are many ways to reach Agarthi. The *Fissures* aren't the shortest way, not during certain periods anyway."

Fer kept its eyes averted and dared to speak.

"But sir, they say the *Fissures* are a direct route to the hanging valley—."

Smug glared at Fer.

"Just who are *they*?" Smug thundered out a demand. "Are you meaning the squat bag of skin, Stenching and his minion?"

"Yes, sir, Mr Smug"

"Then say so!"

"I'm sorry."

"You will be. Nil is on her way here and she's organised for that slimy deceiver, Toke, to join us." Smug was satisfied at seeing Fer chewed its talons. It chose its words carefully.

"See, Mr Smug, the records show the human was accompanied by one guide. There were no additions to the party. See here… Well, the records here are not easily readable. You see, this pen is smudgy and they haven't replaced—"

Smug groaned. Frustrated, he shook his head, his tumour sac slapping.

"Fine! Enough of your cacodaemonaical cacophonies. You have permission to requisition a few pieces of stationery." Smug flicked his gaze up over Fer's head. He saw Nil enter through the doorway leading from the caverns. He straightened at her approach. Fer was so intent on its own misfortune it failed to hear Nil approach. Smug smirked and stared at the space above his head. Fer didn't know whether to laugh or to cry at the sudden good fortune of receiving more stationery.

"Oh, thank you, Mr Smug. Thank you." It lifted the useless pen and looked it over with some distaste. "Now I don't have to put blotches over the records with a smudgy pen. You know when a pen doesn't work properly, things can get messy."

For the first time in some days, Fer became aware of something outside itself. It smelled Nil. Its neck snapped forward and it wheezed out a cowardly plea for mercy. Nil stepped in front of Fer, into the space so hastily vacated by Smug. She looked down into the upturned face of the records clerk.

"Let's see the pen." She grabbed Fer's wrist, placing its hand on the current Book of Records. She stabbed the pen down into Fer's hand, delivering a blow that plunged it through the hand and into the book beneath. Fer began to howl and tug at the pen, which held it captive to the book. Fer couldn't look away. Between its splayed fingers, Fer saw its own words on the journal's pages. Shock crept up and Fer stopped its shrieking. It began to sob. Nil encircled the top of Fer's head with her hand. She tilted its head.

"Well, nothing seems to be amiss with this pen, now; it seems to be working fine, do you not think so?"

She lowered her face further towards Fer's. She flicked out her tongue and tasted the sweaty fear. Looking down at the impaled hand of Fer, Nil saw the grey blood soak into the pages of the record book. She chuckled.

"Smudged enough for you?"

Without waiting for an answer, Nil glared at Smug.

"Where is Toke?"

Smug stood his ground.

"I've put the word out you wish to see him. My associates are professionals, they'll find him soon enough."

Nil displayed her teeth and she licked her eyelids, first closing one, then the other. She opened her eyes and gave Smug a lazy look.

"Never mind bringing him to me. When your minions find him, tell Toke to intercept Stenching and wring all the information the human has blurted to him and report back."

Smug nodded.

"What will that gain, Mistress? We know they're going to Agarthi and the purpose of the visit. What's to know?"

Ignoring Fer's cries, Nil stared at Smug.

"How long has it been since we've had live bait here? You need not answer. I'll tell you how long—long enough that this will be taken by some as an opportunity to make a political move."

Smug seemed puzzled.

"A political move, what do you mean?" He stopped and looked at Nil, realising what she was saying. "Stenching!"

"Correct. If I know him, he'll have the human eating from his scabby hands."

Smug lowered his chin to nuzzle his tumour sac. He listened to Fer's quiet sobbing. Smug spoke.

"What shall we do now?"

Nil watched Fer's distress with some amusement. She watched Smug play with his tumour. She spoke.

"Well if we stand around here—stop flapping that sac!"

With one hand, Smug cupped the sac and cradled it.

"Sorry."

Nil flicked him a cold stare.

"No doubt he has already begun indoctrinating the human—this Tom thing. Soon they'll reach Agarthi and have discussion with the *Grey One* itself. You can watch as Agarthi's media machine propagates their political propaganda."

Smug laughed.

"Hey. That was good."

Nil nodded.

"Yes, it was, but enough. Find Toke and gather intelligence on the current state. Intelligence is not the right word for you bunglers. But just do it."

Smug nodded assent.

"Where will I find you?"

"I'll find you. Inform Toke of this and tell him to select only a few of his minions to attend him at the meeting. You know how big-headed he is regarding his entourage."

Nil glared at Smug.

"*Now* is fine!"

Smug ran from the hall of records. Hurrying through the various departments of the administration complex, he was aware of workers going about their appointed tasks. Several overseers, associates of his, spoke to him as he rushed by them. They were left confused at his hurried exit. Wails from the damned echoed through the chambers as the head of each workstation directed their subordinates to the administering of various tortures. Smug slowed his pace. He'd put enough distance between himself and Nil to feel relatively safe. He'd lost the jitters and now began to stride between the workstations. Here was a place to linger. He thought better of it. Nil would want things to move in her favour. If matters weren't carried out to her satisfaction someone's genitals would roll. Smug shuddered. He knew whatever Nil did to Toke for failure would not be anywhere near what would eventually happen to him. He cupped his tumour sac. He frowned.

No one's taking this from me. No way!

He stopped next to one of the torture slabs. Three workers were administering their own personal slice of Hell to one of the damned. On seeing Smug, they parted to allow their superior a better view of what they were doing.

"What's this?" He snapped. "How many have you done this shift?"

The overseer of the three demonic torturers stammered a reply.

"This is the only one, sir, the only one this shift." He winced, expecting a blow. Instead, Smug nodded with appreciation.

"Good to hear. Spend as much time as possible with one victim at one sitting."

The torturers all had blank stares of incomprehension. The overseer, a great red thing of rolling flesh and suppurating sores, also showed bewilderment. It was obvious he did not understand much of what Smug said. The overseer shrugged its shoulders. The vague response of the overseer angered Smug. He snapped at it.

"Idiot, I mean it's good to hurt one thing for a long time."

The overseer grinned.

"Oh, yes. Yes sir. It's good. I like it."

Screams sounded from the various workstations. Smug sniffed the pain and the terror thick within the air. He smiled and turned to the overseer. Smug pointed to a nearby workstation.

"And what's happening here?"

"Um, it's tooth-nerve scraping and extreme liposuction sir."

Smug nodded and fingered his tumour.

"Oh ho, yes. I've always liked that one, proceed."

He watched while the victim was revived. The overseer and the workers began afresh with their flint knives.

Back in the Hall of Records Fer was wailing anew and was trying to remove the pen stabbed through its hand, but it could not seem to pull it from the pages of the journal. Nil turned and saw a frightened worker staring at the scene. She motioned the creature to her. It cringed as it approached. It looked from Nil to Fer. Nil clicked her fingers.

"Minion, bring another journal, fresh from supplies, and a pen."

Wide-eyed, it scampered from the scene to do her bidding. Nil reached out and patted Fer's head. It looked up at her and tried to smile through its blurred vision. It was lucky enough not to have understood the look on her face. Nil grabbed Fer's throat and dragged it towards the door leading from administration to the ledge above the cavern stream. Fer hopped along after her, the skewered book flapping wildly like some deranged bat attempting escape. The worker returned with a fresh journal and a pen. It tripped over itself in an excited effort to please Nil. She spoke.

"Place them where the others were. Get someone superior to you to summon another clerk."

It nodded and blinked stupidly, gazing furtively at Nil in awe at her proximity. She stared down at the trembling worker.

"And make sure recordings for the past months are available to me. I want to know everything going on here. Sooner we get back online the better."

The little worker ran back and placed the unused journal on the lectern; in the centre of the journal it placed the new pen.

Nil opened the door and jerked Fer through after her. It blinked through its tears and tried to adjust its eyes to the gloom of the cavern. With the book still attached to its hand by means of the old pen, Fer let it hang at its side. Fer turned its pitiful countenance towards Nil. She looked on with glee.

"Don't worry, I'll have the book cleaned up, good as new and stored in the appropriate place." She peered at Fer, her own sight not hampered in the near dark. She smelled the viscous blood seeping from the impaled hand of her minion. Again the great tongue slid from her mouth and licked her eyelids. She looked at Fer and narrowed her eyes.

"Say, you do look tasty."

8

Tom woke to see something flapping along the ground amid the haze. He stooped and gathered up the hem of the dead nun's habit he wore and used his teeth to make a tear; he ripped the habit and made himself a short tunic. He regarded himself for a moment, finally deciding he looked ridiculous. He glowered at Stenching.

"How damned hot does it get?" He plodded on after his annoying companion. More scrabbling sounded from behind.

"Stenching, wait for me." Stenching stopped to let him catch up. Tom fumed.

"Enjoying yourself, are you?" Stenching ignored him and resumed walking.

Tom looked across at his guide.

"So where are all the doomed and damned bodies?"

"Don't mock what you don't know."

"No, really. In the last however many days...hours...I've only heard some weird animals howling in the fog. I've seen a bitch of an overseer, two terrified men running and some *Nuns of Discord*; and I don't want to remember that."

Stenching looked at him and laughed. He spoke as if to a fool.

"Right, you were hunted down and almost eaten. Consider yourself fortunate Nil didn't jump your bones back there. She would have, you know, if your touch didn't make her flesh sting."

"Oh, right," Tom replied with sarcasm. "She might grab you too, eh?"

Stenching scoffed at this.

"You know," he said, "I'll bet even now she's looking for some umbrahumbra oil to protect her skin from you. Then, my hapless Sapien, she'll have you, but good."

Tom sneered.

"Knock it off! I'm doing what I'm allegedly supposed to do. I'm following your ugly self to this Agarthi town. I'm not hassling you about a cab, or a bus. Whatever."

Stenching walked on. He changed the subject, just to hear the sound of his own voice.

"As for the doomed, they're all in the Mines of Sulphur. Occasionally we farm a group out and give them a few years down the shafts and such. Everyone gets a turn."

He scratched at a scab on the back of his head, his flabby arm flesh jiggling. Stenching stopped mid-step. Tom watched his guide watching a rock. Stenching pounced, landing on his knees next to the rock. One hand flicked out and flipped the rock over. Stenching moved quickly and crammed some squirming thing into his mouth.

"Oh. Oh, yes, better." Tom watched with disgust as his guide chewed. Something black writhed from between his lips and waved in the air. Stenching poked out his tongue and shoved the waving thing back inside his mouth. Tom muttered with disgust.

Stenching guided Tom through the rocky terrain, all the while prattling on about irrelevant subjects. Tom groaned, wishing the man/elephant would shut up.

"You know, Tom thing, the boss has a favourite deal for the new arrivals—"

Tom was not impressed.

This flap-eared idiot is hiding his incompetence with all this bravado, he thought.

He shouted at Stenching.

"Shut it, okay? You've been walking for hours and saying nothing important."

Stenching spoke with gusto.

"It's not far now to the House of Black Metal—through this canyon."

Tom's eyes itched. He rubbed them.

"This haze is driving me mad."

"Moan, moan", said Stenching with a chuckle. "Sometimes it rains acid; other times there are volcanic eruptions lasting for weeks—really blackens the atmosphere. Then we have the sweet scent of sulphur permeating everything—good incentive for copulation if ever there was one. Most days though, it's like this. What we have here is mild compared to some days. Why, just the other—"

"Okay. Okay! I hear you."

Stenching smiled and continued through the canyon selecting his route to avoid the sharpest of the rocks.

Tom noticed he did not feel like eating or sleeping. He put his feelings down to a time discrepancy, figuring it had not been hours since he had begun to hallucinate but more likely mere minutes. He looked up and wondered if there was, in fact, a sun. He couldn't be sure, but he suspected somewhere above the haze some sort of orb shone down. He picked his way across the terrain. The pair rounded the shoulder of a clay bank. Tom stopped next to his guide. Together they stood at the end of the canyon, looking out onto a tiny lake edged by high reeds. Tom squinted.

"So, we have had the *Fissures of Myen* and the *Mines of Sulphur* and the *Capybaras of Woe*; so what's this place then, the *Lake of Reeds?*"

Stenching looked at him as if he were stupid.

"No, this is just a flat place with a body of water. It doesn't have a name."

Tom glared at him.

"What a tool."

Stenching stopped, his ears standing at right angles from his head. Tom listened. Then he, too, heard the soundstrident, growing into a raucous type of music. It blared over a low hill on the other side of the lake. Stenching began skirting the lake, making for the hill, his stumpy legs working like pistons. Tom quickened his pace to catch up.

"Hey—"

Stenching held up his hand.

"I know. I know. You want to say to me: 'Stenching, what is that crazy sound I hear?' It's our current touring band."

Tom yelled out.

"Don't put words in my mouth, you stinking Hell man."

Stenching seemed pleased.

"Ahhh, anger", said Stenching. "Good. I'll explain while we walk."

Neither of them noticed the agitation on the dark surface of the lake, as something big stirred in the depths. As the pair walked away, appendages slapped the surface of the water. A mottled shape, driven by hunger, heaved itself from the water and slid out onto the reeds, flattening a large expanse. The creature sensed nearby life as it slithered from the reeds and shifted its bulk out onto the pebbled flatland. It saw with clarity the passage of two animals. It hesitated, then, ravenous, it propelled itself away from the lake. Within minutes the heat of the dry air began to affect it. Appendages waved and something akin to anxiety took hold of the beast. The creature became confused as dehydration dried its outer layer. It crawled after the scent of the potential food. A few moments later, the flopping bulk came to a granite step. It lifted itself a little from the ground. Probing pseudopodia groped to find its progress barred. The air scorched its drying flesh. The haze swirled as the questing predator began to decrease in size. Wounds opened across its surface and yellowish blood spilled onto the packed earth. Small chunks of body mass began to slough from its shrivelling bulk. With a final, desperate lunge it tried to scale the rock step. A shudder ran through its body, stirring dust as the creature shrivelled and died.

Some way ahead and oblivious to the death, Stenching continued chatting, his voice soothing him.

"I was about to say the band is our current black metal act. They're popular—touring here for a spell."

Tom listened to the discordant sound growing louder as he approached. He rounded the base of the hill to the full blast of the creepy stridency of the racket. It was a thunderous crashing of guitars and cymbals. Somewhere through this, a bass guitar droned, the vocals kicked in and Tom thought it sounded as if all of Nil's cousins were converging on the place. Tom gaped when he saw the band. The group was playing in front of a great stone wall, part of a two-storey structure, its rear set to the sheer cliff of a tabletop hill. The electrical leads from the band's instruments were Gaffa-taped together and they snaked away across the ground and up through a metal grille low down on the wall. In the wall next to the grille was a door, its top somewhat taller than Tom. The musicians were vicious-looking, primal in their noise and their posturing. Each was tall, Nordic and skinny and wore corpse-paint makeup. The noise was deafening. Tom could make no sense of the lyrics. Stenching grinned and clapped his hands.

Tom stared at his guide.

He enjoys this…stuff?

The group thrashed to the end of the piece. Stenching spoke into Tom's ear.

"This is what we're into down here. These boys are called *Vulvathoom*, the best touring group we've had here in decades."

Tom gave a derisive snort.

"They tour?"

"Sure. All the best black-metal and doom-grind acts play here. We had *Cannibal Corpse* touring awhile back, they went down a treat. Of course they're all dead now; we reanimate them when we want them to play. We pay very well, you know."

Tom tried to piece together some logic to put things into perspective. There was nothing he could grasp onto. He looked behind him, then turned back to watch the musicians strut their brutal cacophony. What looked like some type of meat seemed stuck to the musicians' faces. Without trying to be obvious about it, Tom stared at the vocalist, watching as the skinny man mouthed his strange words of violence and death. The meat jiggled and it was then Tom realised that these people had offal stuck to their faces. He recognised flaps of crimson liver flapping against gaunt cheeks and high foreheads matted with wet, black hair.

The band started in on another attempt at pandemonium. Stenching moved closer and nodded in time to the breakneck speed of the sinister music. Without a musical cue, the band finished their piece. Tom felt a roaring silence in his ears. He saw the band members as if they were evil scarecrows acknowledging Stenching. Each wore some kind of Scandinavian battle dress —

chain mail, riveted metal shoes and serious weaponry such as broadswords and maces in their belts and scabbards. Tom wondered how they could play their instruments with all that paraphernalia.

One by one, the members left their instruments and walked through the door in the stone wall. The vocalist remained to greet Stenching. Tom heard the sounds of young women's voices coming from beyond the door in the wall, where the other band members had gone. The vocalist strode towards Stenching.

"Ahhh, Stenching, you look like death." At this the vocalist burst into a warlike laughter. Stenching grinned. The vocalist flicked his long hair from his face. He was tall as the door and sapling thin.

Stenching spoke in a Scandinavian tongue. Tom did not know the language, but he was surprised to find he could understand what was said. Stenching clapped the vocalist's back.

"Well, Grimknacker, you demon seed. Good to hear your new work."

Grimknacker sniffed the air and turned to Tom.

"You there, are you here for our show?" He peered at Tom. "You don't seem as if you're into Norwegian Black."

Stenching intervened, grabbing Grimknacker's bony arm.

"Don't talk to him. He's a sarcastic sod."

Tom gave Stenching a rude finger gesture. Was able now to see that the slabs of ruddy liver were stapled to the man's face. He screwed up his nose at the smell of the offal. He left the others, and wandered away in the direction of the door behind which he had heard women's voices. Stenching checked to see where he was going. Grimknacker also turned and looked. Stenching chuckled.

"That's a temporary itch. It's not supposed to be here, a mistake." He brightened. "So, Grimknacker, are you ready for your shows, you old church burner?"

Grimknacker ground his teeth.

"Yeah, your boss will take to the new epic we've written."

The door in the wall was closed. Tom tried to open it, but was unable. He sidled over to Stenching and Grimknacker. Stenching was animated, genuinely interested in the band.

"How long is this epic you mentioned?"

Grimknacker laughed.

"Eleven minutes and six seconds."

Stenching thought about this.

"Clever and appropriate for you guys."

For a while they each played *feed-the-ego*.

After a few moments listening, Tom felt put out at not being invited into the conversation. He chewed his bottom lip. The other band members emerged from the door and began gathering their equipment, taking the gear with them back through the door. Stenching turned to Tom.

"They have a recording studio. We're being invited inside to see them practice."

Tom flinched and whispered out of Grimknacker's hearing.

"Is that necessary?"

Stenching frowned

"Don't be impolite. These people take offence easily."

Tom looked at Grimknacker, who for no particular reason stared wildly back. He knew Stenching was right. Grimknacker looked half crazed already and Tom did not want to see him angry. Stenching nudged Tom.

"Just go along with it. You are my current burden and I'll be glad to unload you. That will make us both happy. Am I right? Am I right?"

Tom nodded. Still half dazed from confusion, he walked with Stenching. Grimknacker opened the door set into the stone wall and showed his guests inside.

Tom found himself in a large studio space, with a wood floor. Against one wall were banks of instrument panels with leads Gaffa-taped to the floorboards. Tom followed to where the leads went and saw they all joined to exit through a hole in the floor. He tried to peer down the hole, found he could not see far, but he did hear a deep hum as if some vast machine was working down in the darkness. He heard women's laughter again. He and turned to see where they were. Further down on the other side of the room was a large Jacuzzi. Tom stared, aghast. There in the Jacuzzi, instead of young girls, four very old ladies sat giggling in bubbling black froth. Grimknacker's band members were splashing in the water with the women. The smell of sulphur was heavy in the room's confines. Next to the Jacuzzi was a low table; scattered on the top were mushrooms, great scarlet umbrellas with white spots. Tom stared at the old women. He blinked, not believing what he was seeing. The women splashed in the noisome water. They giggled with girls' voices. When Grimknacker looked at them, one woman giggled again and each whispered conspiratorially to another. Tom shook his head.

"No, no, no, no, no. This isn't right."

Stenching leaned over and whispered.

"Old people are respected where these guys come from."

Tom winced.

"Yeah, sure, but that's too much respect. I mean *really!*"

Stenching glared at him.

"Shut up. Just…shut up."

Grimknacker walked past the table and grabbed a handful of mushrooms, ate them and sidled over to the Jacuzzi and sat on the edge. He said something that made the old women giggle anew. Grimknacker reached down into the stinking tub water. One of the old ladies jumped, giving a high-pitched squeal.

Tom made a sour face and stared at Grimknacker. Tom had a sudden desire to study the lights on the panels of the recording equipment. He ran his hand over the panels and noticed the gear was very modern. He wondered how it had been brought to this desolate place. He turned back to see what was happening in the Jacuzzi. A couple of the band members were at the food table stuffing the mushrooms into their mouths. He watched them chew.

Stenching walked over and began to laugh at Tom.

"So easily shocked? My, but how crazy is this breakdown of yours? You are insane, you know."

Tom found he could not swallow. The rest of the band emerged from the Jacuzzi and dressed without drying. The old women did not emerge from the frothy black water. They were motionless, almost as if they were robots which had been switched off. Tom watched with a numb feeling as the band picked up their instruments and plugged in. Grimknacker nodded to the others.

An ear-splitting sound rent the previous semi-quiet of the studio. Tom staggered back against a wall. His eyes were very wide for the next 666 seconds as the sonic boom of the band's new epic assaulted his senses. The band thrashed their instruments while Grimknacker began to leap and caper through the rehearsal space. With one hand holding his microphone, he screamed into it while with his other hand he pulled out his cock. He gyrated like a demon over to the Jacuzzi and began to beat furiously on his erection. All the while, he screamed out thunderous passages regarding pagan worship, church burning and an imminent Ragnarok. Grimknacker ejaculated into the black froth of the water and all over the motionless old women. The band slashed at their instruments. Grimknacker howled his pleasure and jerked the last vestige of cum from his shaft. He sank to the floor as the music stopped on a crescendo of death and suggested violence. For a few seconds, Grimknacker moaned. He stood and replaced his shrinking organ into his black clothing.

After the aural assault ended, the corpse faces of the other band members were wet with sweat and they had dripping facepaint splashing onto their chests.

Grimknacker approached Stenching and Tom. Stenching was clapping.

"Good stuff, Grimknacker. What's the new epic called?"

"We call it *Lightning from the void burning upon the ice-veined throne of Umilia Kraken, to dethrone the dragon bitch goddess of the cold wastes: The legend of the Blasted Heath, part one.*"

Tom could not help himself and blurted out the first thing he thought of.

"So, Grimknacker, is that the title of the song or the lyrics for the entire album?" He grinned, but erased the smile when he saw the look on Grimknacker's offal-covered face.

Stenching sighed.

"Fool! These are Norse warriors. You're in the shit. Now it's time to run."

Grimknacker was slow in reacting to Tom's insult, but then he roared.

"You dare to insult the music of Odin!"

The rest of the band answered the battle cry. They ran for their weapons. They stood and faced Grimknacker. Tom was horrified at seeing each man holding either a two-headed cleaving axe or a broadsword. Tom saw Grimknacker pick up a longsword. The eyes under the greasepaint glazed over and spittle was coming from the corners of the man's mouth. Grimknacker's face reddened and he started to gnash his teeth. He shook his shaggy head. Spittle flew, and Tom knew he was in trouble. The signs were unmistakable. The mushrooms had done their job: Grimknacker and the band were berserking.

Tom picked up his heels and fled, realising he was now running for his life. With his tunic flapping around his thighs, Tom heard Stenching shouting.

"You idiot, now they'll be after my hide as well. Look at what you've done to me. I swear I'll get you for this."

With every stride of his long legs, Tom heard Stenching's shouts become fainter as he was left behind. The last he heard of his guide's frightened voice was him screaming faint, far-off obscenities.

Once, Tom glanced behind at the sound of snarling, stertorous breathing and a thudding of feet. Only once did he look back, for close on his heels the frothy-mouthed horror that was Grimknacker, longsword raised, was gaining. Tom shrieked, redoubled his efforts and ran harder. The berserkers were weighed down by their weaponry and were soon lagging behind. Even Grimknacker had lost some berserker stamina and was slowing. With terror giving him speed, it wasn't long before Tom was far in front and gasping for air. He braved another glance behind and was thankful to see he was no longer pursued. He laughed away his nerves. He wondered how far he'd run.

He sat on the ground and got his breath back.

Stenching berated Tom.

"Can't go anywhere without causing trouble, can you? Next time I see the band, I'll have to placate them somehow. I should make you apologise."

"I'm not going back there!"

Stenching nodded.

"Grimknacker will probably chop off your head—you'll be dead and we'll never get rid of you."

Tom retaliated.

"I wanna leave this damn nightmare too. And a strong drink would be good. Anyway, introduce me to your boss and I'm gone."

Stenching smiled.

"Oh, when we reach Agarthi, you'll wish you hadn't said that." He walked on ahead.

Tom felt queasy.

They trudged on. There were bridges, oily rivers, canyons, lakes and the ubiquitous haze. Walking became a plodding semi-dream. He felt his steps were those of an automaton, felt the landscape was repeating itself. He wondered if this, too, was an intended part of Hell. The haze had deepened.

After another hour of trudging over stony ground, the pair walked across an interminable semi-desert. Looking ahead, Tom saw they were nearing some kind of settlement. The haze was thinning. Tom made out stone buildings behind a rock wall.

"We're here," said Stenching. "This is Agarthi—the Ashen Place. This is our own publicity sector. Here it is demon-eat-demon and defecate-down-the-competitor's-throat. It pays to have big ears round here, but don't be obvious."

Tom stopped and looked up the wall to the nearest of the buildings.

"You mean a newspaper-type place?"

"Exactly," said Stenching. "Plagiarism is rife, because only the best ideas get approval and more often than not they are not the ideas of those who suggested them."

Tom felt giddy looking up the wall at the buildings. They appeared to him to shift, stone sliding over stone. Concave became convex and again shifted upon itself. Shadows moved where there was no sun. Tom felt a disconcerting vertigo. He shut his eyes and rubbed them. When he felt a little better he opened his eyes. Stenching was speaking but Tom was not listening. Instead he sat and began removing his shoes. He lifted a foot and sniffed one of his socks. He sniffed again, not liking the odour. He peeled off the socks and looked between his toes. Dark, squishy stuff was smeared between each toe. Tom found a sharp, flat stone. Stenching watched him.

"What are you up to there?"

"I'm cleaning this muck away." He began to scrape the edge of the rock between each toe. He sighed as he worked away.

"Man! Feels soooo good."

Stenching looked on with interest. He eyed the toe jam. It pained him to realise the stuff made him feel hungry. He knew it was something he could never let on to a human. He paced up and down, occasionally looking at Tom's white feet. He felt impatient.

"Hurry up there!"

"Alright, alright", Tom replied from the ground. He picked up his socks and regarded them at arm's length. Stenching spoke.

"Bury those things and cover them good."

Tom nodded.

"Good idea." He used his stone to dig a shallow hole. When he finished he dropped the socks and the stone into the hole. He pushed the earth back in place. He stood and stamped the earth hard into the hole with his heel. He wiped his hands onto his grimy trousers. He wiped each foot onto his trousers and put his shoes back on.

"Good enough for you?"

Stenching scrunched up his nose and flapped his ears once.

"It will do," he answered. "Let's go. Stay close to me and say nothing. Let me do the talking. I have a room here where I can take you. When we get inside, I'm going to set up a meeting with the boss to decide your fate. Oh, I hope they give you to me. I could design a torture specifically for you."

Tom turned on him.

"You know, you and your cronies seem to lack a purpose. I mean, what the hell is the motivation behind making things miserable?"

"You'll find out soon enough."

"I mean, what's your purpose? Where's the creativity?"

Stenching grinned and farted.

Tom stared at his antagonist.

"I know I can hurt you. I haven't figured out how yet. It's going to happen, you know. When it does, look out."

Stenching appeared uncomfortable. He spoke.

"Let's get this meeting over with."

Tom nodded.

"You're scared."

"No, I'm not."

"Oh you are, that's for sure."

"Not true!"

"'Course it is," said Tom. "It's my nightmare and I say you are."

Stenching walked next to the wall, towards an entrance, with Tom calling after him.

"You've got more to lose here than me." He followed Stenching through the entrance and stepped in among the close-set buildings, with their weird sliding stones.

9

Nil sulked as she strode with a heavy tread across dry terrain. Smug strode a little behind, not able to keep pace. Others in Nil's group remained quiet while they trotted behind in an effort to keep up. Nil entered a forest and soon found the path she sought. She slowed a little and stretched wide her mouth, displaying her teeth. Animals ran from her path and she was pleased at their fear. The bone-and-flesh necklace about her throat clacked. She reached up and fingered one of the trophies— Fer's severed left hand. Lifting the grisly item, Nil looked at it and frowned, realising it was not such a good score after all. She licked her dry eyelids and grinned.

Now a trophy from Stenching. Well, that's possible.

She let go of Fer's severed hand and let it drop back to sit at her throat.

Fer followed at a distance, struggling to keep pace. It whimpered and looked at its stump and flicked its wrist. Nil heard movement amid the undergrowth and knew Toke's transparent, information-gathering *Oscolids* were flanking her group. She growled over her shoulder at Smug.

"I see Toke has his lackeys trailing us."

Smug looked up at the forest canopy.

"They're always with us."

Nil was already scheming how to turn the fact to her advantage. She strode into a clearing.

Toke was there sitting under a tree, busily stabbing small, slithering slugs with a twig. He watched each impaled one curl around the twig. Each time he stabbed another slug, the one before was pushed further along the twig. Nil stopped. She turned to watch Smug watching Toke. She sighed at their lack of intelligence. With obvious insolence, Toke did not bother to stand when Nil confronted him.

"Toke?"

"Yes?"

She pointed to the entourage hovering at the edge of the clearing.

"Get those things out of my sight."

Toke complied, making the creatures scuttle away to sit under a nearby tree. Nil looked at Toke's informants. The little gangly-legged creatures had skin allowing light to pass through their bodies. All that could be seen of each was a tiny, beating heart and a dual set of lungs, with a network of tiny capillaries sitting in what appeared to be a jelly-like body the shape of a stick-insect. Nil was envious of their camouflage and detested them for it. She spoke harshly to Toke.

"I suppose you feel safer with your lackeys in tow. Don't you ever get tired of having that motley lot follow you everywhere?"

Toke became defensive.

"They help with gathering information."

Nil pointed to Fer and then to the ground. Fer sat. Nil spoke.

"Toke?"

"Um, yes?" he said, swallowing slugs and wiping his greasy lips.

"Put down that food."

Toke wiped his hands on his stomach. Nil eyed him with distaste.

"No one can hear us. So, explain. No, don't stand up. Talk!"

Toke ground his teeth. He lifted the twig and ate the last slug.

"Well, mistress, it seems the *Grey Flower* is at Agarthi, trying to sort out a problem. I don't know what—"

"Fool, I mean what of that miserable Stenching and his charge?"

"Oh, they're close to the Ashen Place, but their progress is slow. You know how stumpy the wrinkly one's legs are."

Nil smiled.

She looked at the transparent Oscolids, and turned back to Toke, who sighed and picked a handful of sloughing flesh from his stomach and tossed it to the Oscolids, who pounced upon the feast. They ate without noise. Nil leaned down.

"No, don't look at your little bugs. Look at me."

Toke fumed but held his temper. He knew it would do no good to challenge Nil because it would only lead to a quick trip to a torture slab.

Nil looked at her companions. Her head seethed with the outpouring of her fleshy worms from their red, wet nests. The others stared with fascination and ill-disguised lust.

"If we don't intercept Stenching before he reaches Agarthi we will get them on their way out. Whatever they are told about the fate of the human, we'll wring it from them. I know Stenching is plotting something and I know he will attempt to sway the decision of the *Grey One* to his own advantage. I'll flay him, all of them, and the Tom thing, and we'll go from there."

Toke ventured a question.

"But why are we doing this?"

Nil frowned, her greasy head-tendrils thrashing.

"Because, cretin, Stenching is plotting. If I go, you all go with me."

Smug growled.

"Are you sure that's the situation?"

"Yes, I'm sure. Shut up." She glanced down at the Oscolids. "See? See how they creep closer? Toke, put those things to some use." She fingered her bone necklace. "If I don't see action soon, I am going to be wearing your own lungs on this."

At Toke's hand gesture, some of his creatures scuttled away. Nil wrinkled her snout. Toke and Smug looked with trepidation at the pieces of flesh and Fer's severed hand hanging round their boss's throat. But Fer, all but forgotten in the moment, was showing the most interest in the necklace hanging between Nil's corded breasts.

A smooth white tentacle slid from Nil's vagina and caressed her thighs. Toke dared to look. Nil snapped at him.

"If I see that piece of equipment you possess harden, there'll be more than one thing here engorged with your blood."

Toke felt his cheeks flush. He turned and regarded the remainder of his entourage.

"You lot. Make yourselves useful!"

He watched them scatter to do his bidding. Toke felt angry with Smug at having seen the exchange. He jerked his chin at Smug.

"Well? What are you looking at?"

Smug opened his hands and pretended to study them. Toke fumed.

"If I thought you were laughing at me—"

Smug looked at Toke.

"You can do nothing, dim one. You've tried before, remember?"

Toke balled his big, knotted hands into fists. He breathed and relaxed. He knew his colleague was right. There was no sense fighting amongst each other when there were bigger things at stake. Nil watched the exchange with some amusement. She waited for it to continue. When no further argument was forthcoming, she turned to where Toke's minions had been.

"They're not still skulking round here somewhere, are they?"

Toke shook his head.

"No. They don't dare ignore my bidding."

She turned to Toke.

"Nor shall you dare to do so to me. "Looking at Smug, she narrowed her eyes. "Forget what I said before—"

Smug looked puzzled.

"What did you say before?"

Nil reached for him, then drew back her hand.

"What I said before, remember?"

"Forget what I said before. What I'm saying now is… Are you listening?"

"Oh, yes. I'm—"

"Shut up!"

Smug backed away. Nil checked her rising fury. She looked at Toke.

"You, gather your little jelly bugs and take your dangling flesh and whatever else you have hanging on with you. Go and stall Stenching, before he destroys us all. Now, Toke!" Turning to Smug, she studied him for a moment.

"I don't know which of you is more stupid. You, help Toke find Stenching and bring him to me. And I want him and his charge whole, not in pieces."

Smug nodded.

"And you?" he asked. "Where shall I find you?"

"Just find Stenching. I'll meet you near the Agarthi ravine."

Smug looked at Fer's hand on Nil's necklace. He turned and left. Nil watched him. She walked over to where Toke had dropped his slug skewer. She squatted and picked up the twig. With one hand she lifted up a nearby rock and began spearing more of the grubs. She ate and thought things through. She licked her lips and stood to her great height. She shuddered once at the thought of what she had said regarding the *Flower*. Of course she had not intended to include *It* in her threat of flaying, but she had already said the words. She wondered if somehow the *Flower* had overheard her. She swallowed several times and she felt as if there were still slugs lodged in her throat. She turned to Fer.

"You, here with me."

Fer hurried to her. She walked through the forest and hurried on under the thickening canopy of the forest, eager to execute her own plans. Her first task, she knew, was to attempt to get the main computers up and running so as to regain port access to get transport together and be done with walking everywhere.

10

The gates into Agarthi were unguarded. Tom followed Stenching down a narrow lane between stone buildings. Next to a wall of an alley Tom saw a stand holding newspapers. He looked at the front page of the top one and saw it was called *Smoking Dog Gazette*. He took one, reading the headlines of the front page while he followed Stenching. He tapped Stenching on a shoulder.

"So you have computers here?"

Stenching sniffed.

"We do."

"I haven't seen any."

"I haven't shown you."

Tom nodded. "You have a net of some sort, not the old one, the new one, the *Grab?*"

"We have but we don't really need it. We gave you modern tech to keep you distracted from the real issues; keep you searching for trivia to occupy your unused minds with trash."

Tom snorted.

"Not everyone is sucked into that."

Stenching tramped onward.

"I know, but we can't help it if a small portion of your race is intelligent. Still, we even get those eventually."

"Oh", said Tom, "how so?"

Stenching grinned.

"Most of the intelligent ones experiment with illegalities at some point in their otherwise pointless lives."

Tom pondered on this but failed to understand. He gave up wondering what Stenching had meant. He asked a question.

"How come you know so much about what we do?"

Stenching sighed with displeasure.

"I used to be a man, lived in London."

Tom looked at him.

"You? When?"

"It was back in the 1880s. I had to leave in a hurry."

"Why?"

Stenching spat onto the ground, raised his foot and squashed his squirming phlegm.

"Women problems—nothing ever went right for me."

They walked on. Stenching turned down a secondary alley and Tom followed, holding his copy of *Smoking Dog Gazette*. The alley was dark, with leaning buildings almost meeting overhead. Tom looked for signs of industry. He realised this was no place to be walking with this fellow.

"Where's everybody?"

"They are probably brown-nosing up to the boss in the Temple of Shadows."

Tom had heard enough.

"You don't have to make up stuff for my benefit."

Stenching pretended hurt feelings.

"True. There's no temple. Everyone's probably with Azray, wallowing in offal."

"Azray? That your boss?"

"Yes, the Black Light."

Tom shook his head.

"He seems to have more than one name, like you, Jack."

Stenching flinched at the familiar name.

"Careful there," he said to Tom.

Tom spoke sternly.

"Be careful? I'm not a prostitute, so I guess I'm safe enough, eh?"

Stenching showed no reaction.

Careful with this one.

"Azray is known by many names because it dislikes the routine."

Stenching stopped in front of a two-storey stone building with small windows.

"Here." He opened a wooden door. He led Tom inside. They crossed a dirt floor and walked up a staircase. The house smelled of tar. At the top of the stairs on a landing, Stenching pulled a key from a pocket in his grimy suit jacket. Inserting the key, he turned it. A click echoed. He led the way inside. Near one corner, below the room's only window, was a metal bench. Tom looked at it with distaste.

"Not another one of those. Does it heat up?"

Stenching ignored the question and gave Tom an order.

"You camp here for a bit. I'm going to a meeting. We'll soon sort things out."

Tom tested the heat of the bench with his hand. He found it cold so he sat on it under the window. Something flopped from outside against the dirty glass, but Tom did not look up to see what was out there.

"Hey", he said. "I'm not going to have to meet it, am I? You know?" His voice dropped, "Old Nick?"

Stenching glared at Tom.

"You're nothing. It won't see you. I'll explain things and get a decision."

Tom saw Stenching's ears trembling. Stenching left the room, shutting the door after him.

Tom stood and walked to the centre of the room and looked down at the paper he held. He glanced up at the grimy window, then went back to sit on the bench. Opening the paper, he flipped it and read what was on the back page, reading a column heading.

"Sapien special report: genital-biting fish terrorises villagers." He read the first sentence: "Two Papua New Guinea fishermen have bled to death after a piranha-like fish, nicknamed *the ball-tearer,* bit off their penises." Tom looked at another headline.

"Pig bursts into flames during exorcism; priest fried to a crisp." Intrigued, Tom read on. "Ill-fated Father Luis Fontela was trying to exorcise the devil from a raging 800-pound hog when the berserk boar burst into flames, burning both pig and priest to a crisp."

Tom dropped the newspaper to the floor and used his foot to push the thing away.

Should have known what this would be like.

He glanced towards the ceiling. As he stared, something feathery light and leggy ran across his upturned face. He jumped and, in near panic wiped his face and neck, brushing his shoulders in case anything had fallen there. He saw nothing moving.

Uisibility was poor amid the clutter of buildings in the south side of Agarthi. Stenching skulked along a side street and arrived at an alley. A scuffling on the packed earth sounded somewhere behind him. He hurried into the alley, keeping close to the walls of the buildings. The carved stones of the thick walls were grimed with soot and blackened slime mould. He glanced up and saw the walls seemed to lean over him. He ducked lower, as if the weight of those walls was applying pressure. He cursed his cowardice as the embarrassing feeling of trepidation heightened. He knew it was not normal for the place to be so deserted. He realised there would be hidden watchers, noting his progress. At one junction of two branching alleys he had to stop to figure the correct way to go.

Stenching had never been into *The Pit*. He did not question how he knew the way, but followed what he thought were competent guesses; but he also realised he might be receiving subconscious help. He stopped and extended his ears to listen. *Nothing.* He put one hand, palm down, against a wall. The stone felt wet and patches of the wall looked like liver spots. Bending, he licked the wall and found it tasted good. He took a bite from a spongy growth and swallowed. Underfoot, spills of intestine littered the ground. He knew he was close to what he sought. He picked his way amid the spills, trying not to step on anything in case it was someone's food. Pausing to get his position, he turned his head and listened for any sound which would betray a follower. He stepped forward and saw the gap in the wall and the stairs leading underground. Peering around the stonework, he looked down the stairs. He knew there was a door down in the gloom and a series of long galleries and, beyond it, *The Pit*.

With care he descended the stairs and looked for the door. Instead of a proper entrance, Stenching noticed what resembled a cupboard door, at waist height. He grabbed the handle and pulled open the door. Inside was a dark cavity. He climbed up and into the alcove. Standing, he found himself at the head of another staircase. He descended. He counted twenty-three steps before he felt again packed earth under him. For some reason he felt relief at having got this far. He swallowed and held his breath, again listening for any sound that would betray a spy. Hearing nothing did not fool him into thinking he was alone.

He knew the closer he got to *The Pit*, the less he would be able to walk unseen. He expected at any moment to be asked the reason for his proximity to Azray's playground.

Agarthi was honeycombed with sub-cellars. Phosphorescent fungi clung to some walls, refused growth on others. Stenching could smell the first faint odours of *The Pit*. He walked along a widening passageway. He began to notice a sound which was not the rush of blood in his ears. A weight seemed to press down on him. He became disoriented and began to ache, and it felt as if his bones were vibrating. He heard the peal of a bell, sounding thick and leaden—a frightful, heavy thing. He stepped forward, unsure now what was expected of him. His legs weakened. He leaned against a wall and he thought he could feel the clamminess through the fabric of his greasy suit jacket. He waited a moment to allow himself to start breathing normally. A moment later he realised what he was listening to. A gong sounded, making his muscles twitch. The sound came again, metal striking metal. Stenching put his back to the wall and slid down until he sat on the floor of the passage. He felt his nose hairs scratch against the inside of his nostrils. He poked a stumpy digit up one nose slit to alleviate the annoying itch. He extended his ears and moved forward down the passage.

The increasing patches of phosphorescent fungi hung thicker, allowing him to see rusted metal hooks embedded in the walls. The hooks were at irregular heights and from them hung pieces of tissue and more substantial meat packages. The buzz of biting insects filled the place. Stenching looked behind him. He knew he was close to what he sought and his fear grew.

He walked the length of the gallery. The pealing of the bell sounded again, louder. He began to hear murmuring as of many voices. His legs were trembling. He felt ill and wanted to retreat back to the safety of the surface, even if it meant suffering the company of others. His breaths came shallow and rapid. Again he heard something metallic strike the bell. The thrum made his body ache. He lifted his trembling hands and made fists to press against his eyes. He wished he was right now back above and his job was complete and he was on his way back to the safety of the Hall of Records, back where he felt safe. He swallowed and tensed himself for the dreaded meeting.

Something sounded like dry bones clattered across the ceiling. Stenching did not dare look up, for he knew seeing what was there would be worse than hearing it. For some moments he stared at his feet and tried to shut out all sound. With effort he gained courage. He forced himself forward. The sound of voices grew. He followed the sound, which increased at a point where a passage led from the gallery. Walking with senses heightened, he soon entered another gallery. The fungus here was at its thickest and the glow showed him the extent of the cathedral-sized surrounds. He held his breath, exhaled. The gallery was not a natural cavern. The entire space had at some point been tooled to smoothness out of some pre-existing subterranean cave system. Stenching looked up but found he could not see the ceiling. The peal of the bell sounded and he felt like vomiting. Far down to one side of the middle of the gallery he saw the source of the gongs. He stumbled and leaned forward, hands on knees. Again the bell sounded. He forced himself forward and looked at its top. He blinked and swallowed bile. After gaining some composure, he saw a figure sitting cross-legged on top of the bell.

Stenching stood and rotated his shoulders to alleviate cramp. Walking closer, he looked up. The young demon above grinned.

"Hello, Uncle. I heard you were coming. How are you?"

Stenching felt resentment at the fact that one of his kin could dispel his fear. He realised appearances counted, and so swallowed pride and replied with enthusiasm.

"Diabolous. Hello, nephew, what are you—"

"Doing here? I'm doing my new assignment, Uncle. I didn't believe the rumours of the bell 'til I saw it for myself. What d'you think?"

Stenching nodded.

"It's bone-jarring. But what brings you here? When did you apply for this?"

Diabolous held up his hand.

"Sorry to interrupt, Uncle. Have to do this." He lifted a long-handled, metal hammer and brought it down upon the bell. Stenching cringed.

"Is that necessary when I'm trying to hold a conversation?"

Diabolous looked down.

"Sure is. I have one of the damned under here." Stenching looked at the ground next to the gigantic brass bell, as if it would aid him in seeing whatever poor wretch was entombed. He thought of the plight of the pitiful creature trapped. He saw the packed earth, and for a moment substituted himself for the doomed prisoner. Alone in the dark, he would be crouching, with the oppressive weight of the bell over him. He would be crying out in terror, claustrophobia adding to the torture; every few minutes the gong would sound, flesh jarring, reducing his innards to jelly. Stenching perversely allowed himself to imagine the exquisite ingenuity of the torture. He shuddered. He realised Diabolous was speaking to him. He looked up.

"What?"

Diabolous displayed teeth not yet mature.

"Great, isn't it? The idea came from this book." He held it up. "I've borrowed three books from Fer over at records — written by humans. Funny, that. In some ways we've got nothing on them when it comes to dishing out anguish."

Stenching looked up at Diabolous and saw he was reaching for the metal hammer. He held up his hand.

"No, not yet."

Diabolous paused, hammer in hand. Stenching looked at the book.

"What is it?"

Diabolous checked the title, as if he did not know what he was reading.

"It's Octave Mirbeau's *Torture Garden*, a little gem if you ask me."

Stenching frowned. He glanced at the ground where the bottom of the bell met the earth. He shivered and refused to let his fancies take hold once more. He craned his neck to look up. He saw Diabolous was about to strike the bell.

"I said not yet!"

Diabolous pouted, but replaced the hammer next to him.

"What? What now?"

As a distraction, Stenching pretended interest in what Diabolous was reading.

"So, what're the other books, not some of that death porn you like so much, is it?"

Diabolous laughed.

"No, Uncle, not the stuff you enjoy."

Stenching glared at the youth.

"Oh, original. So you're saying it's educational."

Diabolous smirked and held up another book.

"This one's called *Torture Throughout The Ages*. You heard of Messalina? She's from Roman times—a sadistic nympho."

Stenching nodded.

"Yes, third wife of Claudius."

Diabolous was put out at this. He frowned at his uncle. He brightened as he remembered something else he'd read.

"Listen to this. There was this Greek writer, Lucian who wrote of a little-known torture. It tells of a group of men who get together to make plans to seize a virgin and sew her up in the belly of a freshly slain donkey. Great, eh? Anyway, they plan to leave only her head exposed to the sun. They are getting off on this, saying how she will be hot-roasted by the sun and tormented by hunger and thirst. But best of all, they are thinking of her hands being confined inside the rotting carcass, preventing her from committing suicide. Imagine it. Her agony would increase as the putrefaction grew. Writhing worms'd plague her. The book says when vultures came to feed on the decaying flesh of the donkey they'd eat her alive. How 'bout that?"

Stenching stared at Diabolous.

"Does it titillate you just because it describes a woman?"

Diabolous looked hurt.

"A woman's got nothing to do with it. I like reading this stuff. And *you* can talk, what with your legendary exploits with those women in London."

Stenching raised his hands in resignation.

"Long time ago, nephew." He paused before continuing.

"Humans are an inventive lot. Sometimes they make us look unprofessional. Imagine all those billions of meat sacks." He tapped his head. "Their brains are sin containers, transgression machines."

Diabolous chuckled.

"Hey, that's good." He grinned. "Oh, hey, look at this." He held up the last of his books, a great hefty tome. "This is my favourite grimoire."

Stenching looked at the book and saw the extreme age of it.

"And that is?"

"Mysteries of the Worm."

Stenching looked up at his nephew.

"That old thing? I suppose you've read the others?"

"What, the *Necronomicon* and stuff?"

"Yes."

"Sure. I read some of them. They're very rare, you know."

Stenching snorted.

"Rubbish. They're everywhere—full of errors, you know. Anyway, the one you're holding is a fake. See? The cover is made from shaved elephant hide, not the proper stuff." He flapped his ears in annoyance and not a little satisfaction at seeing the grin wiped from his nephew's smug face. Diabolous glanced at Stenching's ears and smiled at the irony of his uncle's statement. Diabolous looked closer at the book.

"So it is, it is made of elephant hide, Uncle. Any chance they are old ears of yours?"

Stenching narrowed his gaze, deciding to ignore the insult.

"So, nephew, where's your father?"

Diabolous spat.

"That old fawner, probably playing the sycophant in *The Pit*. Fool!"

Stenching cackled with delight.

"Still sucking Azray's nipples?" He remembered his mission and felt his fear returning. Diabolous looked down.

"You seem nervous, Uncle—that's reasonable, considering where you're going."

Stenching sighed.

"You young people aren't afraid of anything. But let's cut the chatter. I haven't been here before." He indicated ahead, beyond the bell. "So, which way?"

Diabolous looked along the gallery.

"Not sure, maybe it's signposted." At this he started to laugh. Stenching shouted at him.

"Shut up! Never mind, I'll find my own way. I guess I'll see you soon, I guess." He saw Diabolous pick up the metal hammer, then raised his single eyebrow in question. Stenching glared at his grinning nephew.

"Oh, go on, if you must." He walked towards the branching passageways. The gong of the bell jarred his frazzled nerves, punctuating his exiting from the gallery.

The babble of voices grew louder, and intestines draped thicker from the hooks on the passage walls. Stenching knew he was very close to *The Pit*. He reached a stone archway. He stepped forward and stared with fascination. There, below, in a vast, ill-lit crater, seethed all the abominations he'd been warned of since his arrival from London. The crater was alive with sliding, rustling shapes, conjoined, flesh upon stinking flesh. He heard sucking sounds as body parts separated to morph into still more bizarre forms. Grunts and squeals and shrieks could be heard reverberating throughout the cavern. Great globs of meat and entrails were squelched from between the bodies of the forms below. Stenching stepped out onto a ledge some body lengths above the intertwining throng. He saw what he thought to be overseers sliding against one another, their faces not seen amid the gloom. He felt excited and scared. He looked out across the cavern and saw and gasped. He teetered on the edge.

Directly opposite, Stenching beheld the *Grey Flower* was the present shape of the *Pure Light*. He stumbled back against the wall of his ledge. He stared at the *Flower*. The light was black. He could think of no other way to describe the radiance. His eyes adjusted and he saw the Flower, squatting in the filth of its own faeces. It flapped rubbery leaf appendages, its noxious odours filling the cavern.

Stenching felt a tug at his consciousness and gasped. He felt his thoughts invaded with a numbing, mental cold. He realised he was circling the cavern around the ledge towards the Flower. He sobbed in his terror of the thing and yet could not halt his walk toward the light. The black radiance seemed to dissipate. Stenching was allowed to see more of the Flower. It sat alert, watching everything taking place. It began to defecate from various orifices across its body. It mentally called again to Stenching, beckoning with a promise of reward. Stenching continued his approach. He could now see certain previously unglimpsed details of the Flower. It sat there with myriad almond-shaped eyes set amid the rubbery leaves. Like some vast, stinking Rafflesia, it waited for its minion. Stenching approached, fear now having left him. He stood before the Flower and saw it quiver. Stenching knelt and put his forehead to the floor. He felt the Flower's faeces flow across his fingertips and press against the lids of his eyes. He whimpered as the Flower, Azray's thoughts, invaded his own. At first he could not believe what was being said. Stenching looked up from the floor, muck running down his face. He looked at the monstrous form and he cowered at the sight of Azray's appendages as they reached for him. He tried to be brave as he was lifted from his feet and he began to cry like a tiny child as he felt himself borne aloft into the folds. Azray began to move along the ledge on a ropy mass of tendrils. It picked up speed as it reached the other side of the cavern. Approaching the doorway leading from *The Pit*, seeming to shrink, it squeezed its bulk through. With Stenching in its care, Azray slithered along the outer gallery towards the torture bell.

Although terrified in the grip of the monster, Stenching was elated. He knew now he was destined for great things. This did little to assuage his terror. He sobbed and tried to become smaller in the Flower's grip. He had been vain and he realised he was being mentally corrected. He saw the great torture bell, but now there was no one squatting atop it. Music sounded, as from a great distance. He realised his fists were clenched and his nails were pressing into his palms. He began to bleed from his ears. Shadows flicked across his half-shut eyelids, and he heard a voice somewhere tell him the beginning was at hand.

11

Tom picked up the copy of the newspaper, rolled it up and held it. He turned to the window. A shadow spread over the panes. He stepped back and looked as something scrabbled at the outside grime. He turned away and paced the room, trying to block out the sounds against the glass. He stared at the ceiling. Tilting his head, he began to feel the room had some odd angles making up its ceiling and walls.

The temperature inside the room dropped. By now, Tom was certain the angles of the place were not quite as they should be in a sane world. Remembering where he was, he laughed—a short burst. He got down and lay face to the floor. Turning his head, he shut one eye and stared along the floorboards to see if they had any tilting. He couldn't see anything wrong. He felt like a fool; however, he stayed where he was. It was a few moments before he realised he felt a lot colder. There came a vibrating hum. The noise grew, not so much in volume, but in nearness. The floorboards began to vibrate through the soles of his shoes. He looked at the door. He rushed across the room and put his ear to a wooden panel. He sucked in breath and backed away. The floorboards of the room were springing their nails, the metal spikes clacking off the ceiling. He leaped over to the window. He ignored the frenzied flopping from outside and concentrated on finding a catch. He knew he must not face what he'd heard lumbering up the interior stairs. He noticed the window had no lock, and so rendered him trapped. He sat, terrified, and stared at the door.

Tom could not guess how much time had elapsed when he saw the door open inward. So great was his fear that for a moment his eyes refused to focus. He saw. Stenching was crawling on all fours as he followed the thing, which seemed to grow and to shrink and, once inside the room, grow again to enormous size as it oozed in. Stenching saw Tom and put his forehead to the floor. Kneeling in obeisance, he gave a message to Tom. Stenching grovelled obsequiously.

"The *Grey One*." Tom heard Stenching, but he was looking at the mass bathed in the shining darkness. Out of a patch of black putrescence there grew an enormous plant, topped by a flower, a noisome two-metre expanse of flailing protuberances. Bulbous tubers, wet with mucus, glooped in the muck, giving buoyancy to the plant's weight. The tubers contracted and expanded and fell forward, giving the plant locomotion. From the tubers, stems of flayed animal flesh bulged upward. Towards the top of the plant the stems fused. A viscid substance seeped out. The secondary stem corkscrewed upward to the petals of the flower. Crimsoned and purple-veined, the petals rippled the cilia at their edges. The flower head turned from the doorway, revealing the bloom. Tom cried out and fell off the metal bench. Still he stared. The loathsome thing spoke to him, not in any audible sense, but mentally. And it hurt. A psychic booming bathed Tom's consciousness and he heard the awful tones of the voice.

"Come, walk with me."

Tom blacked out. Somewhere distant he heard sobbing.

He opened his eyes and saw one of the walls of the room now held a vast open door. Tom walked as if in a dream towards that opening. He realised he was being followed by something too great to comprehend. He felt no fear now, only a sense of growing elation. He seemed to be gliding forward without knowledge of how he was accomplishing this locomotion. He found himself in a kind of park or large enclosure. The air was oppressive and the place felt damp, as if it was some grotto in a vast rainforest. Vines and ferns surrounded a large pool of dark water. From somewhere overhead a moon shone, barely lighting the darkening scene with a glow worm effect. He looked down at the water and saw his reflection. The image vanished as a ripple fluttered across the surface of the water, as if something below was rising.

Looking up across the pool, he saw there was no longer a plant, and in its place there was now a light. With eyes widening in wonder, Tom saw the light grow brighter as it shrank in size. He saw the dark brilliance and realised it was so black and beautiful it hurt his eyes. He looked away from the brutal purity. At once he felt a grief rising within him. He shut his eyes so as not to see that wonderful radiance. He felt his heart contract and realised if he did not look again at the light, he would surely die. He felt as if he was growing larger. He stared with rapture on the dark purity before him. From the light, a voice broke the silence of the place. Tom felt as if he was leaving his body. His bones began to ache and he felt his nose start bleeding. He tried to raise his hand to brush away the blood, but he could do nothing other than stand and tremble and listen to that inner voice. The light approached. The ground seemed to buckle, and he felt himself totter back from the edge of the pool. The voice told him of imminent events and Tom stood immobile, appalled at the revelations. At once, the plant began to wither, to melt, the glistening fluids seeping away.

Tom woke still standing and saw there was now no pool. He was again facing the door leading to the stairs. He saw a blank wall where there had been a doorway to the grotto. Turning further, Tom saw Stenching. There were the two of them now. Tom knew the demon flower had made its decision. Tom felt powerful. He looked anew at Stenching. A slow smile spread across Tom's lips. Tom spoke, his voice resonant, authoritative.

"We are starting back, minion."

Stenching bowed his head, his ears flopping forward. He spoke in a whimpering sigh.

"Lord Azray, what's to become of me?"

Tom spoke.

"It's time to get some new laws into place." He lifted his hands and studied the backs as if he had never seen them. He turned round and again faced Stenching.

Stenching whined and began to cry.

"What, what, am I going to do now? No job, no prospects."

Tom said the words.

"Capybaras, my fiendish sycophant."

Stenching lifted his head to face his new master.

"Oh no. Not the cages. Please, not them."

Tom grinned. Stenching fell to his thick elephant knees and began to sob great heaving gasps. Tom gave the order.

"On your feet, pustule, it's a long way back."

They descended the stairs and exited the dwelling. Tom strode through the alleys until they entered the main streets. He walked with authority towards one of Agarthi's gates. Stenching wiped away his tears.

"Sir, what is my first task?"

Tom felt his chin lengthening.

"All in good time, but right now bring me eats, nice treats which squirm and reek; feed me now, before I strip your stinking carcass."

Feeling the power growing within Tom, and realising it was already far too late to alter events, Stenching scurried away to search for his new master's meal. As he searched he knew he was now nothing in the scheme of things. He stopped short. A thought occurred to him.

What if I stick real close to him and become a personal confidant? If I gather intelligence for him, that will give me leverage over the others. What if—

He remembered he was supposed to be gathering food. While he searched his thoughts, he grabbed at several emerging plans. After a moment Stenching saw the perfect food for his new boss, but the food also saw him and flopped away. Claws snicked together as Stenching caught up with the retreating meal. He stooped and snatched up the meal. It slipped from his grip. Thumbnail-sized pores opened on the slimy hide of the retreating animal. Several pairs of its eyes were looking ahead to see where it could escape to, while the remaining pairs of eyes watched the puffing Stenching. It turned and slithered among the trees. Stenching saw the pores on the hide stretch open to allow the young to squeeze from the cavities scattered across the parent's hide. Oily liquid preceded the young's escape from the parent's skin. They dropped to the ground. Stenching scooped up some of the young. He threw them into his mouth. The chase continued, with the food ducking backwards between Stenching's legs. His ears flapped with frustration.

"Stay still!" He raced after Tom's meal. He dived and caught the thing under his chest. Crouching, he gripped the struggling creature and ran back to Tom. Gingerly, Stenching offered the prize to his boss. Tom looked down at the catch. He snorted thickly. Drool dropped from newly grown appendages around his mouth. He snatched the food and pressed it to his throat. The flesh about the throat oozed apart and an orifice formed. Tom laughed. The flesh stretched out and wrapped itself around the struggling food.

Several more of the creature's young squeezed out from the bursting body. Stenching leaped in and crouched, his mouth upturned to catch the young. The meal vanished into Tom's throat with a spray of fluids as it was pressed to death. He looked at Stenching.

"Tasty. Just keep them coming when I tell you." He set off across the flat ground in the direction of the lake, with Stenching in tow, trotting at his heels. Tom looked down his body and saw new growths peeling back his torn clothes. The growths grew before his eyes into bladders, their mucus membranes discharging a carrion odour. Tom liked the smell. The growing bladders changed their hue to match his jovial mood. He felt the beginning of his new brain-stem break through the hair on his head. He strode on, his changing shadow matching his stride.

A while later Tom stopped and turned to stare down at Stenching, who had averted his eyes, his ears hanging flat against his head. Tom spoke, his voice deep and glutinous.

"Oh, yes. There are going to be big changes. All will know Azray has been reborn." He lifted up his head to scan the red haze. Only he could see the shining orb lighting his world. He smiled, slow and crooked. He bared his teeth and opened his mouth. He roared with glee at the feel of his burgeoning power. Tom felt a tickling under his armpit. He hooked a new-formed talon into the space and found another growth. He caressed it.

"Stenching, you will see that the snivelling clerk, Fer, at reception, gets a new pen to write with. We don't want smudges in the ledgers. We'll get the net back up and running. Of course, that is after he is returned from Nil to his rightful position and has his hand reattached. Oh, don't look surprised. I know what's been happening. You will also see to it the Com and Nav systems are back on. Get as many as you need to aid you. Don't look like that. Oh, and you can get any idea of becoming my confidant and personal flunky out of your pea brain, that is not going to happen."

Stenching stared down at the ground and used his tongue to try and dislodge some food from between his tooth stumps.

Tom looked at the orb above his head and then through the haze out across the landscape. He thought of Nil.

Ah, yes, Nil. I'm looking forward to hooking up again with that libidinous overseer. There are containment shafts to be designed, servants to terrify and oh, so many things to make shriek and squirm. My minions will be taught new ways to raven.

Tom raised his head and stretched wide his now huge mouth and roared with delight so all could hear the mighty, guttural utterances of the emerging new Lord of Purgatoria.

12

Stenching watched with grim fascination Tom's body alteration, his gaze centring on Tom's back as it began to split wide. Something was emerging. Tom felt ill as his groin began to ache and he glanced down. With widening mouth and lips puffing like a grouper's, he watched with interest his flesh bubble and smoke, then part. Two blackish-green ball sacks dropped to flop next to the originals. He stared with amusement, all the while muttering things his companion could not understand. Bone slivers began forming in a protective mesh around the new appendages. Tom stared at Stenching and growled at the servant, beckoning the stinking minion to him.

"Why are you standing over there?"

Stenching rubbed his hands together, agitated. He'd found an answer.

"I was staying out of your way for a while. I thought it would be best."

Tom regarded him.

"Wise, but do stop thinking for yourself. That is my job."

Stenching hung his head, ears flat against his wrinkled cheeks. Tom's corded neck creaked like a weighted rope swinging from a tree branch.

"We continue," he said, and began to move along with an odd locomotion, appendages rubbing against one another. Stenching followed behind, marvelling at the eyes opening up on the lower back of his boss. One of the eyes blinked and watched Stenching watching it. Stenching became nervous at this and did his best to act as if nothing out of the ordinary was happening. He contemplated whistling, but refrained.

Tom began a rasping purr, which rattled in his corded chest. He watched Stenching with the open eye. He spoke.

"Talk about having eyes in the back of your head." He laughed, a gurgle sounding like a person drowning.

Stenching swallowed as if in an effort to clear his boss's congestion. Tom rasped out: "We are going to stop at a group of shafts up ahead and have some fun with the inhabitants. I can drop some excrescence down and listen to the wailing. Let's see, how about those child molesters? They are my naughty children. Yes, let's go and molest *them* for a while." Tom continued purring. "Everything here is for me, to use how I see fit. That is right, Stenching. Right, is it not?"

Stenching had begun to detest that staring eye. He coughed before speaking.

"A very good idea, sir."

Tom looked at his minion.

"You'd like anything I say, you obsequious cretin. Now, is it not true I rule all I see? Tell me I'm wrong."

Stenching took a few steps away.

Tom sent down a bunch of newly formed pseudopodia as a balancer and turned his huge form to face Stenching. Gills opened on his throat and he tasted the microbes and pollen from the air as he sifted the mix through. He glared down at Stenching.

"Hmmm, it seems I'm still to have growing pains. I hurt. The unfortunates in the shafts are going to suffer because of this."

Stenching waited until Tom had turned and resumed his lumbering gait. He followed.

At the shafts, Tom gave the inhabitants of each one special attention. Ropy snakes of his flesh inched down the walls of the shafts, the sensitive tips feeling for the prey huddled below.

Strips of wet skin dangled down into the pits, like meat skirts, dripping mucous down on to the molesters. Bone grew from the skin and stabbed the blistered bodies of the shrieking prisoners. Tom purred as he tasted the agonies of his captives. He had never felt so alive. The cries of the molesters were too much even for Stenching to tolerate. He backed further from the scene of Tom's ministrations. Tom toyed with each of the incarcerated, dining on their yelps and pleadings. He sniffed the air and came from his place of bliss. He turned on his pseudopodia.

"Come, Stenching. We go."

Stenching plodded after his master. The heat was intense. Tom parted his grouper lips, boils bursting along their length, and managed a wide, crooked smile.

"Stenching, it is getting hotter. Ah, this is the life."

Stenching realised he was to suffer intolerably at the hands of this thing. He trudged after Tom trying not to look at the great eye staring at him with apparent amusement.

Sometime later the pair entered a forested area. Tom found the going easy as he flowed across the ground, pushing aside small trees and boulders. Stenching looked behind and saw a wide swath had been cut. He turned back to follow his boss and felt uncomfortable under the gaze of that ever-watchful, unblinking eye. A few moments later, Tom left the edge of the forest and entered a semi-arid region. He stopped his forward movement, tentacles rasping together. Tom shuddered, his protuberances jiggling against his oily hide. He stopped and his various nostrils sniffed the air. He looked at a group of rocks, sitting some way off. He remained still as he sent out thought feelers. He knew someone was behind the rocks, watching. Within a moment, Tom knew it was a lowly creature by the name of Smug. He probed further and realised Nil was in the area. Tom grinned as best he could. He knew he was soon to be reunited with Nil. Something in his throat rattled and he gurgled out what may have been laughter.

Sneaking the occasional look from behind his cover of boulders, Smug did not like what he was seeing. He realised the time of change had arrived. He looked behind him. He lifted his head and again peeked over one of the boulders. He saw what had once been the human, Tom, changing shape before his eyes. The spectacle scared him, more so because he could guess what was to come. He began to feel a strange tingling in his thoughts, as if his mind was being somehow invaded. He shut his eyes. The feeling passed. He had watched from behind the rocks as Stenching and the changed human made their way towards him. Now he knew their path would take them to a place not far from the plateau and the ravine where Nil was planning a special greeting. Smug did not dare another look over the boulders. He knew it was time to get out of that place and to tell Nil of the situation.

With no idea Stenching and Tom were close by, Nil was busy organising an ambush for him and his charge. Knowing the area was a major artery for workers, Nil had selected a long, wide plateau. To one side, a small lake lay surrounded by low trees and sandy soil. A short distance from the lake, the great Agarthi ravine snaked through the terrain.

Toke's Oscolids ran to gather intelligence. Smug returned to the plateau. Nil was with Toke and she did not like what she heard.

"Stenching and the man are here?"

"He's no longer that—the change is upon him."

Nil regarded him. She glanced at Toke and back at Smug. She understood what the news meant, and that did not sit well with her. She clacked her jaws shut.

"Of course, it all makes sense. Stenching and the man; the human is not leaving. That's it. He's changing!"

Toke glanced at Smug.

Smug looked at Nil. She regarded them both. She checked her surrounds.

"This changes everything. You two have work to do. Toke, move."

Toke hurried away to find his Oscolids. He knew he was in a precarious position and wondered of his immediate future. If the hierarchy changed, then even with his Oscolids his place was not assured. He began to feel scared. He found his transparent servants on a bare patch of ground. He squatted on the ground and watched them entertaining themselves. His thoughts turned to ways of saving his position.

The Oscolids were gathered beside a large pit in the ground. Each took its place on the rim of the dislodged earth. One Oscolid decided to jump into the hole for a closer look. The creature was snatched from under the loose soil lining the bottom of the hole. It began to shriek in protest. Long, hooked appendages reached out of the earth and encircled the little transparent servant. It renewed its cries and began to struggle with distress. The Oscolid was pulled under the surface, its visible heart labouring at its efforts. When the struggling Oscolid had been completely dragged under the ground by the hidden predator at the bottom of the pit, the other Oscolids looked at Toke, and waited for any type of command. Toke was preoccupied.

Smug left with Nil's instructions, never intending to carry them through. He was planning matters of his own with an ally, one who had of late been keeping a close watch on the comings and goings of the wrinkled windbag Stenching, one even related to the pachyderm. Smug began forming his plan while he went searching for food. He wanted to have something organised, something like a retreat plan, in case of mass demotions being brought in. He knew he was going to lose privileges. He foraged for food. Catching something, he sat with his back to a tree. He ate what he'd gathered, chewed and began to plan a way to maintain a decent position. He finished eating. Seeing Nil standing some way off, her back to him, Smug wiped his hands in the loose dirt of the place. He stood and approached Nil. She turned and pointed at him.

"You will go to Stenching and the Tom thing and ask them for a meeting. Tell them where I wait."

"What, go now?"

"Now, and tell them anything, but make sure they come."

Smug stared at the ground.

"But I think the Tom thing can read my mind."

Nil pondered this.

"That could be true. So if you get close enough, he will know anyway and may wish to have a meeting."

"But Nil, volunteering again, I mean, that last experience was painful."

Nil stepped closer to Smug.

"I'll give you *painful!*"

Smug grumbled, but hurried away. All the while he thought how much he hated his enforced subservience. He began to plan the downfall of a certain few individuals, but he knew in order to do that he needed to escape to where the emerging power lay. And it was with a stooping lope he made his way toward the Power.

The groups met beside the lake. Nil was afraid when she saw what had once been Tom lumber into view. She managed to look away. She saw Stenching and noticed how small he looked beside the hulking monstrosity. She felt a tingling across her synapses. Mental images flitted and pain came. The voice in her head told her to stay away for the moment, told her to be patient. Nil stood tall and flexed her corded arms. She relaxed her massive shoulders. She hesitated, at first unsure. She sat, subdued by the weight of the invasion into her thoughts. She shivered as she realised it was now almost too late to right things into her favour; but she also knew there was still time if she waited for the right moment to launch a physical attack before the final transformation. Nil felt Tom's mental powers and knew they were strengthening, but she realised she was still able to resist his probing too far. She held her mind firm and resisted his efforts. Tom felt resistance to his thought process but could not tell from where it emanated. He gave up for the moment and sought easier minds, thinking to get back to the source of resistance. His plan was thwarted for the moment because he was now so self-absorbed, his new physical alterations interesting him more than outside influence.

Toke and Smug had been inexorably drawn toward Tom, although becoming more anguished as he neared. They lay apart, both on their stomachs, with their faces pressed into the sand by the edge of the lake. Tom ignored them while he watched Stenching watching Nil.

"I will soon feel whole." He felt a constriction in his limbs. He roared his pain. Those nearby shut their eyes to the sound. Nil's wet flesh ropes retreated to their raw nests. She squatted, then sat again as she felt a tiny kick against the inside of her swelling belly. She put a protective hand against her stomach and checked to see if there had been anyone watching her actions.

Smug and Toke kept their heads in the sand. Toke's flesh sloughed faster than he could regenerate; he felt himself weaken and he moaned with encroaching terror.

Tom stopped and turned upon his lengthening appendages.

13

Although no one present knew when the change in Tom would be completed, they watched in fear. Tom oozed across the ground. The air became charged with menace. Red haze thickened along the shoreline. Tom creaked when he moved forward, his wide back slick with runnels of blood where slivers of bone pierced his flesh. Already he sensed bone knitting against bone, new meshes forming. He had a mental vision of his final form—a net of bone with sentient thorns to snare and skewer. He was green, slick and shiny with mucous, sharp ridges scraped across the slick hide, pushing secretions across his pores. Viscous gobs thudded to the earth and a fine spray of urine and blood was discharged from Tom's shuddering form. He raised his upper appendages, and small armpit slits smacked open and the crimson interior of each slit was alive with trembling cilia.

His form had by now altered from a misshapen thing, vaguely human, to a bear-sized, spider-like creature with thrashing, moist tentacles. He moved, fast, on clacking limbs of bone. Under the protective mesh, his body was developing lesions. He felt no pain or fear. He realised they were the sores of health, a final confirmation of his ascendancy. He uttered one final human wail.

A tearing sound came, followed by a sucking sound, and he watched as great flaps of black flesh slapped down to form a wet skirt about his bulging waist. He felt the tremendous weight of the skin pouches growing from his shoulders. His voice lowered in timbre and he began to laugh, a raucous sound now containing nothing audibly human. His eyes bulged from their sockets; the stalks, with their own sentience, seemed eager to get a better look at the Tom thing. His skirt of flesh curled at the edges, new capillaries flushing blue and red.

New bone growth lengthened from the stumps of Tom's hands. Cartilage dropped away and flesh grew from the stumps. Now blue-black, Tom's body changed temperature. Pores stretched wide along the length of the body and a pungent odour surrounded him. He grew a slender tentacle from his chest, where there had once been a breastbone. A mouth opened on Tom's back. Molars ground together. Screams issued from his armpit slits. Urine sprayed the area and the ground shook with the thumping of his ecstasy. In the agony of birth, the spirit of the Flower from Agarthi screamed. The creature flexed appendages, raking furrows into the earth. It turned, stamping the ground. It turned again and with its myriad scattered eyes, it looked at the gathered crowd watching it. Minds joined and at first it was confused as to which of its voices it would use. Extra vocal chords were as yet forming in various parts of the thing. Then bobbing on the limbs, Azray lowered and rested its bulk on the ground. It began to shut down most of its senses. It looked at Nil. Unafraid now, Nil looked back at the new life form. Stenching walked up to stand near Nil. They stared in disbelief at the monster before them. Stenching felt a thought come, unbidden. He looked at Azray and tried to find even a hint of the Tom shape. There was none, but he knew it was Tom who was mentally communicating.

"Grimknacker has written a song and has offered it up to us on this, our day of my rebirth. Tonight we feast and raven. Go. Prepare the bacchanal."

Stenching nodded. He hurried away with a quick glance at Nil.

Tom was gone, absorbed into the new being. Azray heaved up onto strong limbs and veered towards the lakeshore. The gathered watchers moved back from the thundering progress towards the water. Stopping at the edge, Azray turned, bursting with ripe juices and growing larger by the minute. It looked at Nil. Toke and Smug were ignored. Azray spoke to Nil's thoughts. At first, Nil had difficulty in understanding the several conflicting voices she heard from Azray.

"Gather the servants and the higher-ranking workers, we want devices of pain and we want hallucinogens. You know what I mean.

Nil smiled, the first time in a while. She drew a finger across one eyelid. She smiled wider and looked at Azray.

"Pain and drugs", she said with a slow smile.

Azray waded out into deep water. Things lying on the bed of the lake were crushed under the bulk pressing them down into the suffocating ooze.

Azray turned back to Nil, its thoughts now clear to her.

"Bring everything, everyone, to us, here. You will revisit the *Fissures of Myen*. Have Mother Superior brought here. She will be given new instruction and special caresses."

Nil flexed her corded neck.

"What has that woman of discord got to offer you we cannot, Father?"

"The show this day is in celebration of us and it will be a show of many facets.

"And Mother Superior, Father?"

"Superior will eat well and she will learn new torments."

Nil dared to look up across the intervening water. She beheld Azray in the *Pure Light*. She shivered. Turning, she left to do her Lord's bidding. Already those invited were gathering on the lakeshore.

Smug had been scheming, attempting to secure a good position within the new system being put in place. He reasoned that in order to make his position more secure he would need to reach his ally. In the meantime he approached Toke. Although initially positioned above Toke in the old scheme, Smug realised things were now upside down. He knew he had to move, because Nil and Stenching and the others would already be forming alliances. He sidled up to Toke, being careful not to step on any of the now important Oscolids. Toke eyed Smug with necessary suspicion. Toke explained himself before Smug could get a word in.

"There is no way for collaboration, my evil cohort. You have left things too late, don't you ever think ahead? Go look somewhere else for support." That said, and to Smug's anger and indignation, Toke walked away with the Oscolids in tow. Smug snapped shut his jaws and stalked off in the opposite direction in order to find Nil. Some way along the edge of the lake he encountered Stenching. The little stinking man bowed in mock deference and spoke.

"If you are looking to Nil for help, I don't like your chances."

Smug could not help but ask.

"Oh, now what!' he snapped. Stenching smiled and flapped his ears with delight at the sight of Smug's discomfort and frustration. Stenching relished in imparting the news.

"Haven't you heard? Nil has promoted Fer. It seems that odorous little clerk now has a very powerful ally. And I don't need to remind you of his knowledge, what with being a record keeper for all this time. Knowledge is power, Smug. Fer did not know what it had at its disposal. Oh, and did I mention the *Grab* is back up and running?" Stenching chuckled with glee. He rubbed his hands and saw Smug was fuming. Stenching wandered off with some parting words.

"Better work quickly. You're going to need some companions. Be seeing you."

Smug shuddered at the thought and began to feel desperate.

Fer had its own agenda. It knew Nil was a good one to be close to when trouble arose. Fer knew it would be a difficult thing to rid the place of Smug, but Fer also began to realise that with Nil as its ally, it had plenty of time to plot.

Nil travelled fast, her progress across Purgatoria unbarred. She had abducted one of Toke's Oscolids and had it grasped in one of her hands. She maintained her pace as she brought the creature up to her face. She looked at the transparency of the thing. It squeaked with fright. Nil growled at it.

"I need some intelligence on Stenching."

The Oscolid, so far from Toke it had lost all allegiance to him and now belonged to Nil, scampered down her thigh and out across the ground to do her bidding. Nil ran, ignoring the periodic opportunities for sustenance. She realised there would be plenty of time for eating once the gathering had been organised, once the food and the drugs and those to undergo correction had been delivered to the place of celebration.

Within an hour she had reached the hanging valley. Stopping, she looked up at the towering escarpment above. For the uninitiated, the cave entrance would have been difficult to spot. Having traversed this terrain many times, Nil searched the rocky cliff-face and finally saw one of the entrances to the *Fissures*. She smiled and licked her eyes, and began to climb. The cannibal Mother of Discord would not come to Azray without some persuasion, so Nil prepared for the worst.

Smug was now smiling as best he could. He laughed, muttering to himself.

"Yes, yes, that stinking little schemer has no loyalty to anyone, especially his uncle. But now things have changed he has to stop working for himself and form an alliance."

With a bold new plan, Smug went in search of the arch torturer himself, Diabolous.

An entourage had helped Grimknacker and the band to get their gear to the lakeshore. The power supply was sourced from the underground cables. Grimknacker arrived at the site of the gig to see food and other entertainment being delivered. Already a crowd of notables were gathering for the festival. Grimknacker surveyed the terrain. Several workers laid out a long main cable and fed one end into a shallow depression in the ground. Something clicked and power was obtained from underground machinery. Grimknacker watched the gear being set up. Ideas invaded his consciousness. He shouted, got the attention of his cohorts. All turned in time to view the completion of the transformation, as bone ends on Tom liquefied to fuse with new-formed arteries. The throng gathered lakeshore all turned in time to see Azray finally reborn.

Grimknacker stared with awe. He heard the voice.

"You are going to do well."

Grimknacker and the band opened a trunk they had brought with them. Digging inside, Grimknacker extracted a bag of dried mushrooms.

Stenching approached the lakeshore with Diabolous, but they did not speak to each other. Instead they stared across the water at Azray. Standing lakeside and cradling his copy of *Torture Garden*, Diabolous heard the swish and flutter as things scurried away from the lakeshore. Fires were lit and soon smells and sounds of things shrieking as they were roasted filled his consciousness. He patted his book. He knew now that knowledge led to power and knowledge was found through reading. He laughed and scratched his backside. Diabolous narrowed his eyes and smirked. He went off to find some substances to abuse; during this indulgence, Diabolous had come to one major conclusion: Stenching had to be gotten rid of. He wondered if it would be as simple to finish him as it had been getting his own father eaten. He rubbed his hands together. He began contriving a very slick plan. He reasoned if he were to become a respected torturer with innovative ideas, he would need an accomplice who was a master at their art. Diabolous knew if he could accomplish this he would be held in high esteem in the eyes of Master Azray. He realised he would need a powerful ally in this new scheme if he was to gather power. He heard his name being called. At the sound, Diabolous turned and saw Smug approaching. Diabolous saw the look on the newcomer's face and knew immediately he had found his new business partner. He grinned and began laughing as only he could.

Out of breath, Nil had arrived back at the lake. Mother Superior would arrive in her own good time. Seeing Stenching standing close to the water, Nil approached him. He turned and gave her a faint smile.

"It's been a while, sister of mine. You look tired, Mary."

Nil inclined her head to her younger brother.

"Hello, William, or should I still call you *Jack*? You're holding up well, under the circumstances. Is there anything interesting happening in your world?"

Stenching nodded.

"It makes you think." He looked at the ground, then at Nil. "We were conned."

Nil sighed and rubbed her naked belly.

"No. You, me, the others, we fooled ourselves into thinking

that the dying Flower would leave the way open for us. Instead, it simply reinvented itself. While we were working against each other, there were forces exploiting the disunity."

Stenching spat onto the ground.

"I was used. I didn't know it at first. I helped as a guide to bring this about." He looked out across the uneven terrain. "I was going to kill you. And that was supposed to have made me feel good."

Nil laughed.

"You know I got two of the Whitechapel bitches and yet you continue to get all the credit. Your killing days are behind you. Besides, I'm already dead."

It was Stenching's turn to laugh, but there was no mirth.

"I never saw this coming." He stared out through the trees towards the water. "I'm going to lose my position take a demotion. I know it."

Nil nodded.

"Demotion would be a little extreme, under the circumstances. Anyway, we're all vulnerable now. With The Flower, we knew where we stood."

Stenching moved his ears to fan his face.

"I'm not happy."

Nil imagined everything changed at the whim of the new *Pure Light*. She raised her hands, turned them over to look at her palms, she studied the texture. She looked at her brother.

"I don't know what to think yet. We will talk again soon, I guess." She turned and left him, standing, bewildered and unable to think of anything to say. For a while he stood quiet and still, watching his sister walk away.

Grimknacker looked at the enormous being standing in an oily slick in the water. He turned to the band and saw they were ready. Turning back to the monstrous thing in the lake, he introduced his new epic.

"This is dedicated to Lord Azray. It is called *Lightning from the void burning upon the ice-veined throne of Umilia Kraken, to dethrone the dragon bitch goddess of the cold wastes: Legend of the Blasted Heath, part one*."

Stenching jerked his head round to stare at Azray. Grimknacker looked across the water. He heard the question, soundless to all but him. A slow smile spread, shifting the stapled offal a little each side of his nose. He swallowed a handful of dried mushrooms. Inclining his head, he mentally answered Azray.

"No, Great One, the title is not the lyrics to the entire album."

Out of the corner of his eye, Grimknacker saw the boys from *Cannibal Corpse*. He gave them the thumbs up and turned to his band. He screamed into his microphone:

"We…are…*Vulvathoom!*" With that, they launched into their new epic. The amps kicked out a thunderous cacophony spurring those gathered. All present began to leap and to caper amid the fires. Waves lapped up against the lakeshore as the new Thomas Wu thrashed in growing pleasure in the dark water.

Curtain closes